D0915542

MR. MONK
GETS ON BOARD

Center Point
Large Print

Also by Hy Conrad and available from
Center Point Large Print:

The Monk Series
Mr. Monk Helps Himself

MR. MONK
GETS ON BOARD

HY CONRAD

Based on the USA Network television
series created by Andy Breckman

CENTER POINT LARGE PRINT
THORNDIKE, MAINE

This Center Point Large Print edition
is published in the year 2015 by arrangement with
New American Library, an imprint of Penguin Publishing
Group, a division of Penguin Random House LLC.

The text of this Large Print edition is unabridged.
In other aspects, this book may vary from the original edition.
Printed in the United States of America on permanent paper.
Set in 16-point Times New Roman type.

ISBN: 978-1-62899-650-0

Library of Congress Cataloging-in-Publication Data

Conrad, Hy.
Mr. Monk gets on board / Hy Conrad ; based on the USA Network
Television Series created by Andy Breckman. — Center Point Large
Print edition.
pages cm
Summary: "Monk and Natalie board a cruise ship to attend a business
seminar. But when the crew fishes the cruise director's body out of the
water and the ship's doctor declares her death an accident, Monk
suspects murder"—Provided by publisher.
ISBN 978-1-62899-650-0 (library binding : alk. paper)
1. Monk, Adrian (Fictitious character)—Fiction.
2. Private investigators—Fiction. 3. Eccentrics and eccentricities—
Fiction. 4. Obsessive-compulsive disorder—Fiction.
5. Cruise ships—Fiction. 6. Ocean travel—Fiction.
7. Murder—Investigation—Fiction. 8. Large type books.
I. Breckman, Andy. II. Monk (Television program) III. Title.
PS3553.O5166M69 2015
813'.54—dc23

2015020445

To Jeff, as always. Again.

AUTHOR'S NOTE
AND ACKNOWLEDGMENTS

One of the points of pride in the *Monk* writers' room was that we never threw out a script. In eight full seasons, there was never a *Monk* episode that didn't get final network approval. This is rare, probably some sort of record. No matter how much everyone may say they love a story line, most shows produce a script or two every year that gets thrown into the trash bin.

That being said, there was one *Monk* episode that we lost, through no fault of our own.

During season three, someone got the bright idea to put Monk and Sharona on a cruise ship. The USA Network loved it and we turned in a great script. Then came the job of securing a location. Turns out the cruise lines are sensitive about murders on their ships and people falling overboard.

We tried everything to persuade them. We changed the killer's identity, lowered the number of victims, etc. A close friend of mine—and a huge *Monk* fan—was marketing director for Norwegian Cruise Lines. She read the script and told me to get lost. In a last-ditch effort, we contemplated filming on the *Queen Mary*, now a floating hotel in Long Beach. But that fell through.

Over the next five years, whenever we got low on plot twists, we would turn longingly to "Mr. Monk Is at Sea" and make a few calls. It became our white whale, the one *Monk* that never got made. Episode 126.

If you haven't guessed by now, this is that story, the long-lost episode from the *Monk* canon. Although it has been fleshed out with Natalie instead of Sharona, various subplots, and a visit to Mexico to meet old friends, it's the same crazy, unimproved plot twist that six demented writers came up with back in 2004. Our oeuvre is complete.

In beginning this book, I called up Dan Dratch, the writer of record for "At Sea." After spending an hour telling me what it's like working with Charlie Sheen these days, Dan agreed to go into his archives and send me two completely different versions of the old script. Thanks, Dan.

In addition to Dan, contributors to the original include our fearless leader, Andy Breckman; his brilliant brother David, who probably came up with the murder method; Joe Toplyn, who tried his best to keep us within the bounds of reality; and comedy legend Tom Scharpling. I thank them all. Last but far from least, I owe a debt of gratitude to Talia Platz, my editor. The *Monk* books are stronger and cleaner due to her invaluable contributions.

I'd also like to give a shout-out to the regulars at

the Higgs Beach Dog Park in Key West. They had absolutely nothing to do with the book, but every evening they would greet us warmly, ask "Did you get your words in today?" and proceed to fill the next hour or so with lovely small talk. Much appreciated.

I

MR. MONK AND THE KISSING CLOWNS

Opening a business has been tougher than I thought it would be.

I don't mean filling out the incorporation papers or passing my California PI exam. Those were difficult but doable. I mean the actual process of acquiring paying clients and getting the rest of the world to take me seriously.

Before I put you to sleep with my whining, I suppose I should explain.

My name is Natalie Teeger, licensed private investigator and owner of Monk and Teeger, Consulting Detectives, LLC. I like the old-fashioned sound of "consulting detectives," like Sherlock Holmes and Dr. Watson, if Watson had ever decided to become Sherlock's full partner and get incorporated in the state of California. By the way, I am the same Natalie Teeger who used to be Adrian Monk's assistant.

You would think this would be a promotion, going from babysitting a brilliant investigator to being his boss. But since this big change, our world had stayed surprisingly unchanged. Our only regular client continued to be the San Francisco

Police Department. That wouldn't have been so bad except that the department was cutting back. Paying a private detective to do what your own people should be doing was no longer a priority.

It had been nearly a month since our last payday, a two-day case involving a deadly hit-and-run ice-cream truck, which wasn't as much fun as it sounds. The financial drought had made me desperate enough to spend a Saturday afternoon with the Noe Valley Small Business Guild, basically a neighborhood support group for loser businesses that shouldn't exist in the first place.

Right now I was perched uncomfortably on a folding chair in the strip mall storefront that was the headquarters of AmishMingle.com. That's right. Someone had actually created an Internet dating service for the world's Amish population, a religious sect that doesn't even use electricity, much less Wi-Fi.

This is what I've been reduced to, I thought as I sat there. *Sharing tips with an entrepreneur whose last big idea was to reinvent Amish dating.* His only customers so far were first cousins from the same farming community in Ohio.

The brains behind this small-business fiasco was Oliver Petrie. He stood in front of us in his nearly empty store, expounding upon his next brilliant idea. He was supposed to be asking our advice about his business plan, but I was sure he didn't want to hear mine.

Oliver held up a letter-sized flyer. It was a photo of two clowns in full makeup, male and female presumably, locked in a passionate kiss. Across the bottom was the URL in bold black letters: FUNDATE.COM.

"This is so much better than AmishMingle," he insisted. "It's for people who aren't so serious. Get it? Fun dates? I'm going to flood the city's mailboxes with this. Real mailboxes, not the e-mail ones that keep filtering out my stuff and calling it spam."

There were six of us staring at Oliver from our folding chairs. "I'm not sure I'd want this in my mailbox," said Jody Friedlander, squinting at the photo. Jody owned a pair of nail salons and was looking to expand. "It's kind of disturbing."

I had to agree. The photo would have been especially disturbing to my partner, who not only had an aversion to any display of affection, but a top-one-hundred phobia of clowns. If he ever asked me what we'd discussed in the meeting, which he never would, I'd have to make something up.

"Hmm." Oliver seemed to take Jody's critique seriously. "Well, that's why I sent out a test run, to see how people would react. It should be in your mailboxes when you get home. Let me know what your families think."

"In our home mailboxes?" I asked. "You sent us copies?"

"Yes, all seven of you." Oliver pointed to the

13

contact sheet on the business guild's bulletin board. "I trust those are your correct addresses."

All seven? I squinted across the room, as if this would be some sort of memory aid. "You listed your business partner as a contact," he reminded me. "I'd love to hear what he thinks."

Oliver was right. For some perverse reason, I had added Monk's name to the contact sheet, probably to let everyone know that my little agency was important enough to employ a world-class detective. And now this display of clown love was about to show up in his mail.

A chill went through me as I checked my watch. Two twenty. Andrew, Monk's mail carrier, made a point of trying to arrive at exactly 2:22 every afternoon. He didn't always succeed, but it was a game they both liked to play.

"Gotta go," I said, and jumped up so fast that my folding chair skidded across the floor. Within three minutes I was in my Subaru, speeding down Market Street, barely making every yellow light, hoping that Andrew might be running late with his deliveries.

I had no idea how Monk might react when he opened the envelope and was confronted by a flyer of kissing clowns. Actually, I did, which was what made me race through the yellows. At 2:29, I double-parked directly in front of Monk's building on Pine Street. I didn't bother to ring the bell, instead using my keys on both the downstairs door and upstairs on the door to apartment 2-G.

"Adrian?" I stepped into the silence, my ears alert for any faint moans or sobs. It had been only a few months since the big case that had forced Monk to impersonate a dead clown. During that adventure, he'd been kidnapped and almost killed. But that's a different story.

"Adrian, are you home?"

The living room was empty. So was the small dining room—except for the envelope and the creased flyer sitting open on the square oak table. If anything, the kissing clowns looked even more obscene in the midst of all this cleanliness and order. "Adrian, it's all right. I'll get rid of it." I crumpled the offending flyer and stuffed it into my pocket.

From down the hall came the sound of a flushing toilet. I walked forward and stood by the bathroom door. "Adrian, you can come out now." But there was no other sound coming from the bathroom. "Don't do anything rash," I shouted.

Instead, the bedroom door behind me opened. "Natalie?" And there he was in the doorway, a Swiffer in each hand, like long, dust-catching extensions of his arms. "Is the doorbell broken?"

"No," I said, feeling confused. "I just thought . . ." I did a double take, from Monk to the closed bathroom door and back to Monk. "Who's in the bathroom?"

"No one. I don't let people use my bathroom.

Do I look like a hippie?" He opened the hall utility closet and returned the Swiffers to their matching, evenly spaced hooks.

"But I heard a flush."

Monk threw me a thin smile. "I have the toilet set on automatic. It flushes every ten minutes, night and day, just in case."

"Just in case what?"

"In case the unthinkable happens."

I couldn't think what the unthinkable might be, which was probably what made it unthinkable. I knew, however, that Monk loved his toilet. It was the newest Japanese model and did everything from washing and drying your rear end to playing soothing music. It even came with a remote control and automatic settings.

"I'm sorry about the clown picture," I said. "One of the idiots at the business guild sent them out. Don't worry; I disposed of it."

"Why would he send me a picture of people kissing?"

I was taken aback. "They're not people, Adrian. They're clowns." He seemed a lot calmer than I'd expected.

"I know they're clowns," Monk said. "But that doesn't make it right."

Now I was taken aback and confused. "But you're afraid of clowns. They're one of your top one hundred. I spent endless hours trying to get you to solve a murder involving clowns."

"Right. Well, I guess it's over. I wish they weren't kissing."

"What are you saying? You no longer have clown fear?" I reached back into my mind for the right word. "Coulrophobia?"

He shrugged. "One day I was accidentally walking by the Jack in the Box on Geary Street near Union Square. I normally go around to Post Street, but the sidewalks on Taylor were blocked due to construction. I try to avoid Geary Street because of, you know, Jack."

He meant the spokesclown character for the hamburger chain, the guy with the round blue eyes and the red grin and the foam head. "I was all set to close my eyes," he added, "even though I was walking in the middle of a street. And then I realized I wasn't afraid. I couldn't have cared less about that Jack in the Box clown."

"Wow. Congratulations." It sounded like great news, although with Monk, you never could tell. "You've overcome one of your top hundred. Just like that."

"Dr. Bell says the clown case probably acted as a kind of immersion therapy. That's when you slowly immerse yourself in the thing you fear while keeping your mind on other things—in my case, being chained up in a clown lair, trying to survive without food or water."

Dr. Bell was Monk's saint of a psychiatrist, a man who deserved to win two Nobel prizes—one for medicine and the other for patience. Maybe a third for peace, since he had succeeded in making my life more peaceful.

"So you no longer have an irrational fear of clowns."

He nodded. "Now it's just a rational disdain, like everybody else over ten years of age."

"Great. You should use immersion therapy on everything."

"Immersion? No, no, no." Monk shuddered at the thought. And I'm sure he would have continued to shudder if my phone hadn't started ringing. I held up a finger—*hold that shudder*—and answered. "Monk and Teeger, Consulting Detectives. How may I direct your call? . . . Oh, hello, Lieutenant. What's up?"

It was Amy Devlin. Devlin was the number two in San Francisco's homicide division, right under Captain Leland Stottlemeyer, who happened to be one of Monk's oldest and only friends in the world.

I listened as Devlin outlined a rather baffling murder that had occurred the previous night in one of the grand mansions that still grace the stretch of Pacific Avenue that rolls past the edge of the Presidio. I didn't grasp too much of her description, as I was busy throwing Monk a big happy face and pumping my arm in the air. It was a job. Finally. "Interesting," I murmured. "I'll see if I can fit it into our schedule."

I took down the address, promised we would be there two minutes ago, and hung up. "Get your jacket," I ordered my assistant. "Please," I added. "We have a homicide."

Monk went to the hall closet to choose from among six identical jackets, all hung evenly across the bar. I took advantage of the delay to sneak a peek at the three-ring binder centered on the coffee table.

This was Monk's phobia binder, listing exactly one hundred major phobias—the ones that could reduce this genius to a quivering mass of genius jelly—followed by a list of more than three hundred minor phobias that could just annoy him and make my life a living hell. I flipped a few pages into it, past heights and crowds and milk and death.

Number ninety-nine. That's where clowns used to be, followed by aardvarks. I had expected aardvarks to have moved its way up to ninety-nine, followed by something bumped up from the minors. Instead I found a brand-new phobia that I wasn't sure even existed.

Number ninety-nine: *Fear of immersion therapy.*

2

MR. MONK AND THE OTHER CONSULTANT

The Melrose mansion, despite its location in the heart of the city, was an architectural throwback. Once we'd walked up the marble stairs to the double oak doors, we might as well have been time travelers, sent back to solve a case from a hundred years ago. Hmm, time-traveling detectives? That would be a fun read. I'll have to check Amazon to see whether there is such a book.

True to form, a butler outfitted in a black suit, black tie, and gray waistcoat met us at the door and led us up more marble steps to a second-floor library.

Usually when we arrive on a scene, the CSIs are there. More times than not, so is the body. When no one is around except witnesses, the cops, and a bloody stain on a Persian rug, it can mean only one thing: The case was old. Monk hadn't been needed. Not at first. Something must have happened to change this one from a routine homicide to a must-solve.

Captain Stottlemeyer was in the room, ready to air-shake Monk's hand. Stottlemeyer is the epitome of a senior cop, brusque when he needs to be, with thin remnants of sandy hair and a bushy mustache left over from the eighties. I want to use the word *burly,* but his apparent size is deceptive. Not so much burly as substantial.

Lieutenant Amy Devlin is also substantial, in a different way. My mother would call her snippy. But I can empathize with the lieutenant. We're both women in a profession where even the men feel the need to prove themselves. Devlin is tall and thin, with spiky black hair that looks different every time I see it. I want to use the word *wiry.* Can a tall person be wiry? Let's say yes and move on.

"Long time, no see," said the captain. "I keep telling the lieutenant we need to hire you more, just to keep in touch."

Monk didn't reply, but let his eyes roam the room. My partner likes to have a clean first impression. If something is wrong, he can usually feel it right away, even if it takes a week to figure out what it is.

To me, the library seemed even more old-worldly than the rest of the mansion. The side walls were lined with floor-to-ceiling book-shelves, all mahogany, with two library ladders, each serving one side. On one of the short walls was the door, flanked by a pair of marble busts of ugly dead males in togas. Greeks, I guessed. On the opposite wall was a tall window overlooking a lush garden. On each side of the window was an antique framed mirror. One reflected a pedestal, this one without an old Greek on top. The other reflected a leather-bound book on a book stand and a good-looking man in his forties examining the volume.

Stottlemeyer pretended the man wasn't there. "The owner of the house was Lester Melrose," he said. "Fifth-generation San Francisco money. They made their first fortune selling pickaxes to the gold miners." Stottlemeyer pointed to the stain I'd already seen on the Persian. "That's his blood."

"Melrose was sick," Monk said. How he knew this I couldn't tell.

"He was on his deathbed." Devlin made it sound like she was correcting him. "Last night he dismissed his doctor. Fired him. Then he called everyone in and changed his will one last time. He had just a few days to live, he said, and wanted to spend them in peace. When his son went to check on him this morning, his bed was empty. He was in here." She checked her notes. "Bludgeoned to death with the bust of Homer."

"Simpson?" I asked.

Devlin shook her head. "No last name, just Homer. They took the murder weapon to the lab."

"Was he bedridden?" I asked.

"No," Monk answered for everyone, and pointed to something nearly invisible on the Persian rug. "This room was cleaned yesterday by someone who knew what she was doing." Monk was referring to the perfectly straight parallel lines left by a strong vacuum cleaner. "But you can also see two wheel marks, eleven inches apart, going from the door over to the blood."

"And that tells you he wasn't bedridden?" Devlin asked.

I don't know how she could be skeptical after all these years of listening to Monk. As for me, I was once again marveling at how he can see things the rest of us look at but never notice.

"That's the wheelbase of a portable oxygen cylinder," Monk went on. "A common E tank. So, yes, I can tell he wasn't bedridden. Was the cylinder here when you arrived?"

"It was," Stottlemeyer answered. "It was also taken to the lab."

I cocked my head and scratched at my part. "So, someone killed a man with only a few days to live?"

I don't know why this surprised me, now that I think about it. Monk had once solved a case in which someone murdered a prison inmate on death row, a man with just hours to live before his execution. Our current case wasn't that extreme, but it was still puzzling.

"Why do you need two consultants?" Monk asked, looking a little pouty. "Don't you think I can handle this?" He was staring across at the man in the light jacket, who was still examining the old book on the book stand.

"What makes you think he's a consultant?" Stottlemeyer asked.

"Because," Monk explained, "he's wearing a non-police outdoor jacket, so he's not a member of your team or the household. He's been allowed into a crime scene. And his pin says 'ABAA.' It's obvious."

The man had his back to us. But I could see the reflection of a gold lapel pin, the letters tiny and reversed in the mirror but still legible. Okay, I told myself, you're a detective, Natalie. You're Monk's boss. You can figure it out. ABAA. And those initials must stand for . . . I thought and I thought. All I could come up with was maybe the guy was a member of an ABBA tribute band.

"Antiquarian Booksellers' Association of America," Monk whispered, although I was sure the man could overhear everything.

"Don't tell me," said Devlin. "Monk has memorized every single acronym in the world."

"Just the professional and sports organizations," said Monk modestly. "And just the top ten thousand. What would be the point of memorizing them all?"

"Well, you're right, Monk," the captain confirmed. "He's a rare book consultant who's worked with us on art fraud cases. We brought him in to verify the books in the Melrose collection."

Monk nodded. "Which means you're thinking

about a specific motive. Theft. Or the replacement of a rare book with a forgery."

Stottlemeyer nodded. "The Melroses are one of the city's old families. The mayor found the funds to hire a few consultants on this one, including you. Looks like we all lucked out."

As we'd been talking, the four of us, consciously or not, had formed a little semicircle, cutting our book expert out of the loop, at least visually. Now he was directly behind us, still holding the thick leather-bound volume. For the first time, I noticed he was wearing white linen gloves.

"It's genuine," he announced to the room. "A Shakespeare first folio. The first time the Bard's plays were ever printed, seven years after his death. There are two hundred thirty known copies, in various states of disrepair. I can't name you a price, but Paul Allen up the coast paid over six million for a similar one." Wow. No wonder this guy was wearing linen gloves.

I took a closer look at the six-million-dollar book. For being nearly four hundred years old, it was in great shape. I should look so good. It was larger than a normal book, maybe eight by twelve inches and maybe nine hundred pages long. He was holding it open, and I could see the pages were printed in double columns.

"How about the other books in the collection?" asked Devlin.

"Nothing else approaches the rarity of this," said the man. "They've been cataloged, as you know. Everything seems to be here." He didn't come across as overeducated or stuffy. Maybe that was due to the soft Southern accent that I couldn't quite place. I would have to listen to him more if I wanted to narrow down the region.

"Everything here?" Stottlemeyer brushed both sides of his mustache. "That nixes the robbery theory, not that it was a strong possibility."

"I'm Malcolm Leeds," the man said, looking me in the eye and lifting an elbow. His hands were obviously full. Plus, the gloves meant that our hands couldn't touch, although I could tell that he wanted them to.

"Natalie Teeger," I replied, keeping the eye focus. His were hazel, with a little more green than brown. I lifted my own elbow. "Of Monk and Teeger, Consulting Detectives. This is Adrian Monk."

Monk also lifted an elbow. He was always on the lookout for new ways not to shake hands.

"Sorry for skipping the introductions," said the captain. "But now I guess we confirmed the theory of an inside job. Monk, we're going to need you to do your magic here. Mr. Leeds, if you could, please wait downstairs, in case we have any questions."

"Of course." He removed his gloves and dropped them into his faux-leather messenger bag. Very Euro-stylish. "Can Natalie join me?" he asked. This opened everybody's eyes an extra millimeter. Malcolm smiled but kept his professional demeanor intact. "I can fill her in on the whole collection. It may wind up being important."

"It may," I agreed.

Stottlemeyer cocked his head in Monk's direction. "You think you can do this without your boss looking over your shoulder?"

Ever since I'd incorporated our agency, the captain has loved to tease Monk about being my employee. And Monk always took the bait.

"She's not my boss," he said, "except maybe in the legal and business sense."

"What do you think, Natalie?" asked the captain. "Can your guy handle this on his own?"

"Perfectly on my own," Monk said. "All I need is someone to hand me wipes and take care of all the other stuff."

I rummaged through my bag, found a pack of twenty moist wipes, and handed them off to Lieutenant Devlin. "Have fun," I told her.

"I will," said Monk.

The last thing I saw was my junior partner crossing to the library window, his gaze focused on a tiny white scrap of something on the parquet floor right under it. "Pick that up," he ordered Devlin, who snarled—literally snarled—then bent down to pick it up.

• • •

"How long have you guys been in business?"

"We've been incorporated for a few months," I told Malcolm Leeds. "It's been a slow start."

"Know how that goes," he said sympathetically. "I was consulting for most of a year before I started breaking even."

"Louisiana?" I finally guessed. "Say *New Orleans*."

He laughed. "Nuh Or-lens. And, yes, that's where I'm from. Born and bred."

"Sorry," I stammered like a schoolgirl. "It's not an insult. I love your drawl."

He held up a hand to stop me. "Not a drawl. Texans have a drawl. Alabamans have a twang. I have a Southern regional accent. I'll let you call it a lilt."

"I love your lilt."

"Better. Now what were we talking about? Consultin'?" He left off the "g." Very lilty.

"Uh, yes. Consulting."

"And things are a tad slow?"

"It's tough living on murder." I know how callous that sounds. But it was something I'd given a lot of thought to. "Adrian refuses to do divorce work. And when it comes to body-guarding or straight surveillance, there are better companies out there."

"I can't imagine your partner being a body-guard," Malcolm said.

28

"It's not pretty. He once did a bodyguarding assignment where the client actually had to protect him. My challenge is to get people to think of us whenever there's something unsolvable, not just murder."

"Perhaps a law firm could put you on retainer for criminal cases."

"I thought of that," I said. "But Monk can figure out pretty quickly if a guy's guilty. Lawyers don't always like that."

"Do you have much of a financial cushion? If you don't mind my asking."

I didn't mind. It was nice talking to someone who knew what he was talking about, as opposed to the clowns at the Noe Valley Small Business Guild.

Malcolm and I had retreated to the downstairs morning room. A morning room, from what I've heard, is a room with good morning light where the ladies could retreat while the maids were cleaning other parts of the mansion. I had no idea what the maids were up to here, but the butler had brought us tea, and we were sipping it very cozily in front of an unlighted fireplace.

When we'd walked out of the crime scene, I hardly thought Malcolm and I would wind up comparing marketing strategies. After all, he was tall and angular, with a face that was just beginning to show a certain sexy cragginess. Did I mention the hazel eyes?

To our mutual credit, we did spend our first few minutes flirting. Harmless flirting. Somewhere along the way, one of us—it could have been me—suggested we might get together for a drink that evening. That's when we exchanged cards and started talking shop.

"Monk and I got a reward from our last big case," I said. "But I feel guilty about dipping into that."

"Don't," he said. "Feel guilty, that is. You gotta establish yourself. Get out and network. I remember when I started. I took this seven-day, six-night business conference on the *Golden Sun*. Seemed like a splurge. But it led to my first gig with the police department. Best money I ever spent."

"What's the *Golden Sun*?"

"A cruise ship."

"Never heard of it. What line?"

"It's independent," he said. "The ship has seen better days. But they run these business conferences every couple of months. You can meet a lot of clients in a very friendly atmosphere. Plus, it gives you a few days in the Mexican sun. I've done it five times myself."

"Five times?"

"The connections alone are worth the price."

"On a cruise ship?" I had to laugh out loud. "No. I could never get my partner on a cruise ship, especially an old one. There aren't enough antiseptic wipes in the world. . . ."

"Don't take him. You're the business end. Why does he have to go?"

"Go without Monk?" The idea was a shock, a wonderfully appealing shock. "It wouldn't feel right."

"Why not? Can't he survive without you?" Malcolm laughed.

"I know you mean that as a joke," I said, "but I'm kind of essential to his process. The last time he tried solving a case without me, he almost died."

"Wow." His smile crinkled. "I'm impressed."

"Of course, we don't have another case now, not after this one. Sometimes we go for weeks."

"So take the cruise. Look, it's your call. You're the company honcho."

Malcolm was right. It was my call. If Monk didn't want to join me for a seven-days-at-sea business conference, he could just stay home. "You're right," I confirmed. "I am the honcho."

"Natalie?" The word had come from the doorway and was spoken as a high-pitched whine. "Natalie?"

I didn't even bother to look. "What is it, Adrian?"

"You can take me home. I'm ready."

How humiliating. "What if I'm not ready, Adrian?"

Monk snorted. "How can you not be ready?"

Out of the corner of my eye I could see Malcolm stifling a yawn. Oh no. I was boring him already.

"Sorry," he said, recovering. "Still getting over my jet lag."

"Oh, really?" I said, ignoring Monk's impatience. "Where from?"

"New York," said Malcolm. "A buying spree for late medieval medical texts. I actually found one in High German. Most of them are in Latin."

"People really buy those?"

"God, I hope so," he said with a mock grimace. "So, are we on for tonight? Around eight?" He reached into his messenger bag and pulled out a watch. It looked like a Rolex. "Still on New York time," he said, chuckling, and began to wind the stem.

"If you two are done with your chitchat," Monk said, tapping his foot.

"It's not chitchat," I said, perhaps not accurately.

"Well, I'm the one who examined the crime scene and interviewed everyone who was in the house last night and told the captain to drain the pond. What have you been doing?"

"I'll have you know that I have been talking serious business with Mr. Leeds and—hold on. You told them to drain the pond? What pond?"

"There's a pond out in the garden, covered with lily pads."

"Is it dirty? Is that why you want it drained?"

"Yes, it's dirty. Filthy with nature. But that's not the reason. Whatever's at the bottom of the pond is going to solve the case."

"Sorry," I said to Malcolm. "This is what happens when you have a partner."

"Don't apologize," said Malcolm. "You two are fascinating."

I felt like blushing. Instead, I turned to Monk. "Do you know what's down there or are you just guessing?"

Monk twitched his nose and rolled his shoulders. "I'm eighty-six percent sure. We won't know a hundred percent until it's drained."

3

MR. MONK AND MS. CHRISTIE

I felt bad about my behavior that afternoon, at least after the fact. I couldn't remember the last time I'd left Monk alone at a crime scene. We were supposed to be partners, and I should have stayed at his side and helped to figure out who had killed an old man already on his deathbed.

My only excuse . . . Make that three excuses. One, I had felt sure that Monk would do fine. He was already at eighty-six percent. Two, my contribution was mainly on the business end, and that's what I'd been taking care of—networking with Mr. Malcolm Leeds. And three, let me mention once again the hazel eyes.

In my attempt to soothe the guilt, I decided to forgo the latest episode of *Downton Abbey*, which was calling out to me sweetly from my DVR. I had been looking forward to it all day. But this was more important. I needed to catch up on the mystery in this mansion before catching up on the ones in that mansion. I certainly couldn't let Monk solve it without my even knowing the details.

Luckily, Lieutenant Devlin takes good notes—succinct and easy to follow. She had e-mailed them to the captain and me but not to Monk, since he doesn't own a computer and would remember everything anyway, down to the number of red tassels on the curtains in the front hall.

Dinner that evening was a paillard from the freezer, left over from my daughter Julie's visit last weekend, when we spent a few great hours pounding chicken breasts and cooking them and eating together. Tonight, I added some freshly steamed snow peas. Dessert was a printout of Devlin's report, served in the living room in front of the dark, taunting face of my TV. As a side dish, I poured a nice glass of Barolo, then turned off my phone and got to work.

According to the lieutenant, the mansion on Pacific Avenue had been occupied by three individuals that night, four if you count the victim. There had been no sign of a break-in, which was kind of refreshing. Almost every inside job these days seems to involve a halfhearted attempt to make it look like a break-in. In this case, the killer didn't even try. Nothing at all seemed to be missing from the house.

Devlin had included a photo of each suspect, taken with her iPhone and with their consent. The first was the victim's son, Jeremiah Melrose, who wisely went by the nickname Jerry. The man looked to be about fifty, with a large frame and a thin, pinched gray face. The kind of face that always looked hungry.

Jerry had taken over as president of First Mercantile, the century-old family bank. He was rich in his own right and, as Lester's only child, stood to inherit most of his father's assets, including the mansion, which he could probably sell off as a small hotel. Jerry was divorced, had no children, and lived on the second floor, in the wing opposite his father's.

Second on the list was Portia Braun. She was a rare book curator hired by the Melrose Foundation four months ago to catalog the mansion's library. Apparently, the library is not only a pretty room. It's a big deal. At least it was to Lester Melrose. As his final contribution to his legacy, he had brought Portia over from the University of Munich to make some sense of the thousands of old volumes. He had offered to put her up in the cavernous old mansion, and she'd accepted.

From the beginning, Jerry Melrose had been on his guard with Portia. His father was a sick seventy-six-year-old who was now spending half of each day with a German bombshell. Okay, *bombshell* may be an overstatement for a forty-something academic. But from Devlin's snapshot, Portia was still quite attractive, with long blond hair, a trim figure, and a wide, ingratiating smile. And Lester, it seemed, hadn't been too old or sick to notice.

The family soap opera had all come to a head the previous night, Portia's last night at the mansion. Her work on the library was finally complete, and the next day she would be heading off to another job, wherever that might have been. Lester, despite his health and his ever-present oxygen tank, had arranged an intimate farewell in his bedroom—just him, Portia, Jerry, the butler, and the family lawyer.

Yes, I did say *lawyer*. I can just imagine how Jerry Melrose must have felt walking into the old man's room and finding an attorney from Brace & Feingold, who was looking embarrassed and holding a fresh codicil to his father's last will and testament.

According to the butler, Melrose senior said he wasn't giving it away as a frivolous gift, but was doing it for the sake of humanity, for the good of future generations of scholars. What it amounted to was that Portia Braun, a virtual stranger, not to mention a foreigner, was suddenly going to inherit the pride of the Melrose family: the Shakespeare first folio.

Jerry tried to talk his father out of it. And so did Portia, believe it or not. From what Smithson the butler said, she seemed genuinely surprised and, to her credit, more reluctant to accept his generosity than anyone might have imagined. But the ink was dry and Lester was insistent. Smithson and the lawyer signed on as witnesses.

As the four of them walked out of the dying man's room, Jerry had been overheard hissing to the sexy German scholar, "I want you out of this house tomorrow morning. Whatever business you have, do it through a lawyer. I don't ever want to hear from you again."

Smithson later testified that he let out the lawyer, locked the heavy front doors but neglected, as seemed to be his habit, to set the alarm system. The butler retired to his quarters on the third floor, while Jerry went off to his own wing and Portia retreated to a guest room on the first floor.

Given the size and sturdiness of the Melrose mansion, it wasn't surprising that no one heard any noise during the night. You could have played basketball in the library and not disturbed the other floors or wings. The next morning, at a few minutes after seven, Jerry went to check on his father, saw that the bedroom was empty, and walked one room down the hall to find the old man bludgeoned to death with Homer, lying on the Persian carpet.

I put down the pages from Devlin's report and didn't even think about reaching for the DVR remote. This wasn't quite *Downton Abbey*, more like an Agatha Christie novel with a limited cast of suspects. But it was fascinating.

First there was the enraged son, Jerry, aka Jeremiah, who had just seen a family heirloom given away on a whim. Then came the exotic stranger, Portia Braun, who had charmed a dying man to the tune of a six-million-dollar book. Last, of course, was the butler. I was really hoping it would turn out to be the butler.

The only trouble was that none of them had a motive, not that I could figure. And what was the deal with the lily pond? After doing his usual inspection of the library, holding up his hands and wandering around like a movie director, Monk had instructed the captain to drain the backyard pond. I carefully read the rest of Devlin's report but still couldn't figure out what extra detail my partner had latched onto, which, I'm embarrassed to say, is not unusual.

I was beginning to fantasize about all the possible permutations. Was anyone, Jerry or Smithson, having an affair with the German temptress? Had anyone in the mansion opened the door to a late-arriving stranger? Could all of them have done it together?

It seemed obvious that something had gone on in the library, something that had made a sick man get out of bed and roll his oxygen tank in there. What could it have been?

I drained the last gulp of my Barolo, turned my phone back on, and immediately saw I had two messages. Both from Malcolm Leeds. Damn. I had forgotten all about our vague, flirty agreement to get together.

I pressed CALL BACK and spent the next two seconds trying to decide how apologetic to sound. The armchair I was sitting in was close to the front door, and I was stunned to hear a phone start ringing right out on my porch. Why was there a cell phone ringing on my porch?

I figured this puzzle out almost instantly, although it took me a few tries to wipe the girlish grin off my face. By the time I opened the door, it was down to a bemused smirk. "Malcolm."

He was standing in front of me, one hand holding my business card, the other hand holding his ringing phone. His face was also displaying a bemused smirk. "I'm not going to answer this," he said.

"I wouldn't," I said, and pressed END. "I think it's that crazy woman you met this afternoon."

We both laughed, and our rush of apologies tripped over each other. He was sorry for tracking me down at my address. I was sorry for forgetting our drink. He was sorry for not being more specific about this evening. I was sorry for turning off my phone.

I invited him in, then made a quick visual sweep of the living room. Not bad. One wineglass, a raft of printouts on the coffee table, and a folded copy of the *Chronicle* on the sofa, left over from the morning. It's usually worse.

We made our way into the kitchen to find the rest of my bottle of Barolo. Another visual sweep. A lot worse in here, especially the counters. I'm not the neatest cook in the world, even when I'm just doing leftovers and snow peas. Malcolm behaved like a gentleman and pretended not to notice.

"Have you given more thought to the cruise?" he asked as soon as we'd turned our back on the clutter and poured and toasted. "I'm thinking of doing it again. Number six."

Only once before had I been on a cruise, to Alaska to celebrate my grandparents' fiftieth anniversary, along with the rest of our huge extended family. It had been a great experience but might have been even greater without running into a Teeger around every corner.

I had become interested enough to check out the cruise Malcolm recommended online. It was called the B. to Sea Conference, an awkward little play on words—"taking business to sea," as their tagline promised. It was a combination of a few seminars and more than a few chances to network with a business card in one hand and an umbrella drink in the other. Plus a bonus: Malcolm had just said he might go. I couldn't imagine a better venue for a real first date.

"I thought about it," I replied. "But I need to invite my partner. It's only right."

"I'm guessing he won't come." Malcolm stepped a foot closer, tipping down his head to look me in the eyes.

"I'm guessing so, too," I said. Okay, this may sound like a banal exchange, but it was actually quite sexy.

A second later, my phone on the counter did a quick little vibrate-and-ping. Before I could even look, Malcolm's phone did the same from his jacket pocket.

"It's Lieutenant Devlin," I said, reading from my screen. "They found what they were looking for at the bottom of the pond. I have to bring Monk over tomorrow morning to wrap things up."

"I'm supposed to be there, too," Malcolm said, holding up his phone and showing me an identical text from Devlin. "Why do they want me?"

"You're the book expert. Must have something to do with books."

"I told them everything I know." All the flirtation had left his voice. "I don't understand."

"You'll get paid for your time," I pointed out. "And you'll get to see how Adrian solves a case. It can be a memorable moment."

"You mean they're going to arrest the killer? On the spot?"

"If we're lucky." I didn't want to get his hopes up, but this had the earmarks of a classic, with Monk standing in a room of suspects and pointing to the killer. Given the prevalence of DNA and electronic evidence, we don't get many classics anymore, not like in the old days. It would be a sight to behold.

"Sounds exciting," he said, but his expression conveyed something else. Was he just feeling out of his element? A little apprehensive? I can't imagine that antiquarian book experts deal with the arrest of many murderers.

Or could something else be going through his mind, something more sinister?

Please, I said to myself, my heart beginning to sink. *Don't let it be something else.*

4

MR. MONK AND POND SCUM

By nine a.m. we were gathered in the Melrose library. There was the police contingent: captain and lieutenant, looking serious and overworked, with Devlin standing firmly by the room's only exit. There were the consulting detectives: Monk and yours truly. There were the three suspects: Jeremiah Melrose, Portia Braun, and Smithson. And finally the interested observer: Malcolm Leeds, looking just as nervous as the suspects.

All night long, I'd had a bad feeling. I couldn't imagine Malcolm, my tall, craggy academic, being involved. But the truth was, I'd known him only a day. And it wasn't as if I'd never been interested in a man who later turned out to be a cold-blooded killer. It's happened more than once. In fact, it's probably Monk's most reliable way of keeping me single and lonely.

My only consolation was that Malcolm's involvement seemed impossible. He had never been in the Melrose mansion prior to the murder. And he'd never been left alone in the library. But of course, with Monk, the impossible is always possible.

"This won't take long," said Monk to everyone. He was pacing in front of the library's only window, his fingers laced together as if in prayer. Public speaking has never been his strength, except when it comes to murder. Then he can raise his voice and be a powerful presence. It's all about his comfort zone.

"When I was in here yesterday I noticed the petal from a little white flower on the floor under the window." From his side jacket pocket Monk pulled out a sanitary wipe, which was folded into a perfect square. He unfolded it twice. In the middle of the white was another speck of white, a delicate, flowery petal.

"It belongs on that tree," said Monk, and nodded out toward a good-sized tree with gray-brown bark, a few yards to the side of the window. "That's a calabash tree. We used to have one in our yard growing up." He handed the petal and the wipe to Captain Stottlemeyer.

"Thanks, Monk," said the captain, staring at the petal. "I'll have someone reattach it as soon as possible."

"You don't have to reattach it," Monk said. "Well, you could. That would be nice. But you don't have to."

"I appreciate your flexibility," said Stottlemeyer, still with a straight face.

"You can attach it later. I just wanted to establish that it's a night-blooming calabash. They bloom at night," Monk repeated, "and fold up during the day. Like now. No petals." I glanced past him to the tree and could confirm this fact.

We all started to understand around the same moment. That's what he was getting at. It had been chilly for the past few nights, as it often is in San Francisco. And the petal that had drifted inside was not completely shriveled, not more than a day or so.

"You're saying someone opened this window that night," said Smithson. "For a purpose. To let someone in, perhaps?"

"No, to throw something out." Monk pointed to the lily pond, or what used to be a lily pond. It was now a muddy hole, almost centered in front of the window, round and about the size of a baseball diamond. The police draining equipment was still on the bank, all the pumps and hoses.

"I saw that the lilies on the surface had been disturbed," Monk said. "That's why I had it drained. Someone opened this window and threw something into the pond."

Immediately I tried to imagine what it might be. The murder weapon? No, that had been the bloody Homer. Something priceless from the library? No, nothing seemed to be missing. Something incriminating? Maybe. But what?

Lieutenant Devlin, true to her no-nonsense self, reached into a bag, pulled out a huge plastic baggie, and plopped it onto a circular library table. "We pulled this out last night." The rest of us gathered around. I don't know what I'd been expecting, but this wasn't it.

"It's the first folio," Jerry Melrose said, instantly recognizing the book. "But no, it can't be."

It certainly looked like a waterlogged twin of the Shakespeare rarity, with its buckled leather cover and the horizontal row of ridges along the spine. The only difference was that this one was wet and in plastic, and the other was sitting proudly on its mahogany book stand.

Malcolm seemed most intrigued by the find. "May I?" he asked, pulling a pair of linen gloves from his faux-leather messenger bag. Did the man always carry gloves? I certainly hadn't noticed any last night at my place.

With deft ease, Malcolm unzipped the plastic bag, extracted the water-damaged book, and laid it out on a second circular library table. He examined the binding and pried apart the soggy pages. He pulled a jeweler's loupe from his bag for a closer inspection. Finally he looked up and turned to Monk. "It's a very good fake."

"Of course it's a fake," said Monk. "I knew that when it was still covered in lilies."

"You knew a fake Shakespeare was in the pond?" asked a skeptical Devlin.

"Eighty-six percent," said Monk. "It's the only thing that made sense." Meanwhile, the captain and the lieutenant were staring at Malcolm. Staring hard.

At this point, my mind was spinning. I finally meet a sexy, smart, single man and what now? I'm going to have to start visiting him in San Quentin?

"I've never been in this house before yesterday," protested Malcolm. "I've never seen this folio or met Miss Braun before."

"He's innocent," I told anyone who would listen.

Monk shook his head and snorted. "Of course he is. The killer is Portia Braun."

His accusation took the rest of us by surprise, especially Portia Braun.

"This is preposterous," the woman sputtered in her light but distinct accent. "I demand an apology." But no one cared.

From here on everything moved quickly. The German curator was restrained, Jerry said "I knew it" a few too many times, and Monk settled in to explain.

The stumbling block in this case, according to my partner, had always been motive. Lester Melrose had just changed his will. His son wouldn't profit from killing him. The butler didn't inherit. And Portia had just received an immense, unexpected gift. All she had to do was wait a day until Lester died of natural causes.

But the fact that something had been thrown into the pond . . . That had prompted Monk to think in a new direction. What if the motive hadn't been to take something valuable from the room but to return it? And that had led him to his eighty-six-percent theory.

Portia had always had her eye on the prize. The first folio was a curator's dream. It could be sold quickly and quietly with few questions asked. So, during her time in San Francisco, Portia had gone about the task of having a passable forgery made. After that, it would be a simple matter of substituting the fake for the original.

By her last day on the job, Portia had done it and was ready to walk out the door with the six-million-dollar treasure tucked in her luggage, never to return. But then came the unexpected. She'd been too nice to old Lester. He had willed her the first folio. And that was the last thing she'd wanted. She tried to turn down the gift but it was no use.

So here was her problem. When the old man died, any day now, the estate would go into probate, and another hired expert would be brought in and would discover the substitution. Portia's only option was to put the original back on the book stand and wait until she legally inherited it.

She had been in the process of sneaking it back that night, when Lester caught her in the library, red-handed, with two versions of his priceless book. That's why she had to kill him. And that's why Monk hadn't been surprised to find a Shakespeare forgery lying at the bottom of a lily pond.

Once or twice during this process, I glanced over to Malcolm. The antiquarian dealer seemed a little stunned, standing protectively over the original folio, while the rest of us continued with the nitty-gritty police work.

As far as proof went, things were a little skimpy. Monk had revealed no real evidence, and Portia stubbornly refused to confess.

On the plus side, Malcolm would get a few more days of consulting from the department as he narrowed down a list of forgers who might have produced the lily pond Shakespeare.

"Do you think she'll be convicted?" Malcolm asked a half hour later as the two of us strolled out the front door of the Pacific Avenue mansion. Monk was somewhere behind me. I wasn't paying attention.

"Probably," I said. "I don't mean to brag, but the firm of Monk and Teeger has a pretty solid conviction rate."

"For a while you thought I was involved. Why? Because the East Germans are so honest and us Southern boys are all crooks?"

"No," I said. "It has nothing to do with your drawl—accent. I mean lilt. I told everyone you were innocent."

"You said it like you didn't believe it."

"Okay. Maybe I've had a few bad experiences with handsome killers," I admitted. "That happens when you're a PI."

"So you did think I might be a killer. A handsome killer, but still . . ."

"No, I didn't. And if I did for a split second, I apologize. Force of habit."

"I don't accept," he said with a sexy pout. "But you can make it up to me on that B. to Sea cruise you need to go on. If you'd like, we can cut expenses and share a cabin."

The nerve! We barely knew each other. "We are not sharing a cabin," I said. "This is a business trip. I'll pay for my own." And just like that, I made up my mind. I was going on a cruise.

5

MR. MONK
ON CRUISE CONTROL

Ten days later, Julie was dropping me off at the cruise terminal at Pier 35, just a few dozen blocks from home. She had agreed to take care of my aging Subaru while I was gone and to check the house every other day. Ever since I'd found a dead woman floating in my bathtub last year, I've become more cautious about home security.

The interval between the Melrose case and the cruise had not been a tranquil ten days. First there was the "Monk and Teeger" brochure to put together and print, a glossy four-pager featuring a smiling photo of me and an unsmiling one of my partner, plus details from our most famous cases. A lot of the success of this trip would hinge on networking, and I needed to be ready to impress. Second was the matter of culling through my wardrobe and finding some combination of business and resort wear that would be appropriate for all occasions.

Third, fourth, fifth, and sixth was dealing with Monk.

I first brought up the cruise one afternoon after Monk's hardworking washing machine had broken and he was forced to call me, 911, the Center for Disease Control, and the Maytag Service Center, in that order, to help deal with the catastrophe. Normally, I would have chosen a calmer moment to bring up such a topic. The difference this time? I didn't really want him to say yes.

"A cruise?" he said, already shaking his head.

"It's a conference," I countered, "on a cruise ship going down the California coast. Perfectly safe." I felt I had to give it an honest try. Otherwise he would get suspicious.

"A conference on a boat." He laughed in the way that means it's not funny. "That makes no sense. A boat is a mode of transportation. You may as well have a conference on an airplane or a kayak."

"This one is on a boat. Are you coming?"

He thought about it. "Can I can get off anytime I want?"

"No, that's not how a boat works. Think of it as an island. A small island. You've been on an island, right?"

Monk wrinkled his nose and looked disappointed. "You know, you've used the island argument on me before."

"Really?" I remembered exactly when I'd used the island argument, and I'd known that he would, too.

"When you conned me into going on that

submarine a few years ago. You know, the submarine that went underwater and had low ceilings and no place to sleep except a bunk bed surrounded by dozens of snoring men in other bunk beds?"

"Don't forget the murderous captain who locked us in a ballast tank and almost drowned us." This was all worth remembering.

"Exactly," he agreed. "How can you even suggest going on a ship after that?"

"Especially an older ship."

"Exactly," he agreed again. Then he stamped his foot—lightly, so he wouldn't disturb the nap of his living room rug. "I've seen the way you look at that Malcolm fellow. You're just doing it for him."

"No, I'm not."

"He lied to you." Monk was getting desperate now. "Malcolm said he was in New York a few days ago, and he wasn't."

"Adrian, stop it. You're not doing this to me again. Every man tells little lies. It's part of being a man."

"So you don't want to hear about Malcolm?"

"Is he a killer?"

"What? Is that your litmus test? Is that where you're setting the bar? You'll date anyone who's not a cold-blooded killer?"

"Pretty much."

Monk shrugged. "Well, he's not. But he doesn't really like you."

"Shut up." I've never been in the habit of saying "shut up" to Monk. But there are moments . . .

"Malcolm may already have another girlfriend."

"Shut up."

"You can't go on that cruise, Natalie. I forbid it."

My mouth fell open, then returned to speaking mode. "You can't forbid it. The cruise will be good for business and we have the money."

"We?" He was aghast, almost sputtering, except sputtering would be too messy. "You're using company money? I thought you were treating me."

"Treating you? Where would I get the money to treat you?"

Half an hour later, just as the man from Maytag finally rang the bell, Monk was right where I wanted him, apoplectic and refusing to even consider reconsidering his decision. I felt kind of bad. But not that bad.

The next time we spoke was when he called me, minutes before Julie and I left for the terminal. He kindly reassured me that I was on my way to a watery grave, "probably at the hands of an iceberg," he said. After I died, our company would go bankrupt and he would starve and it would all be my fault. Bon voyage!

"Adrian has your number," I told Julie as we pulled up to the curb. My daughter was a Cal Berkeley senior now, busy with her own life and friends across the bay. But she's always had a soft spot for Monk and a real tough-love way of dealing with him. "He won't be afraid to call you."

"No problem," said Julie. "I'm surprised he hasn't called already."

"Maybe that means he'll be fine," I said without believing it.

"What does he think about Malcolm?" Julie asked, turning to me with a wicked grin. "Is he going to accuse Malcolm of murder? Or tell you the man's a leper? That's his usual way of dealing with your boyfriends."

I knew I shouldn't have told Julie anything. When will I learn? "First off, Malcolm isn't a boyfriend. He came over for drinks and we talked business."

"But you like him. And you're going to be spending seven days with him."

"Him and five hundred others," I pointed out.

"Didn't he ask you to share a cabin?"

"It was a joke," I said, even though it probably hadn't been.

The family in the car behind us tapped its horn, hoping to take our place at the drop-off curb. As I undid my seatbelt, Julie leaned over from the driver's seat and gave me a peck on the cheek. "Have fun," she said. "Don't do anything I wouldn't."

It was a familiar scene for us both, only in

reverse. Over the past ten years, it had always been me in the driver's seat, kissing her on the cheek, warning her to be safe on whatever little trip she was taking, then watching in the rearview as she pulled her suitcase out of the trunk . . . Actually, I never just sat there. I always got out and helped and hugged her a dozen more times, which I'm glad she didn't do. Julie hated that part. Plus, the family behind us was already staring daggers.

There was a ton of control points inside the cruise terminal, all of them with lines—a ticket line, a passport line, a line to drop your luggage. Last was the table where I registered for the B. to Sea Conference and picked up my information pack.

"Be sure to put this on," said the representative at the table. He was holding out a red plastic name tag: NATALIE TEEGER. PRESIDENT. MONK AND TEEGER. It sounds silly, but the tag looked so official that I took a moment to gaze at it and be proud. Check me out, president of a company at a business conference. I didn't want to get my hopes up, but this looked like fun.

It was a slightly different matter when I got out to the gangway and caught my first glimpse of the *Golden Sun*.

Malcolm had warned me the ship was privately owned and "had seen better days." When I'd checked it out online, I'd realized this was true. It wasn't one of the new super cruise ships, with climbing walls and three-story waterslides. I don't know how to gauge the age of a ship. I'm bad even with cars. But the *Golden Sun* was at least in its thirties, maybe older than me, heaven forbid. It also had a few more dings than me and a paint job that didn't even try to cover them up.

The *Golden Sun* was built in a classic style, with relatively small decks, a long prow, and three smokestacks, one less than the *Titanic*. Somehow, seeing it in person, floating at the dock next to a cheery white Carnival Fun Ship, made it seem even less inviting.

At least the crew was nice. As soon as I stepped on board, a smiling girl, around Julie's age, welcomed me with a flute of nonalcoholic bubbly, and a photographer asked me to smile. The third person in the receiving line was another young thing, this one labeled MARIAH. CRUISE DIRECTOR. MONTEREY, CA. "Welcome aboard the *Golden Sun*."

"Hi. I'm from Monterey, too," I gushed, as if we should somehow know each other.

"I knew I liked you," she gushed back, and gave me a quick, warm hug. Mariah Linkletter was one of those genuinely bright souls, the kind of woman you can't help liking, even if she did happen to be a tall, willowy redhead with just the right number of freckles. "Monterey High?" she asked.

"Stevenson," I said. I was a little embarrassed to claim the town's snooty day school as my own, so I changed subjects. "Mariah? That's unusual."

"My mom listened to a lot of Mariah Carey when she was carrying me."

"Mariah Carey?" It was a harsh reminder of just how quickly time flies. "You're that young?"

"Not that young."

"But then your last name is Linkletter, like Art Linkletter." I was rewarded with a blank stare. No recognition for Art. "Okay, you are that young."

Mariah laughed, then leaned in to whisper. "There's a hidden bar on the Valencia deck. We'll have to share some Monterey stories when you get a chance."

"Valencia deck," I confirmed. "See you there."

The crackle of a walkie-talkie in her left hand reminded both of us that she was on duty. "Mariah?" a female voice squawked. "We have a guest with eight pieces and no place to fit them."

"Excuse me," said Mariah, and pushed a button. "Ginny? Tell them we can store whatever they're not using at the moment. Will that be okay?"

There was a pause, then more crackling. "He says no. He's got one suitcase just full of bottled water."

"Water?" Mariah laughed. "Tell him the water on board is fine."

"He doesn't believe me."

Mariah laughed again, as if this was all part of the fun. "Some people. Excuse me." She asked for the cabin number of the problem passenger—457—and excused herself again before heading for a staircase and disappearing up to the next level.

I had to laugh myself. It sounded just like Monk, didn't it? Bringing his own water? I felt oddly reassured to see that other people could deal with my kind of problems and maintain a sense of humor.

I actually made it all the way up to my cabin—555—without guessing. I unlocked the door to find my two little bags waiting for me in a charming room for two, just big enough for one, with the sweetest little balcony. I could just imagine myself out there every morning enjoying my coffee and my . . . Then it hit me like a ton of bricks.

What were the chances that, on a ship of five hundred, all of them successful, well-adjusted business owners, there could be another man acting this way, bringing eight huge suitcases and his own supply of bottled water? Damn.

The very last thing I wanted to do was to run down to cabin 457 and help deal with Monk and his luggage. Maybe I could just hide for the next seven days. No, I finally told myself. I had to do it. The sooner, the better.

"Adrian?"

As soon I hit the bottom of the stairs, I could see the commotion halfway down the hall. There were the familiar black suitcases piled up, the ones he kept in his hermetically sealed storage unit two blocks from his apartment. Half a dozen passen-gers were trying to squeeze by in each direction, but somehow I made it through.

"Natalie."

Monk was just inside the doorway of a room nearly identical to mine. Standing with him were Mariah and a distinguished-looking man in a pressed white uniform. In the few minutes since I'd last seen the cruise director, the situation had escalated enough to require the attention of this man, the ship's captain. How mortifying.

"Natalie, don't worry. The captain's going to store my bags in the executive VIP dry cleaning suite. Triple-filtered air and no other luggage."

"That's right," said the captain, with just the hint of a wink my way. "Pick out what you need for tonight and tomorrow, sir, and I'll have a steward take the rest away. You can take out other things as you need them."

"Thank you," I said. And before I could even introduce myself or try to explain my partner's odd behavior, the captain was making his way down the hall.

"That was Captain Sheffield," Mariah said almost apologetically. "He's very busy, but I'm sure you'll get a chance to talk. He's a wonderful man."

I had known the captain for only a few seconds but, honestly, he didn't seem wonderful. He was, to my eye, a smug authority figure who lied way too easily. And I resented his condescending attitude. I'm not saying that people can't be condescending. I'm just saying they should get to know us first.

"He triple-filters his air," Monk said, obviously in agreement with Mariah about the captain.

"I take it you and Mr. Monk are friends," Mariah said.

"We're more than friends," Monk answered, staring straight into my eyes. "We're business partners who share everything fifty-fifty. And one of us would never try to act superior and cut the other out of all the business decisions, although if there was a partner who actually happened to be superior on this team, it would be me."

"Well, I'm glad we got everything straightened out," said Mariah, who then turned to leave. "See you on the Valencia deck," she whispered.

"Valencia deck," I confirmed, with the weakest of smiles.

6

MR. MONK AND HIS CABIN

After Mariah left and we'd managed to drag all eight bags into the cabin, I helped Monk with the task of finding places for as much as possible: his five gray checkered shirts, his ten backup gray checkered shirts, his three dark brown jackets, his six backup dark brown jackets. His emergency medical supplies. His backup . . . You get the picture. We were actually finding places for about half of it, even if the cabin was beginning to resemble a closet.

"I'm glad you decided to come," I said as we were starting to unpack the dozens of bottles of Fiji Water. And I half meant it.

It had been selfish of me to want to do this by myself. This wasn't a vacation. It was a chance for us to learn how a business works, to network, and to get people to think of us when they had special problems. Monk was an essential part of that, the heart of it. And he should be here to represent that.

But I also knew what this entailed. I would wind up babysitting him and apologizing to half the ship for the next seven days. And I probably wouldn't have time to enjoy Mexico or to get to know Malcolm on a more personal level. But as some character said in some *Godfather* movie that Captain Stottlemeyer loves to quote, "This is the business we've chosen." Despite everything, I cared deeply for the obsessive little lug, and I'd chosen to be his partner.

I thought back to life before Monk. There I'd been, the widow of a Navy pilot with a young daughter and a dead-end job, where my biggest challenge was serving beers to tattooed bikers and trying to keep their hands off me. Then came Monk, and I had a reason to get up and get excited again. I was working alongside one of the greatest detectives alive, putting away bad guys. I couldn't let myself forget that.

"You shouldn't have come without me," Monk scolded.

"You're right, Adrian. But now you're on a ship. A few years ago, you would have been kicking and screaming. But you came of your own free will. By the way, how did you get here with eight suitcases?"

"Luther, of course."

"Of course." He was referring to Luther Washington, a young, ambitious, very clean entrepreneur who ran a small limousine company that Monk had bought using the reward money from an earlier case.

"Luther and I have been working on this for days behind your back. I even let him help me pack."

"So this wasn't a spur-of-the-moment thing."

"I didn't tell you, because I didn't want you to talk me out of it again—you and your talk of islands and submarines and old boats. I knew what you were doing."

Monk had me there. All the same, I made a mental note to arrange a serious sit-down with Luther. Luther's help could get Monk into way too much unsupervised trouble.

"It's my business, too," he added, pouting like a five-year-old.

"It's your business, too," I agreed. "I'm proud of you."

"And it won't be so horrible. The ship is barely rocking."

"That's because we're in port."

"And the room's not too small." He looked around. "I can make it work. It was cheaper than your room, you know."

"What do you mean?"

He lowered his voice, even though there was no one else in the room. "You paid for the single supplement and I didn't. I don't know why they try to charge single people extra money. But it's not right. So I didn't check that box, and it saved us a lot."

I was beginning to get that bad, familiar feeling. Here we go!

"Adrian, the single supplement means you get the room to yourself. If you don't pay, the cruise line will pair you up with someone else. A stranger."

He laughed and shook his head in disbelief. "No, that can't be right."

"Yes, it is right."

"They can't make me sleep with a total stranger. It's against the law."

"No, it's not."

"How about maritime law?"

"Adrian, we need to go to the hotel director and get you a single room."

"This is a single room." He pointed to the second bed. "That? That's a cushioned shelf."

"Don't argue. I think the ship is full." I grabbed him by the sleeve, and we were almost out of the cabin when the inevitable appeared in Monk's doorway in the shape of a man, blocking our exit with the sheer volume of his bloated stomach.

You would have thought from the way the man was weaving back and forth that the ship was already at sea. "Whoops," slurred the balding, aging frat boy. "I'm looking for cabin 457. Hey, this is 457! We're all in the wrong room."

"You're in the wrong room," said Monk, clever as always.

"Hey, are you my roomie?" He was smiling and looking at me. "Let's toast. You, me, and my buddy Jack."

"My name's not Jack," said Monk.

"Not talking about you," said the man as he

pulled a half-empty bottle of Jack Daniel's from behind his back.

"You wish," I said, then waited a second until he breathed. The man's stomach was like a wave going out, giving us just enough room to squeeze past him into the hall. "Adrian, come on."

Monk and I took the main staircase a flight down to the lobby. The ship's horn was sounding one long blast. Out of the corner of my eye, I could see the break in the rail where the gangway was being slowly lifted up and away from the *Golden Sun*. I did not point this out. Instead, I led Monk into a sharp left turn.

When we arrived at Guest Services, we were lucky enough to find no one in front of us. "There's been a mistake," Monk blurted out to the man in the ex-Marine crew cut behind the counter. "You gave away half my room." It actually wasn't a bad blurt. I'd expected worse.

"Hello, Bill," I said cheerily to Bill, hotel manager, Santa Fe, New Mexico. I smiled. "How are you today, Bill? My friend here needs a new room. He didn't understand the concept of a single supplement."

"I can't live in the same room with anyone," Monk said. "It's a medical condition."

"It kind of is," I agreed. "We need a private cabin. Whatever you have."

"We have nothing," Bill said. "I don't even have to look."

"Could you look anyway," Monk pleaded, "and then say something different?"

"I wish I could," Bill said with real sincerity. "I mean, this ship never sells out. But this week? Not a free bed anywhere."

"What about the infirmary?" I asked. "You must have a bed in the infirmary."

"It's not really set up for that," said Bill. "Besides, he's not sick."

"What about the morgue?" Monk asked, displaying a hopeful grin. "You've got to have a morgue."

"Sir?" Bill leaned forward and lowered his voice. "Yes, we do have a morgue, but it's not something we like to broadcast."

"Great. Then Natalie can sleep in the morgue and I'll take her room."

"I am not sleeping in the morgue," I said.

"Why not?" Monk asked. "It's clean. It's quiet. It's cool."

"It's a freezer," I said.

"No one will be sleeping in the morgue," Bill said, almost shouting the news.

"Well, then, I need to get off," Monk said. At least that's what I assume he said. You couldn't really hear him, due to the three short blasts of the horn that were signaling our departure from Pier 35. Beneath our feet, the deck began to rumble gently.

Monk didn't react quite the way he normally did in such an emergency. And believe me, I've been through plenty of them. After slowly digesting the news, he settled into a corner of the lobby, his back to the wall, and began with half an hour of deep breathing. Some might call it hyperventilation. I could see he was trying his best to be brave.

This coping process was interrupted by another long blast of the horn and the PA announcement of the lifeboat drill.

From the moment I considered the possibility of Monk getting on a ship, I'd pictured him trying to deal with a lifeboat drill—the orange vests, the lining up next to other people, all the official talk about sinking ships and little boats.

But when it really happened, he was frighteningly calm. He let me put on his flotation vest and followed me to our mustering station on the starboard aft section of the Granada deck. He didn't say a word as one of the waiters explained to our group of twenty the procedures in case of a shipwreck, including the possible need to reinflate our vests by blowing into a tube while bobbing in fifty-degree salt water.

Some might have called his condition catatonic. But it was his way of coping. I knew Monk wasn't processing any of the emergency information. To be honest, neither was I. Neither were half of the other passengers. They were too busy either chatting aimlessly or making *Titanic* jokes.

I knew Monk's calm couldn't last. In fact, I was concerned that it had lasted as long as it did.

Finally, when the drill was over and we were heading back up to our cabins, I made the mistake of talking.

"You can take off the life vest," I said gently.

Monk suddenly came to life. He grabbed at his vest with both hands as if I'd just threatened him. "Over my dead body," he growled. "Over my dead, drowned, bloated body that little fish are going to nibble on the ocean floor, where my bones will scatter and eventually become part of a coral reef." A second later, he was taking the stairway two steps at a time, past his floor and my floor and on upward.

"Adrian, please." I was chasing him and had a sinking feeling—no pun intended—of exactly where he was heading.

When I caught up, he was on the highest level— staff only—and had forced his way past two officers and onto the navigation bridge. "I need to get off," he shouted. His manic voice echoed off the rows of shiny equipment. "It's an emergency."

The entire bridge snapped to a kind of mental attention. "What emergency, sir?" someone shouted back.

"I can't live with my roommate."

The captain was there at the wheel, front and center. To his credit, he didn't laugh or yell or kick us out. Instead, he turned command over to his first officer, then led us into a small communications room next door.

Captain Sheffield was probably still in his forties, square-shouldered, with a military bearing. He was blessed with a high mane of wavy white hair, perfectly groomed, which he obviously considered his best feature.

"You know," he told Monk, "you don't have to keep wearing the vest."

"I do if I want to avoid being a coral reef." Monk had strapped it on so tight that it was starting to affect his breathing. "I need to get off."

"You should have been here half an hour ago," said the captain. "That's when the port pilot went back with his boat."

"What about turning around and dropping me off?" Monk suggested. "Like a do-over."

The captain explained that this couldn't be done, and even if it could, the port of San Francisco would require another docking fee and pilot fee, which couldn't be authorized because of a simple roommate problem.

Monk's other suggestions for evacuation were also rejected. The ship did not have a helicopter. We wouldn't be allowed to commandeer a lifeboat. And, although Monk had learned how to swim years ago from a correspondence course, he wasn't very good at it.

Our next approach was to go back down to level four and try to reason with Darby McGinnis, Monk's new roommate. I checked my watch as we walked. Monk's first little catastrophe had caused me to miss the B. to Sea orientation meeting, and I was in danger now of missing the captain's welcome cocktail party.

Back in Monk's cabin, Darby McGinnis seemed to be a genial, easygoing guy. Instantly, I figured he and Monk wouldn't get along. At the end of their twenty-minute discussion, Darby had—very unreasonably—refused to bunk in the morgue. He'd also refused to swim to shore, since he couldn't swim either and claimed to get panicky even in a bathtub. Why do people like this go on cruises? I don't know.

Darby also refused to sleep in the hall and refused Monk's idea of sharing a room with me on level five. Actually, I'm the one who refused that. But Darby agreed that we would need to at least have a drink first. Everything with Darby seemed to require a drink first.

It wasn't much later, when we were alone again, that Monk made his final plea. "How about you and Malcolm Leeds?" he asked. "I know Malcolm's here. The two of you can shack up in his room and I can have yours."

"We are not shacking up," I said firmly.

"Why not?" Monk countered. "He likes you. You like him. I get to have a room to myself. Everybody's happy."

"Adrian, you are not pimping me out so you can get a single room."

"Pimping?" He shook his head. "Natalie, that is

disgusting. And selfish. You know I'd do it for you if the situation were reversed."

I couldn't help gasping. "You'd do it for me?"

"Yes." He looked sincere. "If the roles were reversed. If you were magically me and I were magically you, I would certainly share a room with a man I liked so that you, meaning I, could have a room to myself."

I knew that in Monk's fevered mind this statement made perfect sense, which was a sign that I should stop arguing with him.

The two of us had wound up at the rear of the Valencia deck, in lounge chairs pressed safely back against the wall. If I craned my neck, I could see past the railing to the last little specks of San Francisco, disappearing in the distance. This was not how I'd imagined spending my first evening on board the *Golden Sun*.

"You didn't respond to my hypothetical argument," he said. "I would switch rooms with you."

"Really? Then let's pretend you did. Thanks for the room, Adrian. I appreciate it." And I got up to leave.

"Where are you going?" he asked. "What about my disaster?"

"I'm going inside," I said over my shoulder. "I'm chilly."

"What room are you in? Natalie?"

I pretended not to hear.

7

MR. MONK AND
THE LIFEBOAT

According to the schedule, the captain's welcome cocktail party would last until six thirty. After abandoning Monk on the Valencia deck, I had time to slap on my red name tag and hurry down to the lobby. Once there, I got my hands on a much-needed glass of white wine and began scouring the room for Malcolm. We had made loose plans to meet here and then sit together at dinner.

As I walked into the lobby atrium with its winding staircase and polished marble, I saw a fair number of the passengers milling among the display of raw vegetables and plastic wineglasses. A large ice sculpture gleamed in the center of it all.

I don't know what I'd been expecting from this at-sea business conference. Perhaps more business? By my rough estimate, about half of the people here were older couples or families with children, none of them with red name tags, and none who might be interested in Monk and Teeger's shiny new brochure.

At a little raised platform at the front of the

lounge was Mariah Linkletter. The captain had just finished with his welcoming remarks, and she had taken back the microphone to tie up the last few details.

"Thank you, Captain Sheffield," she said, as if a king had just deigned to speak. "We are so excited to have you all with us on the *Golden Sun*. I have to confess this coastal cruise to Mexico is my favorite of all of our itineraries. The forecast for the next week looks wonderful. And we're so glad to welcome the B. to Sea Conference. This is their tenth time with us and every time, we all have such great fun."

There was a smattering of applause and a few little whoops. Then Mariah continued, outlining the exciting schedule for this evening and tomorrow. I would try to list the events for you, but honestly, I wasn't even listening.

"I missed you at the B. to Sea orientation." It was Malcolm, a concerned smile on his lips, coming directly at me with a glass of white wine in each hand. I took the larger one.

"I had a little emergency," I whispered.

A serious-looking man in a blue blazer shushed us. We apologized with a nod and stayed shushed through Mariah's cruise director pitch, which ended with a standard plea to please let her know if there was anything she could do to make our voyage more enjoyable. Something about the way she said it actually made you believe. Here was a girl who seemed to treat every little cruise like a brand-new adventure. I knew that was all part of her job, but it didn't stop me from liking her.

At the end, I led an enthusiastic round of applause, then turned back to Malcolm. We toasted with our white wines.

"Did I miss much at the orientation?"

"Yes and no. It was a chance to introduce yourself, which would have been helpful. You said you had an emergency?"

"My phobic, OCD partner decided to join us at the last minute."

"He's here?" Malcolm instantly seemed to understand. "Is this going to be a problem?"

"No, it's not," I said emphatically.

"Good." He sipped at his wine, using the moment to glance around the lounge. "So, what do you think?"

"I thought this cruise was going to be all business," I said, letting my disappointment show.

"I thought so, too. Apparently the organizers couldn't fill the ship. Natalie, I'm sorry. The last time I did this, it was packed."

"It's still packed. Just not with the right people."

"It's going to be great." He slipped his hand onto my arm to reassure me. "I met some contacts already. One's a top-notch defense lawyer. He's dying to meet you."

"You've been talking about me?" What a

simpering thing to say! I could have kicked myself.

"And I hope you talk about me." Malcolm hadn't seemed to notice my simper. "That's how networking works. It's better to build someone else up. You can return the favor for me."

"Right," I said. "Good strategy."

"I'll be sitting at the lawyer's table tonight. I'll save you a seat."

"That would be great," I said, and watched as he waved hello to a man across the floor in a gray, expensive haircut and a Tommy Bahama shirt.

"So I can count on you?" he added. "You have to start making connections right away."

"I'll be there," I said.

A pair of toddlers, dressed identically in polka-dot skirts with bows, started playing a noisy game of tag in the space between us, and when I glanced up again to find Malcolm, he was gone. Just as well. I sipped my wine and pretended to mingle.

I have had my share of standing alone at cock-tail parties. There are certain tricks you can do to make yourself look less pathetic, such as appearing to search the crowd for someone or standing near a conversation and pretending you're taking part.

Captain Sheffield, still looking freshly pressed in his whites, was in one of these groups, and I absentmindedly drifted his way. A woman near his age, stylish and expensively dressed, was

hanging off him, looking attentive. I don't know how I knew this was his wife, but I did. Perhaps it was the proprietary death grip she was exerting on his arm.

"Hello," said the captain as I made eye contact. It took him a second before remembering me. "Did your friend get his problem straightened out?"

"I'm sure he's dealing with it," I said, then took the opportunity to make my formal introduction. "My name's Natalie Teeger." If I was going to make a success of this week, I had to get used to introducing myself.

The captain responded by taking my hand between both of his and cupping it warmly before letting it drift away. "Nice to officially meet you, Natalie."

"And my name is Sylvia. I'm the captain's wife." The expensively dressed woman did not offer to shake. "Did Ms. Teeger have a problem, Dennis? You didn't mention a problem."

"It was just a cabin thing," I said apologetically. "We shouldn't have even bothered him."

"I see," said Sylvia. And within the next ten seconds, she guided the captain's arm and his attention back to the rest of their little group, edging me out of their inner circle. Time for a second drink.

I had just joined the line at the makeshift bar when Mariah fell in behind me. "I see you've met Sylvia Sheffield," she said in an even voice.

"Yes," I said. I never know how to respond to lines like that, so I make a habit of remaining neutral.

"Is that why you need another glass of wine?"

I chuckled. "Probably. Does she always travel with the captain?"

"This is the first time I've met her, so I guess the answer is no."

"Well, I can see why she decided to come. The captain has a very friendly handshake."

"Only with pretty, single women," said Mariah. I was flattered that she seemed to include me in that group.

The white wine was nearing the end of its run. We had our glasses refilled and crossed away in the direction of the casino. Through the closed glass doors, we could see the twinkly lights and the dealers getting ready for our arrival into international waters.

"I was thinking about your friend," said Mariah. "Tomorrow we're docking in Catalina, you know."

Of course I'd known. It was on the schedule. But until this moment it had never dawned on me as an escape route. We'd been so focused on getting him into a new room, we hadn't thought of this. Monk could get off in Catalina and fly home.

"That's a great idea," I said. "I'll mention it to him." I didn't explain that this would entail forcing Monk onto an airplane. One crisis at a time. Besides, he'd been on planes before.

As the lobby started emptying out, I thanked Mariah again for her suggestion and headed out to the lingering dusk and the open air. Dropping Monk off in Catalina? Hmm. How would that work exactly?

The evil part of me wanted to see him gone. I'd have a much better time and probably make a better impression on potential clients. But Monk deserved to be here. He was the essence of Monk and Teeger. And it wasn't totally his fault that he hadn't understood the concept of single supplement.

On the other hand, if Monk got off in Catalina, how would he get back to San Francisco? Would I be forced to get off with him? No, that would be unacceptable. It would mean a huge waste of money and a lost opportunity.

On the third hand, what about Ellen?

Ellen Morse was Monk's part-time girlfriend. I don't quite know how to define their relationship. They had met in Summit, New Jersey, back when Monk and I were doing some work for the Summit police chief, our old friend Randy Disher. Ellen owned a boutique in Summit called Poop, which sold a seemingly endless variety of items made from animal dung—everything you could imagine and some things you were better off not imagining.

For some reason, Ellen and Monk had hit it off, so well, in fact, that Ellen opened a second Poop store, this one on Union Street in the heart of San Francisco's trendy shopping district. She had done it to be close to him, although he didn't always return the love. In fact, he had never stepped foot inside either of her stores. He just couldn't. And he continued to ridicule them every chance he got.

I'm making him sound like a horrible boyfriend. I'm sure he wasn't. But I did wonder if, after the death of his beloved Trudy, there would ever be another real relationship in his life.

So, back to my third hand. What about Ellen?

I knew Ellen was in San Francisco this month. And she was sympathetic to Monk's OCD, having long suffered from symptoms of her own, on a smaller scale. Perhaps she would be willing to fly down to Catalina tomorrow, take Monk off my hands, and let me continue on my cruise. They might even want to spend a night on the romantic little island before flying back, if they could find a hotel clean enough.

I was ambling along the Granada deck on level three, enjoying the ocean's gentle sway. I could only imagine how Monk must be reacting to the sway, wherever he might be. I could almost hear him moaning softly with each little roll of the ship's deck. Wait a minute! I could hear him moaning softly. For real.

I stopped in my tracks and spun around. There was nothing—just me and the deck and the hull of the ship. Plus the railing and the Pacific Ocean. And the lifeboats. A line of orange lifeboats lay evenly spaced on the deck, each attached to a pair of davits that could pick up each rubberized craft and swing it out over the water.

It wasn't hard to isolate the right lifeboat. It was the one with the cover unfastened from its grommets but laid perfectly back in place. It was also the one that was moaning, emitting a steady low hum of anxiety, almost like a sound machine.

"Adrian?" I pulled back the cover and there he was, lying faceup and frozen like a corpse in a coffin, perfectly centered on one of his favorite blankets from home. He was still dressed in his orange life vest. "Are you okay, Adrian? Are you seasick?"

"Seasick?" He thought about it. "No, I don't get seasick. Do you think I should?"

"No. Don't even think about it." Why did I bring that up? "I just wondered what you were doing here."

"Trying to survive," he said, still not moving. "Natalie, I thought I could do this. But the ship and the ocean and all the people. People are everywhere. It's like China."

"Adrian, you can't hide out in a lifeboat. You can't."

"Why not? It's safe. It's clean. And when the ship does decide to sink, I'll be the first one in."

"I'm going to get you off the ship tomorrow," I said. "Promise."

That's all it took for him to sit up and smile. Then he frowned. "Okay, what's the catch?"

"There's no catch."

I sat down on the edge of his lifeboat and explained the plan, about Catalina and Ellen and a quick plane ride back to the safety of his protective Pine Street apartment. He wasn't too wild about the plane ride, but the rest of it must have sounded pretty good.

"You're going to talk to Ellen and have her come for me? Great." His expression turned embarrassed. "Ellen might be surprised to hear I'm gone."

"Wait," I said. "You didn't tell your girlfriend you were leaving town?"

"I thought she might slip up and tell you. It was a very hush-hush operation."

"Fine," I sighed. "I'll straighten it out with Ellen. But you have to promise to go back to your cabin. Darby's not so bad. All you have to do is make it through the night."

Monk agreed to take care of himself, to try to put up with Darby, and, most important in my mind, not to sleep in the lifeboat. Just to make sure, I helped get him and his blanket safely out, then spat in the bottom of the rubberized boat.

Not a big spit. Not a loogie. But any spit was enough.

"Ugh," Monk said, and threw his hands over his eyes. "What did you do that for?"

"To make sure you keep your word. And I'm going to spit in at least two more lifeboats. At random. Just to make sure."

"You would never do something so disgusting."

"You want to bet your hygiene on that, buddy?"

"Natalie, you don't know what you're doing. Now I'll never be able to abandon ship."

"Good," I said. "Meanwhile, I have dinner to eat and some schmoozing to do. See you in the morning."

This was my version of tough love, although in any other world, it wouldn't seem so tough. My partner was on a cruise ship with a full, friendly staff to take care of him. He could survive.

Back in my cabin, I brushed my teeth and hair and changed for my evening of dining and forced smiles. Then I put in a ship-to-shore call to Ellen Morse. It would be expensive but worth every cent.

"He's where?" Ellen said, sounding more upset than surprised.

"On a cruise ship with me," I said. "I'd love to explain every charming detail, but I'm being charged by the second, and I've had only two small glasses of wine."

"I was just about to go over to his place and

cook him dinner," she said. "Meat loaf and peas and pound cake. He knew I was coming. He insisted on the menu."

"Sorry. That was all part of his hush-hush operation."

"Unbelievable."

By the end of the one-minute-fifty-two-second call, Ellen had agreed to grab the first flight down to Catalina Island tomorrow and take full custody. The woman was a saint.

8

MR. MONK'S
CURE FOR SNORING

My first evening aboard the *Golden Sun* could not have gone better. Three criminal defense attorneys from three of the biggest firms in San Francisco had taken my card and expressed a real interest in using us on their most difficult cases, even after I'd explained that Monk wouldn't work for a client who was guilty and that he almost always knew when a client was guilty.

"Glad to hear it," said Gregor Melzer in an accent that was certainly Slavic and probably Russian. He had been the man across the lounge in the gray, expensive haircut and the Tommy Bahama shirt. He had changed into a gray suit that almost matched his hair. "We can use him as a Geiger counter," he joked. "Not that we won't wind up representing them. But it's always nice to know." On second thought, it probably wasn't a joke—or a bad idea.

"As long as you pay us," I said. I handed Gregor a business card and watched as he slid it into his wallet.

After our very successful dinner, Malcolm and I took a leisurely stroll around the Valencia deck, then up one flight and around the Granada deck. I don't know what it is, but there are some people with whom you have to struggle to make any kind of conversation, and others who just make it so easy. Malcolm was one of the easy ones. And his Louisiana lilt didn't hurt. Every time we spoke, about anything, the words just flowed, as if we'd been talking like this for years.

I do have to admit to a little distraction that evening. As we passed by the rows of lifeboats on each deck, I couldn't help checking them for any signs of entry. Nothing. Good. I had not seen Monk at dinner, but to my knowledge he was no longer hiding in lifeboats.

The next morning, I woke up in a good mood. In a few hours, the ship would be docking in Catalina. Monk would be stepping onto dry land and into the arms of his girlfriend—although, now that I think of it, I've never actually seen them in each other's arms.

My mood lasted until after I finished my morning routine, got myself dressed and brushed, and started fantasizing about sizzling bacon and fresh-brewed coffee. That's when I swung open my door and found Monk asleep, nestled in a fetal position right in my doorway like a homeless man on a frigid night. He literally fell into the room just as a family of four scuttled by in the hallway, trying not to look.

"What the hell?" I screamed.

Monk was jolted awake. "Natalie, Natalie, Natalie."

I scrambled to get him off the floor and onto my bed. He was in no shape to stand. "Adrian. How long have you been here?"

"Most of the night. Did you know your room number is 555? Not as symmetrical as room 000, but still a very nice room number."

"You are not getting my room," I said. Then I asked the obvious, although I really didn't want to. "How did last night go with Darby?"

"Darby kind of fell out of sight," Monk said. Turns out he meant that literally.

As Monk had promised, after the lifeboat incident, he'd gone back to cabin 457 to try to make peace with his alcohol-loving roommate. While Monk had been away, Darby had sobered up and ceased to be his easygoing self. He had managed to reclaim his half of the space and made the measurements exact by drawing a line down the middle of the room with a black Sharpie.

Monk's impulse, of course, was to erase the offending line and vacuum the rug. But Darby stopped him. "Keep all your crap on your side," he warned. "And your creepy little noises."

The sink, Darby explained, would be on his side and the bathroom on Monk's, although each would have visitation rights. According to Monk, Darby's side was admirably roomy, except for the scattered clothes and littered beer cans. Monk's side now resembled a child's bedroom fort, with walls and passageways made of neatly stacked accessories, hanging clothes, and dozens of bottles of Fiji Water.

"Where are the backup batteries to my backup alarm clock?" Monk asked as he frantically searched and restacked his fortress.

"You, my friend, are a lunatic," Darby explained. "But you are not going to ruin this week for me. Understand?"

In just a few more minutes, they succeeded in annoying each other enough that they both stalked out of cabin 457. I'm not sure what Monk wound up doing for food that night. As I said, I hadn't seen him in the dining room.

At some point—he didn't recall when—Monk came back and found the cabin empty. He borrowed the bathroom for two hours, then squeezed into bed, pinning himself under the covers, blankets pulled up to his chin. He didn't say so, but I imagine there was some whimpering involved.

Later that night, Darby stumbled his way into his side of the cabin, coming home from one of the many shipboard bars, no doubt. The man collapsed into his own bed and promptly began snoring.

Now Monk doesn't appreciate snoring. Even his own snoring sometimes keeps him awake. Maybe if his roommate's had been soft and perfectly timed like a metronome, Monk could have made an effort to endure it. But Darby's snores were erratic and explosive, and Monk dealt with them as long as was humanly possible—approximately eleven seconds, according to his backup clock.

His first try at a solution was to cross the black Sharpie line and gently shake Darby's shoulder. This did nothing. The man barely moved, and his snorts were uninterrupted. Monk tried a harder shake. Then a harder one and another, until he felt like he was going to dislocate the fellow's shoulder. His final push was enough to send Darby tumbling to the floor.

Monk scuttled into the safety of the bathroom and slammed the door. But he could still hear. Darby's tumble had had no effect on the sounds escaping his lips. Monk emerged in a quandary. Here was a man seemingly impossible to revive. And yet Monk had to wake him. Maybe a good slap to the head. But if the slap woke him up, wouldn't he attack Monk? Most men would.

Darby McGinnis lay faceup on the carpet. The vibration from the snores alone would have kept Monk agitated, so he couldn't let this go on. No way. And then the idea of breath came to him. If this man couldn't breathe, Monk reasoned, he couldn't snore. He would have to wake up.

It took Monk several excruciating minutes to wad up the tissues in just the right shape and size, and long enough so he would never have to touch Darby's face. The first tissue slid effortlessly into the snoring man's left nostril. This had no effect except to redirect the airflow. So it was time for the second tissue into the second nostril.

The result of tissue number two was that Darby's open mouth fell even further open and his volume intensified.

Monk was left with no choice, at least in his mind. He found a washcloth in the bathroom, wadded it into a ball, slipped it into Darby's mouth, then hurried back into his bathroom fortress. Just in case.

It turns out that completely cutting off someone's air supply can have quite an immediate effect. Monk was barely out of the way when Darby, the balding, aging frat boy, began jerking his head and sputtering for breath. He groggily gasped into his washcloth and, when that didn't work, pawed at his nose, and when that didn't work, became fully, desperately awake. But still drunk.

In a matter of seconds Darby was on his feet, his mind not quite aware of his predicament. He grasped at the washcloth and pulled it out. But he was still oxygen deprived and still in a panic and suddenly aware of these foreign objects in his nostrils.

All he seemed to know at that moment was that he needed air. And that led him to stumble toward the balcony and push open the glass slider.

"He just banged up against the railing," Monk confessed to me, his hands flailing. "It wasn't my fault. Those railings are meant to handle a lot more weight than that."

"What? You're saying the balcony railing broke?" I slapped him on the arm. "Adrian."

"Ow." He massaged the arm. "Now you have to hit me on the other one."

"Gladly." And I did. "What the hell were you thinking?"

"Ow. It wasn't my fault. The man was snoring."

"Did he fall?" My mind was reeling. "Did he fall into the ocean?"

"He fell onto the balcony below. Eight and a half feet, by my calculations."

I breathed a sigh of relief. The third-level balconies, as I knew from the ship's map, jut out farther than the ones above them, almost like terraces. "Was he hurt? Did he break anything?"

"I don't know," Monk said. "I ran before I could find out. I've been here in your doorway for hours and hours. Honestly, I expected you to be up before now. You're being a bit of a slugabed."

"Slugabed?" I let that one go, having more important things to worry about. "Okay. Did Darby see you last night when he came in? Did you speak to each other?"

Monk thought for a second. "No. He was skunk

drunk, and I was behind a wall of Fiji Water, pretending to be asleep."

"Good," I said. "Adrian, you stay here. If anyone comes and asks, tell them you were here in my room all night."

"You mean I can stay here? Where are you going to stay?"

"No, you cannot stay here. Just say you did."

"Can I rearrange your room? It really needs it. You'll thank me later."

"No." I said it firmly, then grabbed my little ship's map from the end table before scooting out the door. Infirmary, infirmary . . . Ah, there it was.

The *Golden Sun*'s infirmary was on level two, a small windowless room outfitted with an examining table, a few locked cabinets for supplies and drugs, and an alcove with a cotlike bed. The door was open when I got there. I didn't know quite what I was going to say, so I went with the first thing that came to mind.

"Excuse me," I said, knocking on the edge of the open door. "I was wondering if you had anything for sea sickness . . . Oh, Mariah. Good morning."

Mariah Linkletter and the ship's doctor, Dr. Aaglan—according to the tag on his white coat—stood by the examining table and seemed to be in the middle of a serious discussion. Mariah's face lit up when she saw me. "Natalie? Do you know where your friend is? Mr. Monk?"

"Yes," I said. "He stayed in my cabin last night. On the other bed."

"So, he wasn't in his cabin."

"No. He and Mr. McGinnis don't get along. Why? What happened?"

Mariah looked to Dr. Aaglan, who nodded and took over the story. "The couple in cabin 357 found Mr. McGinnis on their balcony at around three last night. He had apparently fallen through his balcony railing in a heightened state of inebriation."

"Oh my God," I said with convincing shock. "Is he all right?"

"No bones broken," the doctor continued. He was a relatively young man, not much more than a boy, with the hint of some European accent. "Mr. McGinnis was mumbling something about being gagged, but I think that was a reaction to the vomiting."

"Mr. McGinnis vomited quite a bit after his fall," Mariah said. "Probably gave him the sensation of being gagged."

Well, that was one piece of good news. But I wasn't going to tell Monk about the vomiting. Even the mention of the word *vomit* has been known to make him vomit.

"I kept Mr. McGinnis here for an hour or so, for observation." The doctor smiled sheepishly. "Truth is, he was snoring so loudly, I walked him up to his room and put him back in bed."

"We were hoping to learn more from Mr. Monk about the fall," said Mariah. "But I guess he wasn't there."

"No," I assured them. "He wasn't."

I was so relieved that I completely forgot my seasickness. Dr. Aaglan had to remind me and give me a small packet of Bonine from his drawer of pharmaceutical samples.

Mariah and I left the infirmary together, and she walked me back up to level five.

"It's hard to believe the railing actually broke," I said. I was anxious to try to shift the blame away from the human factor.

I was reassured to see Mariah nodding in agreement. "We had a technician check out the balcony. Four of the six bolts that held the railing in place were gone, no sign of them on the upper balcony or lower. He couldn't tell if they'd just been stripped away by the fall from wear and neglect, or whether they'd been removed."

"Removed?" I was shocked. "What do you mean, *removed?* By a person?"

"We sent technicians to check all the balconies on the four hundred level. We called it a standard maintenance check. Four other balconies had the same problem, railings held in place by just a bolt or two. Accidents waiting to happen. Think of it: a young couple posing against a loose railing or a kid swinging on one? We were lucky Mr. McGinnis didn't clear the lower balcony and hit the ocean."

"So it's almost a good thing," I said. "McGinnis wasn't killed, and you can repair the other balconies." I was trying to put a positive spin on Monk's ridiculous stunt.

"A good thing?" Mariah smiled. "I admire your optimism, Natalie." And this coming from one of the most optimistic people I'd ever met.

"Maintenance failures can turn out a lot worse —you have to admit."

"If it was a failure."

"Are you saying this might have been deliberate?" I asked. "Someone sabotaging the ship?"

"Well, we're checking the other levels, and we've found no problem. Not so far. Everything is tightly bolted and shipshape, so to speak. It was just on level four."

"Why would anyone do that?"

"I don't know," said Mariah. "Maybe it's my imagination. But the last thing this old tug needs is a death or a lawsuit. Oops, sorry. I didn't mean that about the old tug. We keep a very well-maintained ship."

"It's a lovely ship."

"It's not. But thanks for saying so." We had reached level five, where I turned left toward my cabin. She was turning right. "I'm glad it wasn't your friend," she added. "The person who fell."

"Me, too. Believe me."

I opened the door to cabin 555, ready to tell Monk both the good news—he wasn't solely responsible for sending Darby McGinnis flying through the railing—and the intriguing not so good news that perhaps someone else was.

I found him in bed, the one that wasn't mine, lying straight on his back on top of the covers, still tightly bound in his orange life vest. He was sound asleep.

And snoring.

9

MR. MONK GETS PICKED UP

The good thing about a breakfast buffet is that you can have a leisurely meal in approximately six minutes. At least I can when I'm hungry. And a morning full of surprise and anxiety had been enough to work up an appetite. I left Monk in his room (also known as my room), walked up to the restaurant deck, had my leisurely breakfast, and still got down to the conference center in time for the first seminar.

The moderator was a senior lecturer from the Stanford Business School, and the topic was "Business Branding." I had circled this one in red on my schedule, an absolute must. How could I make Monk and Teeger the go-to PI firm for all things impossible and mysterious? I didn't want to turn our image into that of a *Ripley's Believe It or Not*, but that's essentially what we wanted. No divorces, no guilty clients, no corporate espionage. But if you or your company has some completely inexplicable mystery, then we're your guys. I took a few pages of notes and asked a few smart questions.

Toward the end of the session—"Any final questions?"—I raised my hand again and found myself beat out by someone in the back.

"Yes," came a male voice. At first I didn't turn around. "What is the best way to manage word of mouth? What do you think is the single best way to translate positive word of mouth into new business?"

Very good question, I thought. And it perfectly summed up one of our problems. I turned around to find out who had asked it and was shocked to see Darby McGinnis standing in the back row, looking sober and alert. A bruise running the length of his left cheek was the only evidence I could see of his overnight adventure. He was even dressed well, in a white pressed polo and black slacks with a crease.

"Very good question," the moderator said. "Do you mind my asking your business?"

"I'm a surgeon," said Dr. Darby McGinnis. "Cosmetic and reconstructive."

My mouth fell open. I swear, you could have knocked me over with the blunt end of a scalpel. Two minutes later, if you asked me what the moderator's answer was, I wouldn't have remembered. I'd been too fascinated by the mental image of this aging, alcoholic frat boy doing facelifts.

It was late morning when the *Golden Sun* dropped anchor in the pretty little crescent of Avalon Bay at the channel island of Santa Catalina, south of Los Angeles. The port was too small to handle cruise ships, even one our size, so the crew used a pair of tenders to shuttle the passengers to the pier in the middle of down-town Avalon, the island's only real town.

I have fond memories of Catalina. I'd been born into a moneyed family along the California coast, so there was always some uncle or cousin with a sailboat and a free weekend. Just twenty-six miles across the sea, according to the old song by the Four Preps, and my cousins would be guiding us onto a rugged little island with rocky inlets and a wilderness preserve. At the heart of it all was Avalon, a fishing village of a few thousand people and a few dozen bars. Arriving here from the hectic world of the mainland was, for me, like stepping back in time to the days of John Wayne and Howard Hughes.

When I got out of the meeting, Monk was no longer snoring in my cabin. He was waiting for me at the level two disembarking point, wearing two life vests this time, the second one undoubtedly being mine. His eyes were glued to the tender, a large rowboat with an outboard motor, bobbing in the water with the last two places just waiting for us.

"Come on, Adrian," I said as casually as I could. "Ellen is on the pier."

And there she was. Good for her. As we motored up to Green Pleasure Pier, we could see her, tall and blond and all in white, a very clean and welcoming vision of womanhood. "Adrian. Natalie. Hello." She waved at us and we waved back.

Monk was so happy to see—and to step onto—dry, steady land. I'm sure he would have hugged her if the man weren't so opposed to public displays of affection and private displays of affection and touching.

"I'm not in San Francisco," he confessed. "You probably noticed." That was his way of apologizing.

"I know," she said, which was her way of accepting. She pointed to a picnic basket at her feet. "I brought your favorite, meat loaf sandwiches, no crust, Fiji Water, and bananas." Bananas were Monk's all-time favorite fruit because they came naturally wrapped.

"This isn't going to be a picnic, is it?"

"No, we'll find a nice place indoors with a table." Ellen picked up the basket and took him by the crook of his arm. "Come on, let's spend a few hours together. Then we'll come back and get all your stuff off the ship."

"You can take off at least one of your life vests," I suggested.

"Maybe in a little while," said Monk. "Are we going back to San Francisco?"

"Tomorrow," Ellen promised. "You and I are spending the night at the Avalon. Adjoining rooms. Ground floor. No view. Ranked the cleanest hotel on the island." The woman seemed to have all her bases covered. "And I'm paying," she added. Perfect.

"Thanks, Ellen," I said, and kissed her on the cheek. "Adrian, if I don't see you before you leave, I'll see you back in the city." And that was it.

I walked away from the pier with mixed emotions. I felt bad for Monk. He had really wanted to be part of this conference, enough to confront a few of his major phobias. And who knows? If he'd paid his single supplement, it might have worked. I would miss him now, to be honest—the way you miss a good friend or the way you miss an earache when it's gone. Both ways equally.

It was a bright, breezy day in the mid-sixties. I started out with a nice walk along the shoreline to the Casino, a huge, romantic Art Deco theater that juts out on the northern tip of the harbor. It's always a wonderful stroll. Then I headed back to the Pavilion Hotel on Crescent Avenue, where they have the only Internet café on the island, with a combination Wi-Fi hotspot and actual desktops for rent.

On my way in, I recognized a few other passengers on their way out, including tall, angular Malcolm with a tiny MacBook tucked under his arm. I was going to go up and say hello but decided it was more important to race for the last computer in the last booth before someone else could grab it.

It's not like I'm addicted to my e-mail or to Facebook. No more than the average person, I'll bet. But it's always nice to sit down with a good latte and check in on the world for a few minutes. And by "the world" I mean cute puppies and political opinions that happen to mesh perfectly with my own.

The connection was nice and strong, although nothing much was happening on Facebook. Last year, I had somehow reconnected with two childhood pals who, to my delight, always share links to the best videos and photos. But both these friends were devout Catholics and last month both had given up Facebook entirely for Lent. Forty days without a single cute post. It didn't seem right that I should have to suffer because of their religious affiliation. But apparently I did.

Next, I checked Julie's Facebook posts. There had been a time when I could keep up with her life this way. But then one day I commented on a photo of a late-night party. I didn't post anything too motherly, just "I hope you weren't driving last night." Ever since, either her social life has become incredibly boring or she's no longer posting the evidence. I choose to think the former.

Last came my e-mail. Right away, I noticed something from Amy Devlin, but not from her personal account. It was from the SFPD and was written in her usual style of trying to mix business with . . . something else—I'm not quite sure what.

Natalie,

Hope all is going gangbusters. We haven't been able to connect with Monk. Is he with you? Stottlemeyer says it's more likely he's been kidnapped by terrorists. LOL. (All laughing aside, if he's not with you, tell us.)

My real reason for bothering you is Malcolm Leeds. He's not answering his phone or e-mail, and we need to confab on the Shakespeare book. He gave us some leads for the forger, but none of them panned out. Portia isn't cooperating, so the case against her could collapse.

Anyhoo, we need Leeds on this ASAP. Maybe he'll answer you.

Thx, Amy

It's surprising how dependent we've all become on instant communication. One day at sea with Monk and we already had the SFPD homicide division in turmoil. I shot Devlin a quick note, telling her Monk was with me but would be back tomorrow. I also told her why Malcolm had been out of touch. This was probably unnecessary, since I'd just seen him walking out of the Internet café with his MacBook.

After my online fix, I still had the rest of the day to re-explore my childhood stomping grounds. I bought a touristy sunhat made from green palm fronds at a roadside shack. And since cars and taxis are few and far between, I rented a bike at Brown's Bikes and pedaled my way up past the Casino to Descanso Beach. Back in the day, this was a half-deserted little strip of scruffy beach. Now it was a private club with white sand, a beachside bar, and a restaurant open to the public.

When I got there, it was early afternoon and a few hardy souls were lying out. Most of the patrons were enjoying the bar or having a late lunch. I found a small table for two on the beach and filled half of it. It was a little breezy, but I wanted to be on the sand, and the only other option was the little white cabanas with curtains on the side that could be closed against the wind. The tables in the cabanas were set for four. Occupying it with two people would have been fine on a slow day like today. But one would have been pushing it.

"What are you doing here?" a man's voice demanded out of nowhere. The voice startled me, putting me on the defensive. *Why shouldn't I be here?* Then I realized it had come from behind the white cotton curtain of the nearest cabana.

"I just want to make sure you tell her." This was a woman's voice. A younger woman, I thought. I couldn't be absolutely sure just by hearing a few of her words, but the voice . . .

"She's here, you know," the man hissed back. "She's going to see you."

"Your wife's in the ladies' room," said the young woman. "Dennis, the last thing I want to do is put you at risk."

"How did you find us? Have you been following us?"

"You said you would tell her months ago."

"I'm home one week a month, for God's sake. What do you want from me?"

"Well, now she's here and there's no excuse. If you don't tell her, I will."

"I'll tell her. It'll all be settled tonight. Now get out of here."

I have this theory about eavesdropping. If people don't want you to listen, they shouldn't be talking. After all, we were in public and I was innocently sitting at my table for two, looking at a menu, trying to catch the waiter's eye. Or rather, I had been trying to catch the waiter's eye. Now I was eavesdropping.

I pulled my new sunhat down over my eyes and turned away just as Mariah Linkletter scooted out of the cabana and back up toward the bar.

It wouldn't have taken a Sherlock Holmes or even a Monk to determine who the male voice had belonged to, especially two minutes later, when Sylvia Sheffield, the captain's wife, made her way to the same table in the same white cabana.

"Was that Mariah I saw?" she asked. I could almost hear her pointing back up to the bar.

"Mariah from the ship?" her husband answered.

"Yes, Mariah from the ship. How many Mariahs do you know?"

"I wouldn't know which Mariah. I didn't see her."

"Yes, you did. Is that girl stalking us?"

"Sylvia, please. We're on the same ship, docked in the same town. So what if it was her?"

"I don't like her," Sylvia said, lowering her voice, but not enough. Believe me, I have good hearing. "I want the girl fired, Dennis."

"I agree," said the captain. "This is her last trip."

"You agree?" If anything, his acceptance of her demand made her even more suspicious. "Why? I thought you liked Mariah."

"Mariah's fine," Sheffield said. "She's a good worker and people like her. But if she upsets you, then she has to go. I'll tell her tonight."

"Good." Sylvia's voice regained its warmth. "That's very nice of you, dear. I didn't expect it."

"Have you decided?"

That last voice was actually the waiter, my waiter, now standing by my table, waiting for my order. I glanced at the menu and chose the first thing on the first page. "The yellow snapper sandwich, grilled," I whispered. "And a glass of iced tea, unsweetened."

"Good choice," he whispered back as if the two of us were part of a restaurant conspiracy.

10

MR. MONK
WAVES GOOD-BYE

After picking at my snapper and drinking my tea and paying the inflated tab, I spent the rest of the afternoon in a haze, cycling around Avalon, venturing up and down little dead-end streets and hardly paying attention. The good part was that it's difficult to get lost when nearly every road leads to the coast or back into the brushy wilderness.

Perhaps if I'd been a normal woman with a normal job, this scene might not have bothered me. It might have seemed like just a dishy piece of gossip. An affair between a captain and a cruise director. A jealous wife who can't help seeing their mutual attraction.

But there were other elements going on, ones that I'd seen dozens of times at least. Mariah was holding out some implied threat. "Tell your wife or I will." Could the captain really fire her, just like that, and expect her to go away? The answer, by the way, is no. Not unless he was ready for a scandal. Or not unless he was planning some way to shut her up. Like murder.

Okay, I know that sounds dramatic. But this is

what I see every day, what I do for a living. It's probably no different from a plumber driving by your house and knocking on your door and saying that he noticed from the look of your lawn that your septic system was on the verge of failing. That's a detail he's been professionally trained to see.

What makes my job unlike a plumber's is that there are human lives at stake. In this case, the life belonged to Mariah Linkletter, a woman I liked, although I barely knew her. She was sweet and young, with her whole life in front of her. All of this was going through my mind as I dropped off my rental bike at Brown's and walked out on the Green Pleasure Pier to catch the four p.m. tender back to the ship.

Malcolm Leeds was waiting there as well, a tote slung over his shoulder and a shopping bag labeled C. C. GALLAGHER at his feet. Standing beside him was a quiet couple in their seventies, holding hands. They'd probably been holding hands like this for half a century. Lucky them.

"Fancy running into you." From the way he said it, I could tell that he'd missed me.

"Sorry," I said. "I've been dealing with Adrian."

"We could have spent the day together."

"I know," I said, matching his wistful tone of voice. "Totally my fault. But we still have five more full days."

"Five more full days," he repeated. "It's a date."

"Did you get in touch with Lieutenant Devlin?"

"Devlin?" Malcolm asked. "Why? Has she been trying to contact me?"

"You didn't get her e-mail?"

"I haven't checked e-mail," he said. "Or my phone. I suppose I can get reception here."

"You didn't check e-mail?" This was very strange.

"Not yet. But there's a business center on the ship. Did Devlin say what she wanted?"

"Um, no. She didn't say."

I used to be very direct when people lied to me, almost confrontational. Malcolm was definitely lying. I could see the outline of his MacBook, bulging in his tote. But over the years, I've learned to play things a bit closer to the vest. If Malcolm wanted to lie about not getting Devlin's e-mail, that was his business. For now.

The arrival of the tender was delayed—4:20 by my watch—and the two crew members running the boat were full of apologies. "Sorry. We're down to one boat," the taller, older one explained. He and his partner had just tied up and were ready to help us on board.

"The other one capsized," said the shorter and younger.

"Capsized?" By this point, seven more passengers had joined us, and I think we all must have said it at once. Everyone took a step back.

"Josh?" the taller crew member said in a warning tone.

"They're going to find out soon enough," said Josh. Then he turned to us, smiling brightly, as if he were telling a joke. "Everyone's fine. Just a little wet. We don't quite know what happened. The boat started taking on water and . . ."

"There was never any danger," said the taller man.

"Although there was one woman," Josh said, continuing his joke. "She was crawling all over this guy, just to stay afloat. And he couldn't swim to begin with. I had to pull her off him. Pretty funny. Anyway, welcome aboard."

"We do insist you put on life vests," his partner advised, pointing to the orange vests on the benches. "I mean, we always insist on that. It's the rule."

I couldn't help wondering how Monk was reacting to the news of the capsized tender. If Ellen had any sense, she would keep this from him until he and his baggage had left the ship for good.

During our short, uneventful ride out of the harbor, everyone sat quietly, vests in place and securely tightened. I don't know what they were thinking, but I wasn't feeling good about any of this.

I added it up. First there were the accidents, two of them: the missing railing bolts last night and the capsized boat today. Then there was the overheard scene in the beachside cabana that made my mind wander to the possibility of murder. And last, and probably most trivial, Malcolm's lie about not checking his e-mail.

These were not monumental events, each one taken alone. Taken alone, each was ignorable. Except maybe the chance that Mariah's life was in danger. And except maybe the two potentially lethal accidents. And except maybe the cute rare book consultant who suddenly left San Francisco and wouldn't respond to repeated phone calls or e-mail messages.

You can see how this would be unnerving to a plumber like me. Things were in play here, bad things, although I had no idea what. And the worst part was that I would be left alone on the ship to deal with them, me and the ship's tiny, unsuspecting security staff. Could I do it? I wondered. Could anyone do it except Monk?

It was ironic that I hadn't wanted Monk to come along in the first place and now I was almost afraid to let him go.

As the tender began to circle around to the docking area, I could see Monk and his twin orange vests, standing back against the wall, waiting for us to pull up. Ellen, still lovely in white, was at his side, and the eight pieces of black luggage were piled around them, waiting to be loaded for their evacuation.

I was the first one off. I walked up to Monk and Ellen and waited wordlessly until the other passengers had spilled around us and disappeared into the ship.

"Well, I guess this is good-bye," said Ellen with a sad smile. She gave me a warm little hug. "Have a good trip, Natalie. Learn some things."

"Don't drown or die of dysentery in Mexico," said Monk.

"Adrian, you can't go." God help me, it just came tumbling out. I knew what I was asking from Monk and from Ellen and from myself. But I had to do it.

Ellen was the first to react. "Natalie, what are you talking about?"

The two crew members were still in the tender, so I stepped aside, pulling Monk with me, and lowered my voice. "I think there's going to be a murder. We have to stop it. And there's something going on with the ship. And Malcolm . . . I don't know about Malcolm."

"Do you want us to load the luggage?" shouted Josh in our general direction.

"Not yet," I said over my shoulder. "Can you wait a minute?"

"A murder?" Monk's face brightened. "It's not Darby, is it?"

"It's not Darby," I said, and watched his face fall. "It's Mariah, the cruise director."

"I like Mariah," Monk said. "Are you sure it's not Darby?"

"I thought you wanted Adrian to leave," said

Ellen, looking at me, mystified. "I canceled everything to fly down here and help." She pointed to the suitcases. "We spent the last two hours repacking him."

"It doesn't matter. I don't have a room," Monk said. "I can't stay on the ship without a room."

"You can have my room," I promised. "To yourself. I'll find somewhere else."

"Where?" he asked. "The morgue?"

"If it's still empty by tonight." Ouch. I shouldn't be thinking like that. Bad karma. "I'll find somewhere to sleep. Just stay."

"Really?" Monk was impressed by my self-sacrifice. "This is for real."

"Very real."

"You're not just feeling lonely for my company?"

"No."

"Natalie, please." Ellen was speaking in that calm voice that means *I'm trying to be reasonable.* "I think you might be overreacting. There aren't murder plots everywhere you go. I know how sometimes it seems to you . . ."

Monk ignored her. "The captain or his wife?" he asked. He was already working it out.

"Captain," I said. "No doubt."

"Then he's already arranged an alibi."

I hadn't thought of that. Monk was right. If Mariah was like most women, the affair was not a total secret. Someone knew. After her death, the captain would become a suspect and would need a foolproof alibi. In case you didn't know this, no one is better at breaking foolproof alibis than my brilliant partner.

"I think it's tonight," I said. "From the way he was talking."

Monk scowled. "We're definitely at a disadvantage. The captain controls the ship, the security, the schedule. He'll have the upper hand."

"Mariah's going to be my new best friend," I pledged. "I'm not letting her out of my sight."

"Maybe there's a place for you to stay in the crew quarters," Monk suggested. "That way you can be closer to her."

"I can ask." It wasn't a bad idea if there weren't any rules against it. It wouldn't be as comfortable, of course, but that wasn't the point.

"Did you bring your Glock?"

"No." I hadn't even thought about bringing my gun, which wouldn't have been allowed in the first place. Not legally. "Do you think he'll try it in U.S. waters or international or Mexican sovereign?"

"Not U.S.," said Monk. "International. Unless he's planning an accident."

When it comes to crime, Monk and I have a kind of verbal shorthand. I can understand how it might be annoying to the outside world.

"You're actually staying?" Ellen said in disbelief.

"I don't want to," Monk said.

"Yes, you do. Look at you. You're practically giddy."

"Not giddy," I said, answering for him. "Working. I'm sorry, Ellen. But if Adrian leaves and this girl gets killed . . . I couldn't live with myself."

"What if it's all your imagination?"

"Then we'll be lucky," I said. "I couldn't be happier."

Ellen shook her head. "So that's the way it is? Every time you see something a little suspicious, you throw everything else aside? Your friends? Your life?"

"It's just this once," I said.

"No, it's not," Ellen almost shouted. "It happens all the time. And the rest of us are just supposed to fly back home and wait—until the next time you're bored or you need us."

She had a right to be angry. On the other hand, it wasn't like we were asking people to murder one another just to keep us busy. "If you knew this girl . . . ," I said.

"Look," said Ellen. "I'm sure Mariah is a wonderful girl. And if you can keep her from getting killed, that's what you should do. No doubt. But there's always going to be another Mariah, isn't there?"

Monk is not very eloquent as a rule. And when the moment does come, it's fleeting. "Ellen, this is what I do. This is me."

He was right. *For better or worse, this is the business we've chosen,* I thought, quoting Stottlemeyer quoting someone from *The Godfather.* Monk and me.

"Excuse us," said Josh. He and the taller crew member were still in the tender, looking up at the three whispering weirdos and their eight pieces of luggage. "We gotta take the boat back for the last pickup. If any of you guys want to leave, now would be the time."

Monk and I just stood there side by side, facing Ellen, saying nothing.

"I'm going," Ellen said to Josh. "Don't worry about the luggage. It's just me."

Monk and I stood in the docking area, watching the crew members helping Ellen board the tender. She sat down near the front, facing Catalina, and didn't look back. I felt so horrible.

"I'll bet he lied about triple-filtering the air," Monk said.

"What?" I had no idea what he was talking about.

"Captain Sheffield. He said my luggage would be stored in the VIP dry cleaning suite with triple-filtered air. But I think he was lying. Murderers lie."

"Yes, Adrian. Murderers lie."

He stood there stoically, watching as his girlfriend faded away in the distance. "That's okay," he muttered. "I can buy new luggage."

117

11

MR. MONK GETS A ROOM

Looking back on that moment, I've never felt closer to Adrian Monk, or more depressed about Natalie Teeger.

What was wrong with us? I had just asked Monk's girlfriend, a generous, loving, patient woman, to fly down and rescue him. Then, after she made the trip, I persuaded him not to leave. And Monk agreed without a blink. I wouldn't blame her if she never wanted to see either of us again.

On the other hand, a young woman's life was at stake. But back to the first hand . . .

It's probably no accident that I haven't had a serious relationship since I started this job. I'd always told myself that it was the memory of Mitch that had made me skittish of getting close to another man. But what if it were more? What if our work had changed both of us? What if the victims—even the killers—had become more important to us than anything else? Any normal woman has girlfriends who aren't cops. Any normal man has male friends who aren't police captains.

Was it somehow easier or more satisfying for Monk and me to deal with the lives of the dead than with our own? That was a scary thought and one that I didn't want to focus on too much. For right now, all I could focus on was that a young, vibrant woman might be killed tonight.

The Valencia was one of the two upper decks that ran around the entire ship, with little inlets here and there to accommodate special features, like an outdoor bar, protected in a nestled cove with space heaters projecting from the wall in case of a cold snap.

I'd been meaning to join Mariah there ever since she invited me to yesterday, when I first stepped on board. Was it yesterday? It seemed like a world war ago. She had mentioned it more than once, which made me guess I could find her here at some point during the two-hour interval the grown-ups in my family used to call the cocktail hour.

Sure enough, she found me there waiting, an hour after we lifted anchor in Catalina, as I was nursing my first white wine of the evening.

"Natalie, fancy running into you." She leaned in, kissed me on the cheek, then settled onto the stool beside mine. "Welcome to my hideaway. Do you mind?"

"Not at all," I said. I'd chosen the far end of the bar and had been lucky enough to get several empty stools next to me.

"Charlie," she called out. "My usual. My new usual."

Charlie grinned. Everyone seemed to grin when Mariah arrived. Charlie finished delivering a pair of beers at the other end, then grabbed a highball glass in one hand and the bar gun in the other. I'd been a bartender long enough to see that her new usual was club soda.

"How was your shore day?" she asked as she took her first sip. "Did Mr. Monk's girlfriend fly down to pick him up? Did it work out?"

I had rehearsed this conversation a dozen different ways. The best way, I figured, was to get her, not me, to bring up my housing situation. "He decided not to get off."

"Wow." Mariah was obviously surprised. "Does that mean he got everything worked out with his roomie, Mr. McGinnis? So cool. It renews my faith in human nature."

"Don't get too renewed," I said. "There was no reconciliation. I gave Adrian my cabin instead. And no, we're not rooming together. I don't know where I'm sleeping tonight."

"You're kidding."

I lifted the wineglass to my lips, just to let the dead air hang.

"There are no free rooms, Natalie. And you can't sleep in the public areas."

"Are there any extra beds in the crew quarters?" I asked, as if the possibility just occurred to me.

"The crew quarters? That's not allowed. What are you going to do?"

I took another sip and gave her a little more hang time. Whatever solution we came up with had to come from her. And I knew, or at least strongly believed, it would. She was that kind of caring, involved person. And a problem solver.

"Why in heaven did Mr. Monk change his mind?"

"He had a fight with his girlfriend and she left without him." All true.

"That's too bad. You hate to see that happen. I suppose . . ." Okay, here it came. "Giselle, the ship's accordion player . . ."

Okay, this was unexpected. "What accordion player?" You'd think I would have noticed an accordion player.

"She was let go after the Alaska cruise. She used to wander through the tables in the dining room and play requests. Really sweet girl. Wonderful musician. I say 'girl,' but she must have been in her eighties. Anyway, the company has made some cutbacks."

Thank goodness for accordion cutbacks, for the sake of the diners and my housing situation. "So, her room is free?"

"Giselle actually bunked with me. I suppose we wouldn't get into too much trouble if you . . ."

"I would love to bunk with you, if that's possible."

Hurray! This would be the best imaginable solution, I thought. I'd have a place to sleep, I'd be able to keep a better eye on Mariah, and we could become closer. I might even be able to warn her about Sheffield.

"It's not going to be as comfortable," she said. "We're below the waterline, so there are no windows. And the rumbling of the engines can be annoying until you get used to it."

"Sounds perfect. I mean, except for the rumbling. I think we'll get along great. And you'll be helping Adrian so much."

"It's not the trip you signed up for," Mariah said. "And it hardly seems fair. You're the one who paid the single supplement."

"I don't mind, believe me. As long as it doesn't get you in trouble."

"Don't worry about that. The captain can't fire me."

"He can't?" That's not what he'd told his wife.

"I mean he wouldn't," she demurred. "He's a great guy. He'll understand. Just the same, it's probably a good idea not to tell him."

Charlie the bartender was making his rounds. I waved him off, but he took Mariah's highball glass and refreshed her club soda. "Your new usual," he repeated. "At least it's cheaper on the house."

"Thanks, Charlie."

All right. Are you ahead of me here? You could be. Because this was the exact moment when it hit me. The reason behind her new usual cocktail.

Mariah's old usual had probably been an alcoholic drink. Let's start with that assumption. Mariah liked to sit at bars, at least this bar, which is a no-no for recovering alcoholics, at least in the early days of recovery. So let's assume she wasn't a recovering alcoholic, just someone who had recently given up drinking. She was also someone who could put pressure on her captain boyfriend to leave his wife—or else.

Somehow I just knew. Mariah Linkletter was pregnant, which was bad news for the captain. And probably for Mariah's life expectancy. Suddenly I had a renewed urge to stick by her side all evening.

"Can I eat at your table tonight?" I asked, my voice rising just a tad. "It'll be fun. We'll get my things and move them into your cabin. Then we'll have dinner and maybe do something afterward." I knew I was sounding desperate right now in a *Single White Female*, stalker-girlfriend kind of way.

"Sure," said Mariah with a little hesitation. "Sounds great." The pocket in her skirt buzzed. "Sorry." She pulled out a phone and spent a few seconds checking a text. I couldn't tell if she wanted to smile or not. She did neither.

"Let's get your things right now," said Mariah. "Then I'm afraid I have some work to do."

The crew quarters were not as cramped or as depressing as I'd been led to believe. True, at the doorway leading down into the ship's bowels, all the nice carpet and woodwork stopped and were replaced with thin green carpeting and steel walls and, as Mariah had warned me, no windows.

The narrow corridors were lit by overhead lights and wound around oversized pipes and other bits of ship machinery I couldn't begin to figure out. As Mariah led the way with one of my bags, I followed with the other and worked hard at remembering each twist and turn.

We passed only two other crew members. Mariah said hello but didn't introduce me, and no one asked. Good. We soon came into a series of corridors with dozens of cabin doors on each side. Mariah used her electronic key card on one of them.

Our cabin was perhaps half the size of the guest cabins, painted a cheery light yellow, with a ceiling that curved gently over a pair of bunk beds. Mariah, I could see, had taken the upper, probably in deference to Giselle, the eighty-something accordionist.

"Is the bottom okay for you?" she asked.

"Perfect," I said. "And I just want to thank you again for coming to my rescue."

"No problem. If you want to know the truth, I miss having a roomie. Giselle was a hoot. Did you know the song 'Lady of Spain' was written by Englishmen? It's true."

Despite the close quarters, the built-in cabinets

had hooks and drawers for everything—a Winnebago was wasteful by comparison—and I had no problem squaring myself away. Mariah ended the orientation by handing me Giselle's key card, coded to open both the general crew passage and our cabin.

Mariah checked her watch, the fifth time she'd done it since we arrived. "I gotta go," she said, sweeping her long copper hair back over her shoulders. "Make yourself at home. You remember the way out?"

"Of course," I said, meaning *maybe*.

"Good. I'll see you at dinner." She spent the next ten seconds checking her hair and freckled face in the mirror.

"Where are you going?" I asked.

"Just business," she said over her shoulder. And she was gone.

Why didn't I follow her, you're probably asking. Stupid Natalie. Or warn her. I could have sat her down on the edge of my bunk and explained what I'd overheard at the beach club. But I knew how she would have reacted to such a crazy warning. And as for following her, I tried.

After the door closed, I counted to three, then eased it open and turned right down the corridor, retracing our steps. I went as quickly and as quietly as I could, making all the turns just as I remembered them, seeing all the landmarks I'd noticed on our way in: the crew lounge, the cafeteria. But as quickly as I walked, I never found her.

When I got to the stairway going up, two cabin stewards were blocking the way, chatting in Spanish. They stepped aside as soon as they saw me, not in the least curious about this unknown intruder in their private space.

"Excuse me," I said. "Did Mariah come by here? Mariah Linkletter? Cruise director? Red hair? Did you see her?"

Both of them seemed to understand. And both of them shook their heads.

12

MR. MONK AND THE ALIBI

"It only took two hours to get everything cleaned. And I only used two maids. Two maids plus me, so I guess that's the equivalent of four maids."

I felt a little insulted. "Adrian, I spent all of one night in that room."

"That's what I'm saying. I'm surprised it only took two hours. Can't you take a compliment?"

"Thanks."

"Oh, and I'm sorry you spilled a bottle of Chanel No. 5. I know how expensive that is."

"I didn't spill anything. I used a drop or two last night behind my ears. Is that a crime?"

"Getting rid of the smell took the maids half an hour. Don't worry. I paid for it."

"That's so generous."

"Well, I think it's a fair trade for you giving up your room."

"Are you sure I don't owe you anything?"

"We'll call it a draw."

I didn't respond. Monk squiggled his nose and watched as I toyed with the three tiny lamb chops on my plate. He had been given the same food and had spent much of the dinner moving it around—

just like me, but for hygienic reasons rather than emotional ones. "You know, you're paying even less attention to me than normal," he said.

"I'm trying, but you don't make it easy."

It was a semiformal evening in the dining room, with the women in elegant dresses and the men in suits and ties. I was in a long, lavender affair, a little off the shoulder, a reworking of a bridesmaid dress from six years ago. Monk was in his usual checked shirt and brown jacket and orange life vest. It was still drawing its share of stares.

We had situated ourselves at a table with an unobstructed view of the dining room's double doors. It was a table for four, but we'd been saving a place for Mariah, as I promised, and no one had taken the fourth spot. Every minute or so, I would glance over to the doors, hoping to see her walk in.

"I shouldn't have let her out of my sight," I said. "At least the captain is still here."

Captain Sheffield was seated at the large circular table in the middle of the dining room, next to his wife. He was once again in his officer whites, and his wife was in what we used to call a cocktail dress, black and strapless with a cinched waist. For a woman a little north of me in age, she still had quite a figure.

"Yes," agreed Monk. "The captain's still here." His tone was not reassuring.

"What does that mean?" I asked.

"Probably nothing."

"Will you let me know when it means something?"

"You'll be the first. Actually the second, after me."

I tried turning my attention back to my lamb chops, but they were cooling on the plate, and Geraldo, our waiter, was beginning to make wide circles like a vulture hungry for a few more dirty plates.

"You missed the five o'clock talkback seminar. Both of you."

That was Malcolm, of course, walking up to us and looking disappointed.

I'd seen him at his table across the room, laughing and eating and drinking with a circle of two women and five men, including Gregor Melzer, the Russian lawyer who'd taken my card last night. All of them seemed important and well-connected in their shiny red name tags.

I felt a pang of guilt. I hadn't even remembered to put mine on. And I knew Monk would never wear his, not unless he had a name tag for each lapel and a level to make sure they were lined up straight.

"Did we miss it? I'm sorry." I vaguely remembered a seminar in the schedule, happening around the same time I was unsuccessfully chasing Mariah in the crew quarters.

"I think you were the only ones not represented," he went on. "Everyone else got up, said a few words about their company, answered some questions, and tried to make a good impression."

"We'll do better tomorrow," I half promised. "Today just got away from us." How embarrassing. Not that I regretted how I'd spent the time. We were on a case. This is what we did.

"I'm sorry, too," Malcolm lilted. "I shouldn't scold you. It's your business. I'm just trying to help."

"And I appreciate it," I said. "I really do. It's just that—"

"Shh."

Monk had a finger lifted to his lips, and a finger from his other hand gestured at the captain's table. Something was happening.

"What's he doing?" asked Malcolm, staring at Monk.

"Nothing," I said softly. "Sorry." But when it looked like Malcolm was going to speak again, I doubled down with a "shh" of my own. He shushed.

In a previous life, when I'd worked for two years in a Las Vegas casino, I used to make a game of isolating voices. I would stand at my croupier station, taking bets and spinning the roulette wheel, but I would really be focusing on an overhead mirror, trying to hear what my pit boss, a woman, might be saying to the floorman, her unhappily married boyfriend. It was the most entertainment I had all shift, until one day when I heard them discussing me and the fact that I seemed to be distracted all the time. That had put a stop to my fun.

I was still pretty good at isolating voices. And so was Monk.

"Dear, I have a headache," Sylvia Sheffield was telling her husband two tables away. She had stood up and was reaching for her Gucci clutch bag hanging from the back of her chair. If you're wondering how I knew it was Gucci, you must be a guy.

"Stay for dessert," the captain said, his voice solicitous but firm. "Kathy was right in the middle of a story, weren't you, Kathy?"

The tablemate to the captain's left, a blowsy, flowery woman in a Lilly Pulitzer, sputtered and said how it wasn't important and how dreadful it must be to have a headache on a moving ship. "I totally understand," she told Sylvia. "Feel better."

"You should stay," the captain said, more firmly than before. Then he checked his watch, a subtle movement of the eye and wrist. "I hear it's a wonderful dessert."

"But you never eat dessert," Sylvia complained.

"Tonight we'll make an exception."

Monk leaned across the table to me. "That's the third time he checked his watch. I've been counting."

I had missed the first two, to be honest, and had barely caught the third. "What does it mean?" I whispered back.

"He's establishing an alibi. For him—and his wife."

"What are you talking about?" Malcolm asked, more annoyed than curious.

"Establishing an alibi?" It took a second for me to understand what Monk meant. "Oh my God. It's happening now?"

I was up from the table so quickly I nearly knocked down Geraldo, who was passing behind us with a towering tray of chocolate somethings. Monk was up a second later, and we both headed for the double doors. "Sorry, Malcolm," I called out over my shoulder. "Sorry, Geraldo."

Monk was right behind me. We stopped in the foyer and faced each other. It was crazy to think that the smiling captain was at this moment somehow killing his mistress. But things like this happen in our world. "Where do you think?" I asked.

"Suicide in her room?" Monk suggested. "It needs to be an enclosed, controlled space."

"An accident?" I suggested back. "Nearly everyone's at dinner, so there's little chance of witnesses."

This was another part of our shorthand. When the killer goes to such lengths to give himself an ironclad alibi, then you're probably looking at a "suicide" or "accident."

"I'll check her cabin," I said. "You check the decks."

Monk winced. "I'm not that fond of open decks and oceans. Maybe I'll check my room."

"Adrian, she's not in your room. Go." I pushed him toward the stairs going up. "Check the lounge or the game room or anywhere. Go."

I took the stairs going down, fumbling in my pocket for my key card. I didn't want to think about it, but there was a chance Mariah was already dead, her body lying somewhere, waiting to be discovered.

No, I told myself. She had to be alive. Sheffield was checking his watch, which meant he was waiting for something. What could it be? A certain time? A message? A phone call? All these possibilities went through my head as I tumbled down flight after flight until finally using my key card on the door to the crew quarters.

I don't know how I found our cabin so quickly. I certainly wasn't counting doorways and turns. But there it was: "Mariah Linkletter," handprinted in the little cardholder. I took a deep breath, steeled myself, swiped my card, and pushed open the door.

Nothing. Just our bunk beds, neatly made up, and a few personal things on the tiny tidy desk. I'm not sure if I was happy or sad. At least she wasn't dead in the room.

I was deciding what to do next when an alarm bell began ringing far away, several levels away.

Seconds later, other alarm bells were triggered, and the constant rumbling of the engines underneath me turned into a grinding sound, metal on metal, and died. The ship had been stopped, dead in the water. This was not good.

Through the open door I could see several stewards putting on their life jackets and running in the direction of the stairs. "What is it?" I shouted to no one and everyone. "What's the alarm?"

"Man overboard," someone shouted back, and kept running.

"Mariah." My heart sank. Whatever had happened, I suddenly knew we were too late.

I followed the line of scrambling crew members, at least until we got to the Calypso deck, the lowest of the outside decks, divided between a few public spaces and crew spaces. There they split up, going to whatever assignments they'd been given for an emergency like this. My emergency assignment, as always, was Monk.

At some point, as I raced from deck to deck, from room to room, I heard the engines rumble back to life. Probably in reverse, I thought, back to approximately wherever we'd been when the alarm had sounded. A minute or so later, the engines stopped. I must have been near the bow at the time because I could hear the heavy anchor chain start rolling off its spool.

From then on it was a simple process of following the people and the lights.

Most of the action seemed to be toward the front of the Calypso deck. That's where I found Monk. He was off to the side, sheltered by a lifeboat, trying not to be crowded by the other thirty or so onlookers, all held back by a pair of hard-faced stewards. Beyond them all, the ship's front searchlights were panning the wide expanse of moonlit water.

Monk caught my eye but didn't speak. Instead, he pointed to the captain, leaning over the starboard railing, binoculars up to his eyes.

"There," shouted another officer with binoculars. The man pointed. It took a few more seconds for us to make out the body, fifty yards or so away, just a head bobbing in the gentle swells, looking so peaceful. Even from here we could see Mariah's hair flowing around her face, like a halo of crimson seaweed.

"She's dead," Monk said flatly.

"No," I protested. He didn't even seem to be looking at her. "You can't know that for sure."

Four crew members came running in our direction and politely shooed us out of the way. Within seconds the lifeboat was being lifted from the deck and swung out over the side.

"Don't look at her," Monk said. "Look at the captain. His attitude. His stance. His shoulders. The man knows she's dead."

Monk was right, of course. Damn it.

13

MR. MONK AND THE GUY

She was laid out on the examining table, the girl named after Mariah Carey, cold and in rigor, her copper-colored hair tucked behind her ears and under her shoulders. I was surprised to see her freckles had disappeared. Perhaps they were still there, under the blue of her new skin tone.

"I need to put her back in the morgue," said Dr. Aaglan. He could barely look at her without tearing up. "People need the infirmary, and I can't have a dead body here."

Monk was still examining Mariah. Naked living women can cause him to run away in horror. Naked dead women have no effect. That's just the way it is.

He inspected the gash on her left temple, probably caused when her head hit the ship on her fall into the ocean. From there he moved his focus to her fingers and toes, which could tell him approximately how long she'd been in the ocean. There was a greasy stain an inch wide on her left side, running most of the length of her pearl gray dress. I didn't know what that meant, and I guessed Monk didn't know, either. I took pictures of everything on my iPhone.

The previous night we'd learned nothing, except for a few rumors. A relatively small ship like this can be like a family. And Mariah, a lively and warmhearted cruise director, can seem like everyone's sister. The crew quickly closed in around the tragedy, excluding the passengers from any hard information. No one cared that the famous Adrian Monk was on board, willing to investigate. I had even given my brochure to the ship's security officer. He treated me like he would any ambulance chaser trying to turn a horrible accident into a job.

By morning, things had loosened up slightly, and Dr. Aaglan proved willing to let us look at the body, provided we didn't tell the captain, which was perfectly fine with us. More than fine.

"Did you take a postmortem temperature?" Monk asked, still fingering the long, mysterious grease stain.

"No reason to," said Aaglan, a little defensively. "We know when she fell." He was right. Even I could see—from the condition of the body and the lack of bloating—that she'd been in the water only a few minutes.

"Was there water in her lungs?" Monk asked.

"I don't have the means to do an autopsy," said Aaglan. "Even if I could cut her open, I wouldn't. Besides, it makes no difference."

He was right. Again. The blow she suffered before hitting the water could have been enough to kill her instantly. Even with an autopsy, no one could say for sure if she'd been killed before her fall or after.

"The alarm was pulled in the crew area of the Calypso deck, near the bow," the doctor continued, telling us what we already knew. "The bow is always more bumpy, especially on an old ship design like this at the speed we were going. And there was a large wet patch on the deck. My guess—I shouldn't call it a guess, because it's going in my report—is that she'd had too much to drink, slipped on the wet patch, and fell."

"Wait," I said. "Mariah didn't drink. I was at a bar with her last night. She had club soda."

"Mariah drank," Aaglan countered. "Many an evening, we tossed back a few brews at the Valencia bar." The doctor had a slightly odd way with American slang. For some reason I was thinking Dutch or Danish.

"No. She stopped drinking," I insisted.

"You're wrong," said Dr. Aaglan. "We have the equipment on board to do basic blood work. For employee drug tests. There was alcohol in her system. It was one of the first things I checked."

"Well, you made a mistake. Mariah didn't drink. She was pregnant." I don't know how I was so sure of it. But I was, so we'll just leave it at that.

"Pregnant?" asked Aaglan.

"Why don't you check?" Monk was obviously

annoyed with the doctor's work. "It's too late to check body temp or lividity or to time the onset of rigor. But you can still do a pregnancy test."

"Of course," said Aaglan. "I'm just surprised Mariah didn't tell me, if it's true. We were friends and I was her doctor."

"Mariah Linkletter didn't tell you about her pregnancy," whispered Monk as we stepped out onto the Calypso deck. "You can't fool me. You guessed."

"The same way you guess with your eighty-six percent or your nineteen percent."

"Those aren't guesses."

"I'm putting this one at ninety-two. You want to lay odds?"

Monk didn't take the bait. "We'll find out soon enough." We both were nursing bad moods, but mine was worse. I was upset with myself, with the world, mostly with Captain Sheffield.

"It certainly increases the motive," Monk said. "Even if Sheffield didn't know about the pregnancy, Mariah would have been pressuring him to leave his wife."

We had left the infirmary and gone straight to the Calypso deck, to the spot that, just between us, we were calling the crime scene. We checked for passersby—no one—then unhooked the chain that read CREW ONLY and let ourselves in. Nothing had been changed since the night before, except that the lifeboat was back on deck, hanging from its davits.

"Do you think we should call Stottlemeyer?" I asked.

"Jurisdiction," Monk said simply. "Plus, no official crime. Plus, the man legally in charge of your floating island is our bad guy."

I sighed in exasperation. This was a relatively narrow space, just a dozen yards or so before the starboard and port sides met to form the prow. With the ship moving, there was a constant, buffeting wind. It would be easy enough to fall.

"What was she doing up here?" Monk asked. "Why wasn't she at dinner?"

"I'll ask around," I said. That was one part of the job I did better than him, asking questions without people hating me or becoming scarred for life.

It felt odd to be investigating a scene without yellow tape or gloves or plastic booties. It also felt odd not to have Monk circling the scene, holding out his hands in front of him, framing the scene. Monk was currently using his hands to hug the wall behind him.

"Do you want me to walk around and frame the scene?" I volunteered.

"What good would that do?"

"I don't know what good it does, period. Just thought I'd offer."

"Let's get this over with," Monk said. "The front is one of my eighteen least favorite parts of a ship." I had no clue what the other seventeen parts were, but I assumed they added up to the whole rest of a ship. "Where's the alarm?" he asked. "The one that was pulled?"

I found it five feet away, on the same wall he was hugging. Like all the others around the ship, it was red, about four feet off the deck, with a handle below and a bell on top. The bell was large, about the size of a honey bun, with an old-fashioned hammer poised about an inch and a half away. Above it was a sign, also in red: MAN OVERBOARD. EMERGENCY USE ONLY.

"Shouldn't it be 'person overboard'?" I asked, crossing back to where Monk stood. "Just to be correct."

"Bird, bird, bird," Monk said. "Bird, bird, bird."

"Bird overboard?"

I turned back in time to see a gray-and-white plover with horizontal stripes across its chest, like a feathery inmate. It stood directly below the alarm, drinking in little gulps from a puddle on the deck.

Monk's normal disdain for nature quickly turned into fascination. "Do those things drink salt water or freshwater?"

"I don't know," I answered. I knew from a childhood spent near the beach that seagulls drink salt water. But a lot of other coastal birds don't. I wasn't sure about cute little plovers.

"Shoo," Monk said, and jerked his head just

enough to scare the bird into flight. "Good. That's better. Natalie, go taste the water. I want to see if it's salty."

I looked at the puddle, then back at him. "You want me to taste the puddle?"

"Yes. I'd do it myself, but I'm germophobic."

I almost laughed. "You would not do it yourself, not if the puddle was hermetically sealed and filled with Fiji Water."

"That's why I'm asking you. You're not germophobic, are you?"

"No, I'm not germophobic. But I'm not an idiot."

"I never knew you to be afraid of a little water. Just taste it. On your finger."

"No," I said. "It's water on a dirty deck that a bird was stepping in. Besides, it has to be salt."

"We'll know for sure if you taste it."

"I am not tasting it."

"Does that mean you're ornithophobic? An irrational fear of birds? Even I'm not ornithophobic, and I'm everything."

"Then you drink the puddle," I told him.

"I'd love to, but I'm germophobic."

It was almost a relief when Captain Sheffield caught us, forcing us to stop our annoying banter. He was dressed in his blues today, perhaps his form of mourning, and came walking around from the port side. He stopped when he saw us. "Mr. Monk? Miss Teeger?"

Out of five hundred passengers, we were two he remembered by name. I wasn't sure I liked that. "This area is restricted to crew," he informed us.

"Captain. Good morning." I turned on the charm. "So sorry. I guess we didn't see the sign."

He looked past us. "You mean the sign on the chain you had to take down in order to get in here?"

"Natalie just wanted to see the spot," Monk said. "She's got this morbid side to her. Don't you, Natalie? Do you have any idea why Ms. Linkletter was on a slippery outside deck in the dark, instead of in the dining room, Captain?"

"I don't know why she was here. No one does."

"Someone does," Monk said. "I mean, the girl wasn't alone. Someone must have seen her and pulled the alarm. Unless she did that herself."

"Yes. We were wondering about that," Sheffield said with a thin smile. "Who pulled the alarm?"

"And do you know?"

"As a matter of fact, it was a passenger. Teenage boy. He came forward this morning. Poor kid was afraid of getting into trouble for being in a crew area. And then the whole trauma of the death scared him."

I was taken aback by this revelation. This could change everything. If someone innocent had seen the whole thing, then how . . . "Did this boy actually see Mariah fall?"

"He didn't actually see it, but . . ." The captain

143

had steely blue eyes, which were now piercing my watery brown ones. "What are you implying?"

"We would like to speak to this witness," said Monk, "if that's okay."

The captain squared his shoulders. "You're free to speak to any passenger, of course. I can't stop you, as long as you don't annoy them to the point they complain, which you undoubtedly will, given your history. But this is not a police investigation."

"An investigation?" I tried to laugh it off. "Who said anything—"

"I have informed the San Francisco authorities of the accident. If Ms. Linkletter's relatives want an autopsy, that's their right. This sort of event is tragic but hardly unique. The cruise industry has systems in place to deal with accidents."

"So that's it?" I found his attitude more than a little callous. "Life just goes on?"

Sheffield pursed his lips and shook his mane of white hair. "I know who you are, Ms. Teeger. Mr. Monk." Then from out of a jacket pocket he pulled one of our glossy brochures and unfolded it.

"Where did you get that?" I asked. *Probably from his security officer,* I thought. *Little snitch.*

"You two are private detectives, trying to drum up corporate clients. Isn't that why you're here? Isn't that what you're trying to do now, create a big, flashy case out of a poor woman's tragedy?"

"No." Monk glared my way. "I'm here because my ex-employee suddenly thinks she's my boss and wanted to take this stupid, useless trip without me. Hold on. Is that a brochure? Natalie, we have a brochure?"

"Yes," I confirmed. "We have a brochure."

"Why didn't you tell me?" Monk grabbed a corner of it for a closer look. "Is that a four-color process? It looks expensive."

"Adrian, the brochure will pay for itself."

"Does that mean we don't have to?"

"No, we still have to pay for it."

"Thought so. How many of these did you make? How many did you hand out already? Maybe we can get our money back."

"We're not getting our money back."

"My God." Sheffield pulled back the brochure. "You two are like amateur hour."

The captain had a point. Not just about amateur hour. About everything. To an innocent man, it might appear that we were trying to take advantage of the death to impress a captive audience. But Sheffield wasn't innocent. He was, in my expert opinion, a cold-blooded killer trying to shame us into stopping before we even began.

"Who is your number two on this ship?" asked Monk out of nowhere.

"What? My number two?" The captain seemed thrown.

"The person who takes command if you're

incapacitated," Monk explained. "You know, sick or dead. Or arrested for murder."

"Arrested for murder? What murder?"

"Let's say, for the sake of argument, a crew member."

"What kind of insanity is this?" The captain's face turned red, which I find often happens when people are bellowing at full voice. "First off, Mariah Linkletter was not murdered. And if by some chance she was, it wasn't me. I was with you in the dining room, in full view of hundreds of people."

"Yes, you were," said Monk.

"Damn right I was."

"Meanwhile, you checked your watch every few seconds and pretended to want dessert and waited for the alarm to go off." Monk had stepped up. He was toe-to-toe with Sheffield now. Good for him.

"I believe it's the first officer," I said. "He would have the authority."

"I knew that," said Monk. "Don't you think I know? It was a rhetorical question."

"It didn't sound rhetorical."

"You two are crazy," said the captain, and started to cross away. "No wonder you're so desperate to drum up business."

"Did you know she was pregnant?" That was me shouting it into the back of his uniform, trusting my ninety-two percent instinct.

The captain stopped and turned. "Pregnant?" His face was no longer red.

"Dr. Aaglan's confirming it now," I said. "I thought you might like to know."

"That makes it even more tragic," Sheffield said slowly, separating each word.

"When we get back, I'll get the police to do a DNA test," Monk said. "It will tell us who the father is."

"I'm not going to let anyone swab my DNA. Out of the question."

"We didn't ask you to," said Monk with a sly grin. "Unless you think you're the father. Do you think you're the father, Captain? Because we never even suggested that."

I stood there with Monk, waiting until Captain Sheffield was through yelling his profanities at us. Then we watched him leave, past the CREW ONLY chain and up a flight of exterior stairs.

I wanted to be the first to say it. "He's the guy."

Monk scowled. "That's for me to say."

"We're partners now. I have just as much right to say it as you."

"Okay. Let's start from the beginning," said Monk. "He's the guy."

"That's what I said."

14

MR. MONK ARRANGES THINGS

So here we were. Monk and me. Ignoring whatever else might be in our lives and trying to get justice for a girl who'd done nothing worse than fall in love with the wrong married man— not that there ever is a right married man.

I don't want to make us sound like saints. Focusing on our own lives is certainly more important in the grand scheme. But moment to moment, we always choose something else. For example, I could be having a poolside piña colada with Malcolm Leeds. Instead, I was in the cafeteria, having lunch with a teenage boy with acne and braces and a doting father.

Barry Gilchrist was the chief operating officer of Ethersafe. According to the B. to Sea folder, it was a security company with a mandate to protect the secrets of its big business clients. This was a man I'd probably want to meet anyway. Who knows what kind of problems we might be able to help his company solve? But the reason I had sought him out and sat at his table was his son, Gifford.

In the past few hours, Gifford had become a

minor celebrity on board, the thirteen-year-old who had pulled the alarm and tried to save Mariah Linkletter. "Are you a real detective?" he asked, putting down a greasy Tater Tot and picking up my card.

"Natalie and her partner are famous," said Barry. "And she's proud of you, buddy, for pulling that alarm." The man was being so solicitous. All the clues pointed to a divorced dad taking his boy on a business vacation and hoping to survive the week.

"Very proud," I improvised.

"Is your partner joining us?" Barry asked. "I've read a lot of articles about Adrian Monk."

I glanced across the cafeteria to the massive circular buffet, where dozens of diners were pushing their trays along and reaching under the glass for plates of brown and white and faintly green food. Monk was right in the middle, pushing his empty tray, every now and then reaching in a hand, then pulling it out, as if he'd just touched fire. I think he and his orange vest were on their sixth time around the endless circle, and still his tray was empty.

"He's trying to join us," I said. "But I'm not sure he'll make it." They say a cat will starve itself to death rather than eat something it doesn't like. Monk wasn't that bad. He'd find a way to feed himself.

"Natalie wants to hear your story," Barry prodded his son. "Tell Natalie."

"Da-a-a-ad." According to Gifford, the word has five syllables.

Barry explained. "I was worried when Giff stormed out of the dining room last night." He lowered his voice. "But if he hadn't gone out on deck and happened to see . . . you know, the accident . . . it would still be a mystery. The poor woman would have just disappeared, never to be found. It was lucky."

"Everyone was wondering who pulled the alarm," I said. "Why didn't you come forward?"

"I didn't want to get in trouble." Gifford looked at his father and rolled his eyes. "But Dad kept bugging me. 'Where were you? Where were you?' I had to tell him something."

"So, you were in the crew area," I prodded. "Exploring the ship. I understand. And you saw Mariah fall."

"I didn't actually see her." Gifford shifted his little brown eyes away from mine. "I mean, I couldn't tell you what she was wearing. Or how she fell. But I heard a splash. And I looked over and I saw someone in the waves. A woman with red hair."

"Was she conscious in the water?" I asked. "Was she still alive?"

"I don't know," said Gifford. "It happened so fast. Anyway, I pulled the alarm. That's what matters."

"Good. That was fast thinking," I said. "Was it hard to pull? Did it take a lot of strength?"

"Strength?" He thought about it. "I don't know, you know? Sort of medium. Not hard, not easy. It was like, you know, loud. Very loud."

"I'll bet," I said. "I've never pulled an alarm like that."

"Well, I did."

When I glanced up to the space between father and son, I nearly jumped. There was Captain Sheffield heading straight for us across the cafeteria. He had plastered on a broad smile. "If it isn't our little hero," he said, hands spreading wide toward the thirteen-year-old. "I guess everyone wants to hear your story."

"Yes, I do." It wasn't my wittiest line but it got my point across.

Papa Barry was beaming. "Hey there, Captain."

Young Gifford rolled his eyes. "It's no big deal. I wish people would stop asking me."

Sheffield turned suddenly serious. "Is Ms. Teeger asking too many questions? Do you want her to stop?" He turned to Barry. "It's probably not wise to subject a young boy . . ."

"No, no, not at all." Barry Gilchrist laughed. "We're honored. Do you know who this woman is?"

"Yes. She's a criminal investigator." The captain had managed to make it sound dangerous and sleazy, both of which it can be.

"I help catch bad guys," I explained.

"What do you think, Gifford?" said the captain

playfully. "Are you a bad guy? Is that why she's asking so many questions?"

"I'm not a bad guy."

"Glad to hear it. Just be careful." And just like that, he walked away. It had taken Sheffield just a minute to undo any progress I may have made.

"I wish I never pulled that stupid bell," Gifford grumbled.

"Giff, you don't mean that," his dad scolded.

Gifford shrugged. "Maybe."

The teenager shifted his eyes again. I chased them with my own, just fast enough to see them flit by a table of teenage girls also in the thirteen-year-old range, huddled together. They were gossiping as only teenagers can, with a pretty, sandy-haired girl in the middle of everything. She glanced toward Gifford, and her conspiratorial look told me all I needed to know.

"I want more Tater Tots." Gifford pushed back his chair and sauntered over to the food carousel.

"Excuse me," I told his father, pushing back my own chair. "I need Tater Tots, too."

I caught up with Gifford in front of the potato trays, just a few yards from the trio of girls. "You weren't on the crew deck last night," I whispered in the boy's left ear. "You didn't pull anything."

Gifford looked shocked. "I don't know what you're talking about."

Aha. My suspicions were confirmed. People say "I don't know what you're talking about" only when they know damn well what you're talking about. "You were with a girl, weren't you? What's her name?"

The thirteen-year-old gasped and abandoned his empty tray on the buffet line. I watched as he headed straight out the door, onto the deck.

"Have you seen any wrapped cookies? Oatmeal is preferable. The machine-made kind. Chocolate chip is okay, although I find the randomness of the chips unsettling. When will the cookie-making industry learn?" It was Monk, on his eighth or ninth time around the buffet carousel, catching up to me. So far he had snagged one bottle of water, a wrapped pack of saltines, and a hard-boiled egg. "Maybe I'll go around once more and see if they have any."

"You do that. Good luck. Meanwhile, I'll just mull over my conversation with young Gifford, the bell ringer."

I waited in the same place on the food carousel until Monk made one more complete circle, searching for his precious wrapped cookies.

"What did you talk about?" he asked, picking up the conversation right where we'd left off.

"I reminded Gifford that he didn't pull the alarm."

Monk was puzzled. Human motivations often puzzled him, especially in young people. "Why would he lie about that?"

"Because it makes him a hero. And it stopped

his dad from bugging him about where he'd really been."

"You mean with a girl?" Monk asked, shuddering at the thought of anything even remotely hormonal.

"He was with a girl," I confirmed. "Trust me. I know the signs."

"What signs? Do you think Julie ever lied to you about boys?"

"Probably. I lied to my mother about boys."

"I never lied to my mother. At all."

What could I say? "Not everyone's as well adjusted as you."

Monk frowned. "So if this kid didn't pull the alarm, who did? Why haven't they come forward?"

"That's for you to find out."

"Right," he agreed. "But first, I need to find a cookie."

And he headed around the carousel one more time.

Today was a full day at sea, as we sailed down the Baja California coast to our Mexican port of call. With every passing hour, the *Golden Sun* swam its way into warmer waters. A Jamaican steel drum band played out by the pool and gave a sense of tropical climes, even if it did seem to be lost on the wrong side of the continent.

There was a seminar going on in the conference room, but I'd made up my mind not to feel guilty about missing a few meetings. A lot of attendees had started cutting class after the first two days and were just enjoying the slower pace and the nice weather. My excuse was that I didn't want to split my focus. I didn't want anything to keep me from figuring out—okay, helping Monk figure out—how Sheffield had done the impossible.

I hadn't seen Monk since lunch, but he seemed to be adapting to shipboard life. In his own way. He kept alive by drinking his precious Fiji Water and eating packaged food during the day, plus enough bananas to give a monkey constipation. Yesterday evening, he'd joined me for dinner, but we'd both been understandably distracted, and I'm not sure if he ate anything or just rearranged his food into neat, nontouching piles.

As much as he wanted to spend the rest of the time in his cabin, he did have an assignment. Captain Sheffield knew this ship forward and backward and must have used some of this special knowledge to perform his little magic trick last night. I told Monk that he needed to learn the ship until he discovered the trick.

I was taking a few minutes on a chaise on the balcony level above the pool, feeling a little tropical despite the distractions. The steel drum band had just finished a set, and I was closing my eyes—in order to think better, I swear, not to take a nap.

It couldn't have been more than a minute later

when I was awakened by a piece of performance art going on in the open space below. I like to think of Monk's spontaneous shenanigans as performance art. I find it helps me cope.

Someone was shouting: a shocked, outraged woman. That's often how these performance pieces start. "What the hell are you doing?"

"You'll thank me later," came the familiar reply in the familiar voice.

I dragged myself to my feet, went to the railing, and looked down to the pool. There he was, my problem-child genius, standing out in his orange vest. Behind him a dozen plastic lounge chairs had been perfectly lined up an equal distance between pool and railing, exactly the same distance apart from one another. They might as well have been wearing a sign: MONK WAS HERE. In front of him was his biggest challenge: an immensely overweight woman in a gray one-piece swimsuit and an off-centered chair. She squirmed like a fish as Monk tried to drag her, lounge chair and all, to line up with the others.

"You have to be the same," he ordered her. "Look at the others. They're perfect."

"Let me go," the beached woman yelled back. "I moved my chair here to get sun."

"No, no. That's a common mistake," said Monk. "You'll feel better when you're lined up with the other chairs. And your tan will be more even. It's a scientific fact."

"Who are you?" She shielded her eyes to get a better look. "I want to talk to your superior."

"I don't have a superior," Monk said.

"That's hard to believe."

Monk was still trying to drag her into position. "I mean, I don't work for the ship. I'm a consultant." The metal legs screeched against the wooden deck, and the poor chair looked in danger of collapsing. "Are you aware how much you weigh? I'm no expert, but I'd say exactly two hundred and forty-seven pounds." It was the textbook example of adding insult to potential catastrophic injury.

"No, I don't."

A few other passengers were starting to come to the woman's rescue, crossing around the half-deserted pool. "Sir? Sir? Ma'am? Is everything all right?"

"No, it is not all right," Monk and the woman said in near unison.

"I do not weigh two hundred and forty-seven pounds," the woman felt obliged to add.

Just to make things more interesting, Monk's old roommate Darby McGinnis had stumbled over from his regular post at the poolside bar to join the bevy of Good Samaritans. He had even put down his frothy white drink with the umbrella—that's how annoyed he was.

"You again," Darby barked. The wound on his left cheek was healing nicely, I was glad to see. "Is this jerk bothering you?"

"It's not her so much. It's her chair," Monk said. "Come on. Help me move it."

From my perch, I could now see Teddy, the assistant cruise director, coming through a door on the run. He had obviously been alerted, probably by a cocktail waiter.

"Teddy," Monk shouted. "Thank God. Maybe you can talk some sense into this woman."

"Mr. Monk. Good to see you, sir. You make the jokes again, I see. He's a very funny man," he added for everyone else's benefit. "Professional comedian."

Teddy had introduced himself to us last night while Monk spent twenty minutes trying to pick the right table in the dining room. He was a sweet, patient Cuban immigrant who instinctively knew how to defuse that situation and get Monk seated. I later found out that he had spent three days on a raft on his way to Miami, dealing with sharks and dehydration and drowning. I judged Teddy almost qualified enough to deal with Adrian Monk.

I know I should have gone down and joined the performance. But I didn't. I would have just gotten in the way. To be honest, I didn't even stay until the end. I'd seen it before, performed all over the world with larger casts and more exciting sets—not that I have anything against theater on cruise ships. But the original San Francisco production is always better.

And Monk would be fine.

15

MR. MONK GETS TO WORK

The play was still in full swing when I decided to end my moment in the sun and go down to the crew quarters. If there was one place to ferret out the details about Mariah and the captain, this was it.

On my way through the lounge, I happened to pass by the ship's overly pricey business center. For a second I thought of going in and shooting an e-mail to my daughter, Julie. But I didn't want to worry her about yet another murder. And I didn't want to say that everything was fine when it wasn't.

I also toyed with the idea of contacting Lieutenant Devlin, just to see if she'd ever been in touch with Malcolm about the Shakespeare case. But I didn't have to. Malcolm was right there, his tall, angular frame emerging from the cubicle closest to the door and coming out just as I was walking past.

"Did you answer Devlin's e-mail?" I blurted out. Wow, look at me. I was becoming another Monk. No hellos. No niceties. Just spitting out whatever's on my mind.

"Nice to see you, too, Miss Teeger," he said with

exaggerated Southern courtliness. "Are you having a pleasant day?"

"Sorry. It just popped out. Hello. Nice to see you."

"Thanks. And since you asked, I did talk to the lieutenant. Everything's fine."

"Good. She was worried about their case against Ms. Braun."

"All taken care of," he assured me. "I made a few calls and got a few more names of possible forgers. But the murder case seems pretty strong without them."

"Really? That's great." It was certainly a load off my mind.

Monk will often make brilliant deductions on very little evidence—a misspoken word; a button out of place. This has become more and more of a problem in the courts, especially with juries who watch too many *CSI* reruns. Now they all want a mound of DNA evidence, like neon lights pointing to the killer. Our easiest cases are the ones where someone is so overwhelmed by Monk's brain power that he or she confesses. "Did Portia confess?" I asked.

"Afraid not," said Malcolm. "But they have enough physical evidence to hold her to trial. That's what Devlin said."

"Good. One less thing to worry about."

"Worry about?" His eyes creased at the corners, but in an attractive way. "What are you worried

160

about? You mean the accident last night? That was terrible. You knew her, didn't you?"

"A little," I admitted. "Mariah had a few problems. But she was a wonderful girl. She didn't deserve to die."

"No one deserves to die. Well, maybe some people do, but . . ." The creases framing his eyes deepened. "Hold on. Are you saying there was something sketchy about her death?" Malcolm lowered his voice. "Is Monk looking into it?"

"We're both looking into it."

"Sorry. I didn't mean to imply . . . But Monk's the one bad guys have to worry about."

"They can worry about me, too," I said. Then I straightened my shoulders, stretched my spine to my full five feet, five inches, and strode off across the lobby. I wasn't really offended, just a little disappointed. Malcolm Leeds was looking less and less like the soul mate of my dreams.

I was almost at the door to the crew quarters stairwell when the overhead lights flickered, just for a second. I didn't think much about it until the walkie-talkies began to crackle. A pair of maintenance workers rushed past me, almost knocking me down, and I was sure I heard one say something about the pool deck.

Pool deck? What had Monk gotten into now? Had the lounging woman been injured? Was he being restrained in a straitjacket? I could have kicked myself for being so complacent about his performance piece. Damn. Leave him alone for a minute . . .

When I got back up to the pool, Monk was standing off to the side, an onlooker this time. He wasn't dead or injured or surrounded by villagers with torches and pitchforks. "What happened?" I asked him.

"I got the woman to run away. Then I straightened her chair. It didn't take long."

"No. I mean, what happened over there?"

I was referring to the area by the poolside bar. Two passengers in swimsuits, both male, both in their twenties, were laid out on the deck. They were moving enough to set my mind at ease. Four crew members with emergency kits knelt over them, asking them questions and checking their vital signs.

"You didn't have anything to do with that?" I phrased it as a question. "Please say no."

"Electrical shock," Monk explained. "After that woman stopped making such a fuss, people went back to the bar. I saw those two sit down and put their naked feet on the footrail, which is not very sanitary. Someone should tell them."

"Forget the footrail, Adrian."

"I don't think we should. It was charged. I can't tell from this distance, but I'm guessing the culprit was the outlet that feeds that row of drink blenders. They all stopped as soon as it happened." He cocked his head and rolled his shoulders. "Do you think I should offer help?"

"I'm not sure that would be appreciated."

Darby McGinnis walked by us with an empty glass, probably on his way to refill his piña colada. He looked our way. "Did you have anything to do with that?"

"No," said Monk. "Why does everyone keep asking?"

"Because you usually do," said Darby, who walked off and began his quest for a new favorite bar.

The first officer had also arrived on the scene by the pool. I remembered him from that day on the bridge. He was a small, slender wisp of a man— East Asian, I assumed—who always looked too small for his uniform. He'd been on his walkie-talkie, which he now reattached to his belt. He spoke to a young bartender, who suddenly turned and pointed directly at Monk. "He's pointing at you," Monk said.

"I wish."

"Mr. Adrian Monk?" The first officer was half-way across the deck. "Can you come with me, please?"

"Why does everyone think it's me? It's not me."

"The captain would like to see you, sir. In his quarters."

The captain didn't live below the waterline like the rest of the crew. His little suite was on the

163

bridge deck, starboard side, which they tell me is a naval tradition for captains. It had a little living room with an office setup, plus a pantry off to the side. Behind a closed door was what I guessed to be a bedroom.

"You can't blame Mr. Monk for what happened," I said as soon as we'd been ushered in. "It was an accident."

Months ago, I had switched from calling him Mr. Monk to calling him Adrian. Monk hates it. About once a week, he still asks me to go back to Mr. Monk, but I feel it's important for full partners to be on a first-name basis with each other. On this occasion, I made an exception. I thought a situation like this could use a little more formality.

The first officer didn't leave, but took his position by the captain, who had remained seated at his desk. The officer whispered a lengthy monologue into the captain's ear. Sheffield paused and smiled.

"This has nothing to do with whatever escapade you were up to with the loungers at the pool, Mr. Monk. It's about vandalism, maybe even attempted murder."

Murder? Another one? All right, he had our attention.

"Someone rigged a drink blender," Monk guessed.

"That's right," said the first officer. His gold name tag described him as SOLOMON LAO.

164

FIRST OFFICER. SINGAPORE. The man chose his words carefully. "The bartender left his post when you were having that disagreement with . . . well, with everyone. While he was gone, someone sneaked behind the bar and substituted the blender body with a new one. It had an extra wire that was attached to the footrail. When the bartender returned and someone ordered a piña colada . . ."

"The bartender was wearing rubber-soled shoes," Monk guessed again.

"Correct," said Solomon Lao. "He escaped injury. But the two gentlemen at the bar were barefoot. Luckily, they were young and healthy with good hearts. Otherwise, we could be dealing with two more deaths. The last thing this ship needs."

Sheffield winced at the sentiment but didn't object. "The *Golden Sun* is not part of a cruise line," Sheffield explained. "It's an older ship, not as popular or as easy to fill. We don't have the luxury of letting something go wrong."

"And things have gone wrong," I said.

"Correct," said the captain. "Ever since we left San Francisco. You're already familiar with most of the events. There was the balcony railing incident. That affected five cabins. Luckily, only one injury occurred, Mr. Darby McGinnis. Thank you, by the way, for keeping that incident our little secret."

"Your secret is our secret," I said. Monk stood beside me, wriggling uncomfortably, his lips sealed.

"There was also the incident of the tender," continued Sheffield. "A hole had been bored near a bottom seam. Luckily, our crew caught it early, since some of the guests couldn't swim. Then there was the near electrocution at the bar. Anything I'm forgetting, Mr. Lao?"

Lao cleared his throat. "There was Mariah Linkletter's death, sir."

"Of course," Sheffield said. "But that event isn't connected. It was a tragic accident."

"The others looked like accidents, too," I pointed out.

"True," said the captain.

"There were a few other things." The first officer took a small notepad from his jacket breast pocket. "There was a drink blender yesterday stolen from the Valencia deck. Now we know what happened to that. It was rigged and used at the pool. And there was an ice sculpture vandalized in the lobby."

"Ice sculpture?" Sheffield snorted. "Mr. Lao, I don't think anyone's concerned with some youngster hacking off a corner of an ice sculpture. Next you'll be talking about a missing after-dinner mint."

"You asked me, sir," said Officer Lao, and slid the notepad back in his pocket.

"Sorry. Quite right," said the captain. He raked his fingers through his white mane and turned to face Monk. "And that brings me to the point. Mr. Monk, would you consider doing a job for me?"

"What kind of job?" I asked.

Before he could answer, the door to the bedroom swung open. "You'll actually be doing it for me," said Sylvia Sheffield. The woman had been listening in and chose just the right moment to make her entrance.

"Sorry, dear," said her husband. All the hot air seemed to drain out of him. "I thought that, being the captain, I would be in a better position to ask."

Sylvia trained a wary eye on Monk. "Is there an emergency drill?" She pointed a manicured finger at his vest.

"He likes to be prepared," I said. "Like a Boy Scout. A paranoid Boy Scout."

"Not the worst idea on this ship. I'm Sylvia Sheffield." She stepped forward and held out a hand. Monk reluctantly shook it. Then he slipped his arm behind his back, where I seamlessly handed him a sanitized wipe from my pocket.

"Mr. Lao, you can leave us now," snapped the captain to the only person in the room he could still boss around. The first officer did as he was told. The rest of us relocated ourselves from the desk to the little living room.

"I own the *Golden Sun*," Sylvia told us. "It's the only asset left from my father's estate. I came on this trip with Dennis to try to see why we're losing money on the old tub."

"We're on an old tub?" Monk whispered in my direction. I could see a little panic attack forming behind in his eyes.

"I'm sure she didn't mean it," I whispered back.

"Perhaps it's not a tub," Sylvia conceded. "But the ship has nearly bankrupted me, so you'll forgive a little hyperbole."

"Is it a tub or isn't it?" Monk demanded. "It's important that I know right now."

"He doesn't like tubs," I hinted.

"It's not a tub," said Sylvia firmly. "But these bits of vandalism or accidents or whatever . . . They're not helping. Someone is trying to sabotage the *Sun*. One good lawsuit and our insurers will drop us. We'll be dead in the water."

"Dead?" Monk gulped. "Like drowning?"

"Don't say *dead in the water*," I cautioned her. "Adrian, don't listen. It's just an expression."

"It is just an expression," the captain confirmed. "The *Sun* is safe, I assure you. But we need to find out who's behind this and stop them."

"Do you know anyone who would want to bankrupt your company?" I asked.

The Sheffields looked at each other and shook their heads. "We're not a threat to anyone, business-wise," said Sylvia. "No one's trying to take us over." She laughed. "I wish they were."

168

"Has anything like this happened on previous trips?" I asked.

"Nothing," said the captain. "I suppose it's rather lucky we have you on board. I showed your brochure to my wife." He pointed to the coffee table where it lay, my marketing triumph, unfolded and still glossy.

"Very impressive," said the captain's wife. "Mr. Monk. Ms. Teeger. I would like to hire you to investigate these acts of . . . let's call it vandalism for the time being. We'll pay your usual fee plus a reasonable bonus for a satisfactory outcome. Agreed?"

"I'm sure we can draw up a quick little contract," I said. I had never drawn up a quick little contract, but I had taken an evening class covering just this thing. "Oh, and we'll need free access to all communication links—Wi-Fi, ship-to-shore—for our inquiries."

"Of course," said Sylvia. "Does that mean we have a deal?"

"We have a deal," I said.

"Not so fast," said Monk. "Excuse us." He leaned over and cupped a hand to my ear. "Natalie, we already have a case."

"I know," I whispered back. "But this will make it easier to snoop around. Plus, we'll get paid."

Monk nodded and took an extra few seconds to wipe his hand. It had been a little too close to my ear. "Deal," he agreed. "But I need to have absolute freedom. To talk to anyone, look anywhere on the ship . . ." He was gazing directly at the captain.

"Anywhere within reason," said Sheffield.

"No. Anywhere," said Monk. "And I need to be able to look into Mariah Linkletter's death."

"Mariah." Sylvia pressed a red-tipped hand to her heart. "That poor girl. I still can't believe it."

"Her fall might have been part of the vandalism," I said. Of course, Monk and I knew that it wasn't.

Sylvia seemed taken aback. "Are you saying her death wasn't accidental?"

"Of course it was," said Sheffield. "Mr. Monk, there's plenty to investigate without dragging Mariah into it." He appealed to his wife. "Sylvia, if that girl's fall turns out to be a wrongful death, it will leave us open to all sorts of lawsuits. As captain, I can't allow it."

"Then I can't take the case," said Monk.

Sylvia Sheffield took a moment to think over his ultimatum. I saw her eyes wander from Monk's face to her husband's to the brochure lying on the coffee table.

"Well, I guess that's that," the captain said. He tried to look disappointed.

"Investigate whatever you need to," said Sylvia, still eyeing the brochure. "You're professionals. You've done this hundreds of times. Dennis, I think we're in good hands." And, as if to illustrate, she opened her hands in our direction and smiled. "Monk and Teeger. You're hired."

"You won't be sorry," I said, all smiles. They couldn't know I was using the singular, not the plural. Sylvia wouldn't be sorry; no one likes being married to an adulterous killer. But we were going to work hard to make sure he would be. Sorry, that is.

"Very well," said the captain. "First Officer Lao will be your point man. He has all the information. But if you get results, I want you coming directly to me."

A minute or so later, as we were walking out of their quarters, I couldn't resist a little poke in Monk's side. "You see? Brochure already paid for itself."

16

MR. MONK AND THE BILL

It felt odd and sad, coming back to Mariah's cabin, seeing her clothes stuffed in the tiny closet and her things on the bathroom shelf, as if she'd just walked out without a care and expected to return, which was pretty much what had happened.

The night of her death, when I came back, I had slipped into detective mode and searched through everything. I don't know what I'd been expecting. If she had indeed been pregnant, her affair with Captain Sheffield would be easy to prove, thanks to the wonders of DNA. I didn't even worry about her laptop and getting into her e-mail. All of this would come out. The mystery wasn't in the motive. It was in the captain's ironclad alibi.

Since yesterday I'd been sharing her cabin, and I was grateful that no one had questioned me, not even the two lounge performers next door, who seemed to come and go at all hours. Perhaps they thought I was some stowaway friend. Or perhaps they assumed I was employed by the ship, which I guess I was now.

I felt good about our agreement with Dennis and Sylvia Sheffield. This would be our first nonpolice job as an incorporated business, my

172

incorporated business. Dennis had not wanted us on the case—that much was clear—especially not with an all-access pass approved by his wife. And that made me feel even better.

I guess I'd been surprised to learn that Sylvia owned the ship, but not shocked. If anything, it made the captain's motive clearer, his situation more desperate. Poor, love-struck Mariah. Did she really believe he would give up all this for her and their unborn child?

As for the B. to Sea conference, I was ready to forget the whole thing. I know. What a waste. But with two cases to investigate, I didn't really have time to sit in a conference room and find out how to drum up new business.

At four that afternoon, I knocked on Monk's door, ready for our strategy session. We've never had formal strategy sessions. Ever. But a book I'd just finished reading, *Business Management for Idiots*, had suggested it, and I thought I'd give it a shot. Monk had shuddered and made several faces and finally agreed.

"Adrian?" I kept knocking and calling his name until I realized I'd been stood up. *Well, this is annoying,* I thought. Monk doesn't forget appointments. He doesn't forget anything. Either this was part of some defiant power play, which didn't bode well for our working relationship, or he was distracted. Or he was in trouble. Or dead. There was always that possibility.

I started scouring the ship in an orderly fashion, trying not to take his absence too personally. The halls and decks were full of passengers enjoying their lazy day at sea. But nowhere could I spot the owner of a brown wool jacket topped with an orange life vest, not until I passed the window to a small meeting room on the lounge level, just beyond the jewelry shop and the T-shirt boutique.

Because of the design of the neighboring boutique, this room was built at an angle, with a little foyer bending off to a larger area set up with folding chairs. As I looked through the window, I couldn't see much of the rear section. All that caught my eye was Monk's vest hovering over a table covered with a pot of coffee and two perfectly even stacks of paper cups. The vest seemed even brighter than before, and I'm sure it had been disinfected within an inch of its life.

When I moved for a better view, I saw that he was tearing open one cellophane envelope after another and popping the contents into his mouth. Somehow I just knew these were machine-made oatmeal cookies.

"Adrian," I hissed, pushing open the door. "Stop that."

It was like catching a kid with his hand in the hermetically sealed cookie jar. "They were just sitting here," he mumbled through the crumbs.

"But they're not yours."

"They're everybody's," he said. "A cruise ship is like a big socialist commune."

I shushed him again just as a few heads turned from the folding chairs to see us. "Come in," a sweet-faced African-American man whispered with a friendly smile. "You're welcome to join us."

I was all prepared to say "No thanks" and drag Monk away. But there was such a look of appeal in the smiling man's eyes. Plus, Monk was standing there with two wrapped cookies in each hand and at least two in his mouth. "Um, sure," I wound up saying.

As I was dragging Monk into the room, we passed by a white plastic sign holding a row of plastic sliding letters: FRIENDS OF BILL W. 4 P.M.

Monk had also seen the sign. "Is that Bill? We're not his friends."

"Well, you're eating his cookies," I said and kept dragging. We found two chairs in the back and slipped in without a fuss.

A woman was at the podium, in the middle of a speech. She was thin and stylish, more so than most of our fellow passengers, and reminded me of my mother. She had that preserved, pulled-together look that hints strongly at cosmetic procedures and defies you to guess her age. I would have put her between fifty and death, but I could have been a little off on either end.

"This week has been particularly hard. But as

they say, take it day by day." She was in obvious distress, choking out the words. "My best friend passed away a year ago. This is Tuesday? It'll be a year ago tomorrow. I've always blamed myself. If only I'd been kinder . . . If only I hadn't allowed her to go through what she went through . . . My husband tells me it's not my fault. I realize that's true. But it's still hard to forgive myself. And impossible to forgive . . ." She wiped away a tear and returned to her original theme, how important it was not to blame yourself and how you must rely on your friends and family for support.

At the end of her remarks, the dozen or so people in the folding chairs applauded warmly, and the woman was replaced at the podium by the sweet-faced man who had welcomed us with his smile. "Thank you, Daniela. Very moving. And now it seems we have two newcomers joining us. Faces we haven't seen before this week. Would you mind introducing yourselves? Don't be shy." Everyone in the room turned in their chairs and stared.

Why do I say the things I do? I don't know. All I can tell you is that, in the rush of the moment, the following seemed perfectly appropriate. "Hi," I said, standing up slowly. "My name is Natalie Teeger and I'm an alcoholic."

"Hi, Natalie," said the dozen or so people in unison.

"You're what?" Monk hissed.

He was probably confused because here he was, this great detective, and he'd had no idea that his partner and friend of ten years was an alcoholic. Neither did I. But I threw him a quick look, the kind that says: go with me on this.

"Um, yes, she is," Monk said, finally getting one of my looks right. "I've seen her drink wine. Natalie is a stinking drunk. A sloppy, stinking drunk. She tries to hide it from people, but . . ."

I jumped in as soon as possible. "Used to be. I haven't had a drink in five months," I said, just picking a number.

"Five months?" Monk shook his head. "Don't believe her, Bill W. I saw her drinking last night."

The smiling man was no longer smiling. "Sir, we are not judgmental here."

"Well, she's the one who started it," said Monk. "Saying she's an alcoholic out of the blue like she's proud of it, then lying about it a second later."

"Sir, please. This is a safe environment. We're all alcoholics. That's why we're here."

"No, you're not. You people are serving coffee and antiseptic cookies. Real alcoholics serve wine and liquor. It's common knowledge."

I finally had to say it. "Adrian, please. This is Alcoholics Anonymous. Friends of Bill W. is just another name."

"Alcoholics?" His eyes went wide. "You

177

dragged me to an Alcoholics Anonymous meeting?"

"No, Adrian. You dragged me."

"Adrian," the man said, a little more sternly now. "Perhaps you would like to introduce yourself."

Monk stood, straightened his vest, and boldly faced the group. "Yes, Bill. My name is Adrian Monk. I'm not related to Natalie in any way. And I'm not an alcoholic."

"It's all right," said the man who Monk insisted on calling Bill W, whose name turned out to be Bill Matheson, a recovering alcoholic of fifteen years who looked like he was ready for a drink right now. "This is a protective environment, Adrian. If you're not ready to speak, no one's forcing you."

"Ready to speak about what?" Monk asked.

"About the issues in your life." Bill did his best to be diplomatic. "I know from my own experience how alcohol affects one's behavior, especially toward a loved one like Natalie. How long has it been?"

"He's not this way because of alcohol," I said, coming to Monk's defense. "This is normal."

"I'm not a drunk," Monk confirmed. "In my whole life I've had only a few drinks. The only time I was ever drunk, it was part of a murder, which doesn't really count. So there's no way you can call me an alcoholic."

"He's right about the murder," I said. This particular adventure had happened many years ago at a small hotel in the Napa Valley, just as I was first getting to know my eccentric boss. But that's another story. "And it wasn't his fault," I added. "Someone else killed the guy."

"Murder?" I'm not sure who said that. They all had the same look on their faces.

Even Monk, as socially inept as he is, could see it wasn't going well. And since he was already on his feet at the back of the room, it was an easy choice for him to turn and flee. My last sight of him was in the alcove, where he snatched up a few more cookies before disappearing out the door.

After our little display, the AA meeting was pretty much over. What else was there to say? Bill made the usual reminder about small donations for the future cookies and coffee. Then we all repaired to the alcove—to find most of the refreshments missing in action.

"It must be hard having an unsympathetic friend," said the thin, stylish woman of indeterminate age. She had come up to me, nibbling half a cookie, which she had split with someone else. "I'm Daniela Grace." She held out her hand and we shook. "Do you have a sponsor on board the ship?"

Sponsor? I had to think. An AA sponsor is another, more experienced member you can call on twenty-four/seven for emotional support to help you stay sober. "No," I said. "It's just Adrian and me. I'll be okay."

"You are not okay," said Daniela. "You want a drink now. I can see it in your eyes." She reached out for my hand. "Let me be your sponsor, Natalie. I won't take no for an answer."

"No," I answered. "You have enough to deal with. The anniversary of your friend's death . . . that must be hard."

"Yes. But being here for you will help take my mind off it." That's when she took a small calfskin-bound notepad from her purse and wrote down her information in a precise, feminine script: *Daniela Grace. Cabin 432.* And her cell phone number, which wouldn't be of much use out at sea, but might come in handy on our days in port.

The most important part of the note would turn out to be her cabin number.

17

MR. MONK MAKES AN ALLY

We never did have that strategy session, the one recommended in the book for idiots. Maybe next time.

After leaving Daniela, I went straight to my symmetrically numbered ex-cabin, 555. Monk was there, of course, hiding out. He didn't bring up my recent bout of alcoholism and neither did I. "Are you ready to face the world and get to work?" I asked. "Have you stolen enough cookies? We can always go to another meeting tomorrow."

"No. That was enough fun for one cruise," Monk said. He straightened his jacket, shot his cuffs to their perfect length, and reached for the door handle. "Although if you need to go back for personal reasons, Natalie, I would love an extra ten cookies."

Our first stop was the bridge of the *Golden Sun*. Our arrival was perfectly timed, at the moment we knew Captain Sheffield and his wife would be busy smiling and shaking hands at yet another cocktail reception. That would give us a chance to be alone with Solomon Lao.

The captain had assigned First Officer Lao as

our point man, so there was nothing secretive about us showing up. But from the way we'd seen Lao interacting with the captain, Monk and I felt—okay, Monk felt, but I agreed—that there was something brewing under the man's calm, obedient exterior. We needed to find out what.

Solomon Lao was at the wheel. He saw us come through the door, motioned us to wait, then turned the controls over to some other navigational officer standing by. A few seconds later, he was leading us into the communications room where, just two days ago, Monk had requested a helicopter to take him back to San Francisco.

"I've been expecting you," Lao said. He had the spit-and-polish attitude of a navy man, which I liked, having been married to one. Lao reached into a folder on the main console. "I cataloged the vandalism in the order the events occurred, at least the ones we know of. There could be others that haven't come to my attention. I included as much detail as possible."

I took the printed, paper-clipped sheets and glanced down the subject headings: Balcony Railing. Passenger Tender. Ice Sculpture. Mariah Accident. Bar Electrocution. Each one was followed by the relevant information in bullet points. Monk read it from over my shoulder. "Tell me about the ice," he said. "The captain didn't seem to feel it was a related event. You did."

"I'm not saying it was," said Lao. "It's just

never happened on any previous trip, so I felt it should be included."

"How big was this chunk of ice?" I didn't know why Monk was ignoring the big things and fixating on the least important one. But then I'm not Adrian Monk.

"About the size of my fist." For a small man, Lao had a decently sized fist. "This happened on our second night."

"The night Mariah Linkletter died," I pointed out.

"Yes," Lao confirmed. "The chef does the sculptures himself. He's very proud of them. On the first day, he sculpted a miniature version of the ship. It was on display in the lobby from midafternoon until after dinner, when he took it back to the freezer. On the second night, he used the same piece of ice to carve a dolphin jumping in a wave. On the third night, he was going to sculpt it down into a Mexican sombrero. So he was more than a little upset to come back after dinner and find a chunk of it chipped away. Right where the brim was going to be."

I clearly remembered the ice ship and the ice dolphin. The sculptures had been beautifully done and added a cheery touch to the lobby displays. On the third afternoon, which was today . . . "Didn't I see an ice cowboy hat?" I asked. "I was wondering why someone had created a cowboy hat for a Mexican cruise."

"The chef did the best he could," said Lao. His mouth came as close as it could to a smile.

"Was it an ice pick?" asked Monk. "The tool used to chop out the missing ice?"

"It had to be something substantial like that," answered Lao. "That's why I don't think it was a kid."

"And was it freshwater or saltwater?"

"You mean the sculpture? It was fresh. We have no facilities for making ice out of salt water, not without contaminating the kitchen. Is this important?"

"I was just worried about contamination," Monk said, then smiled slightly and wriggled his shoulders. Bingo. I could tell that some light-bulb had just gone off in his brain, while my brain was still loitering in the dark.

The next question was from me. "Was there anything else unusual last night, besides the ice and Mariah's death?"

"What do you mean?" asked Solomon Lao.

"I mean in the running of the ship. Anything odd happening on the bridge or in the normal routine? For instance, did Captain Sheffield give any orders that he normally didn't give? Was he behaving oddly?"

The first officer stared into my eyes, then glanced behind him to make sure the door was closed. "You think he killed her, don't you? Pushed her over."

Wow. Had we been that obvious? And how should we answer such a question from someone who worked every day with the captain, a man he took orders from and who might well be his friend?

"He killed her," said Monk. "We just don't know how."

Lao studied Monk's face. "But he wasn't there."

"Technically he wasn't," I admitted.

"Are you saying he left dinner for a few minutes, killed her, and came back?"

"No," I said. "He never left."

Lao scratched his head. "So you're saying what? He pushed her off before dinner? What about the witness who saw her go over? And Mariah's body? It would have been fifty miles behind us."

"You leave that to the firm of Monk and Teeger," I said. "We're working on it."

"How can you work on it?" asked Lao. "It's impossible."

"Technically, yes."

Lao kept his voice low. "Mariah was a sweet girl. I could see Sheffield was getting involved. You can't hide that from your first officer. Dr. Aaglan says Mariah was pregnant."

"She was," I said. We hadn't yet received confirmation. But obviously, the doctor had done the test and hadn't been able to resist spreading the news. I suppose no harm had been done, although it did point out that we were outsiders in what was probably a very tight-knit community.

"Sheffield's baby?" Lao asked, then answered his own question. "Of course. Poor Mariah. She must've thought he would leave Sylvia. That wasn't going to happen."

"Do you think he had an accomplice?" I asked. "Someone who actually did the dirty work?"

"I don't see how," said Lao. "He's the autocratic type, not close to any of the crew. And the hotel staff is international, most of them below minimum wage. I can't see him trusting them with this kind of life-and-death secret. Plus"—and here his eyes seemed to mist up—"people loved Mariah. It's easier to imagine her getting an accomplice to help kill him than the other way around."

So much for an easy solution to the case. Accomplices, we've found, are always a weak link, and we've broken more than our share of them.

"Captain Sheffield's a smart guy," Lao added. "He knows every inch of this ship. And his word is law. All the same, no one can be two places at once."

"Hard but not impossible," said Monk. "Were you driving the boat when the alarm went off?"

"We don't say *boat* or *driving*. But, yes, I was at the wheel." He pointed through the window separating us from the bridge. "When a clapper makes contact with an alarm bell, it not only rings—it triggers a light on the console. I saw immediately it was fore starboard Calypso. From that second, we did everything by the book. I noted our position, checked the security camera. . . ."

"Wait," I said. "You have a security camera on that deck?" I asked. "Why didn't anyone mention—"

"It wasn't working." Solomon Lao shrugged apologetically. "At any given moment, one or two cameras are out. This is an old ship. It's hard to keep up on repairs."

"How long had this camera been broken?" I asked.

"That was the first time I noticed it," he said. "When the alarm rang."

Lao went on, outlining the next several steps: ringing the general alarm, cutting the engines, sending crew members down to the Calypso deck, then reversing the engines to bring us back to the coordinates and dropping anchor. They took the overboard alarm system very seriously.

"Captain Sheffield reviewed the protocols right before we left port," said the first officer.

Yes, I'm sure he did, I thought. There must have been something about those protocols—something even Monk couldn't see, not yet—that had allowed Sheffield to get away with it.

"Can we look at the other tapes?" I asked. "From the other cameras? They might help us pinpoint Miss Linkletter's whereabouts during dinner."

Lao crossed to a small monitor on the aft wall of the communications room and fiddled with a wall-mounted keyboard. Monk and I both knew it would be a waste of time.

"He erased them," Monk whispered in my ear.

"Of course," I whispered back. "Anyone smart enough to arrange this would be sure to cover his tracks."

"Then why did you ask?"

"So Mr. Lao can see for himself what we're up against. It's called psychology," I said.

"It's called a useless question."

"I don't get it," the first officer murmured, his back still to us. "It should be here." He was hitting keystrokes and pressing ENTER, but the small monitor was staying blank. "The cameras are on a forty-eight-hour cycle. The footage shouldn't be erased. I don't understand." We stood behind him and watched, empty screen after empty screen. "It must be a glitch."

"He erased it," Monk said.

"He can't have erased it," Lao protested.

"Obviously he can," I said. "He did."

"That's impossible." I could see Lao's thin face reflected in the little black screen, his expression slowly turning dark and serious.

"Is there a security officer monitoring the cameras?" I asked.

"That was something we had to cut back on," said Lao. "The cameras feed into here. If there's a crime or emergency, we have a forty-eight-hour window to find and save the tapes." When he finally looked me in the eye, I knew we had him, the one ally on the ship we really needed. "I'll do whatever you need."

"Good," I said. "We may need you to take over the ship. Not now. When we have proof."

He didn't balk or even blink. "I'm not sure how that's done. I'll have to check maritime law. It's not something the captain does regular drills on."

I wasn't sure how it was done, either, but I pretended. "We have a working relationship with the San Francisco police. Once he's in custody back home, they'll figure out the jurisdiction." I held out my hand and we shook. "Thanks for helping."

"Thank you," said Lao, and extended his hand to Monk. "If you weren't here, he would get away with it. Now at least we have a chance."

"That's what we do," I said.

A minute later, I was handing Monk a wipe as we walked side-by-side down an exterior set of stairs. "He was going to help us anyway," Monk said.

"Maybe. But now he's extra committed. You don't have to say thank you."

"Good."

I refrained from smiling. "So what's the deal with the freshwater?" I asked.

"What do you mean?"

"You asked about the ice sculpture being made of freshwater. When he said *fresh,* you got that look in your eyes. That look. I've seen it a million times."

"It's nothing," Monk said. There was a familiar tone of false modesty in his voice. "Not like I solved the case. I just figured out how he pulled the alarm while he was at dinner."

"You mean the captain? He pulled the alarm?"

"Uh-huh," Monk confirmed but didn't explain.

"Adrian?" I hated when he did this, saving his little secrets like he was some kind of magician, which I suppose he was. "Adrian, we're full partners. You have to keep me in the loop."

"If we were full partners, you'd have figured it out yourself."

"So you're not going to tell me?" How annoying and how typical. "Adrian?"

"If you go back to Mr. Monk, maybe I'll tell you."

"I'll figure it out on my own."

18

MR. MONK AND THE DRUNK

Okay, the chances of my figuring it out were slim. I'm no Adrian Monk. On the other hand, I am Natalie Teeger, which is nothing to sneeze at. Plus, Adrian Monk had just given me a clue to the clue. According to him, Mariah's death was connected to at least one of the mysterious acts of vandalism: the ice sculpture.

Back in my tight, lonely quarters, I read the report Solomon Lao had printed out. After reading it three times, I couldn't even begin to see how any of this might be related to Mariah's fall. The only thing I did see, on my third time through, was that one of the tampered-with balconies was cabin 432, the one occupied by Daniela Grace, my well-meaning AA sponsor, which simultaneously reminded me that I wanted a glass of wine and made me feel guilty about wanting it.

According to an announcement on the PA system and numerous notices around the ship, dinner was being pushed back from its regular seven p.m. slot to seven thirty. No reason was given. But even if I couldn't figure out the ice sculpture clue, I could figure out this one. And I knew just where to go.

At a few minutes after seven, I made my way to the front of the Calypso deck and past the sign reading CREW ONLY. About fifty ship employees, hotel and navigation both, whoever wasn't working, were gathered at the fateful spot, each one clutching a red rose. They listened, some stone-faced, some teary-eyed, as Teddy, Mariah's ex-assistant, spoke to whatever celestial spirit might be listening, telling Mariah how much they would all miss her. I took one of the last roses from the ice bucket near the hanging sign and tiptoed up to the back of the group.

Captain Sheffield was there, impressively solemn, although his wife Sylvia was notable in her absence. Also present was First Officer Lao, which left me wondering for a moment who was "driving the boat," as Monk would have phrased it.

The captain was the next to speak, but I was too angry to listen. I'm sure his words sounded heartfelt and appropriate, and tried hard not to betray any connection that might seem too intimate.

Three more crew members followed, including Geraldo, our waiter, who called Mariah an angel. He'd get no argument from me. And then, for some inexplicable reason, it was my turn. Actually, it wasn't inexplicable to me. This, I felt, would be the perfect time to ask my question.

I approached the space by the rail, clutching my

rose and apologizing profusely. "I know this is a private memorial," I said. "I shouldn't be here. I'm sorry. I'm just a passenger. But in the two days that I had the pleasure of knowing Mariah Linkletter, I feel we grew quite close. She told me a lot about her personal life." That wasn't true. But it made Sheffield flinch, so it was worth it. "In fact, I might have been the last person to see Mariah alive."

I gave this a moment to sink in. "Mariah and I were together around six thirty, just a little before dinner. She got a text, so maybe she went off to meet someone. Maybe one of you? Did anyone see Mariah after me? It would be comforting to know. After six thirty? Did anyone speak to her? I'd like to think she spent her last hour or two laughing with a good friend. Anyone?"

Okay, that was a little clunky. But you try saying it better.

No one raised a hand or replied to my appeal. The fifty or so mourners all stared blankly at me and at one another until I slunk away and made room for someone else. Two other coworkers spoke briefly and eloquently, at least by comparison. Then Teddy, the new cruise director, stepped up to the rail and tossed his rose into the Pacific. We all followed suit and watched the red dots get quickly swallowed up in the churning wake.

"Natalie, how goes your investigation?" I hadn't

made any attempt to escape. Perhaps I should have. "Working hard?" Captain Sheffield wasn't scowling, but was close to it.

"Working hard," I stammered back. "I mean, this isn't part of it. I just wanted to pay my respects. I'm sure we'll have some results by tomorrow or the next day."

Out of the corner of my eye, I could see First Officer Lao walking by, looking as concerned as I felt.

I had seen Malcolm Leeds for only a minute all day, just in passing. I was reminded of this when we met a second time at the doorway to the dining room. I was there with Monk, who was busy trying to scope out exactly where to sit. The rumbles from his stomach hinted that he might even put some food in there tonight.

"Natalie." Malcolm smiled, his hazel eyes twinkling as he leaned in to give me a peck on the cheek. "Rumor has it you're investigating something on the ship."

"Um, yes, we are," I whispered back. This place was like living in a fishbowl. "But I'm not at liberty to reveal exactly what. . . ."

"That's fine," he said with a laugh. "I think it's great. Solving a case in front of a hundred potential clients? Best publicity in the world. You guys are savvier than I gave you credit for. Mr. Monk?" he added, tipping an imaginary hat in

Monk's direction before heading inside. "Good to see you."

Monk didn't answer. He was still scanning the seating arrangements.

"Malcolm's an expert when it comes to business promotion," I told Monk, feeling a little full of myself. "He's done this conference six times."

"No, he hasn't," Monk said absently. He was zeroing in on a half-empty table, far from any bothersome windows. "He's lying."

I sighed dramatically. I couldn't help it. "You always say that about him."

"That's because it's true. This is Malcolm's first time on this ship."

"You're wrong." I don't know why I said that. He's very rarely wrong. "How is he lying?"

"I noticed Malcolm Leeds when he first came on board," said Monk. "He asked Mariah Linkletter where the public bathrooms were."

"So?" I chuckled, a little relieved. "Not every-one memorizes where the bathrooms are in every building." Monk did that, not because he ever intended to use them, but so he could avoid going near them or accidentally opening a wrong door.

"Well, they should. For public health reasons. He also asked her if the ship had a casino."

Okay. This was a little worse. "So?" I said. "Maybe he forgot about the casino."

"He also asked where his luggage was. Even I know they automatically deliver the luggage to

195

your room. Remember when they tried to deliver my eight pieces, and they couldn't fit them all in? Fun times."

I remembered. "No, Adrian, that's ridiculous. Why would Malcolm lie about being on this ship?"

"I don't know why, but he did." Before I could object again, Monk raised a hand and cut me off. "I found our table. Come on, before someone grabs it."

Monk would have preferred a table for two, which the dining room didn't have. The next best thing was a large table for four in a windowless corner.

Monk took a few moments to wipe down his chair, then reached into my bag to take out his own silverware, place mat, and napkin. Meanwhile, I distracted our tablemates by introducing ourselves. The other two, Ruth and Ralph Weingart, seemed friendly and well-off in a not very showy way, even though they resided in Hillsborough, one of the toniest suburbs in the Bay Area. As with many middle-aged couples, she was a little more groomed and stylish, while he was a little fleshier and more comfortable.

"Adrian," said Ruth, trying to make eye contact. "Nice to officially meet you. I've seen you walking the halls." I didn't know what exactly she was referring to, but I'm sure she was being diplomatic. "We're in 444. Your cabin's down the hall."

"I used to be down the hall," Monk explained. "I moved to a more symmetrical room on level five."

"More symmetrical?" asked Ruth, still smiling and under the impression she was speaking to a normal human being.

"It's not as good as your room, which has the advantage of being both symmetrical and even-numbered. Did you have to pay extra? Do you want to switch rooms with me?"

I took this opportunity to flag down Geraldo and order a glass of the Barolo. It arrived with merciful quickness.

"Do you know if there is a room 000?" Monk asked. "Because that would be the best room."

I had barely taken my first luxuriant swallow of the pale red when I glanced up to see the sad, disapproving eyes of Daniela Grace hovering over the table. She looked like she was about to cry. "Natalie, dear. What are you doing?"

Caught red-handed with a gulp of wine barely down my throat. "Just one glass," I said, sounding to all the world like a boozehound. The glass shook as I put it down. "It's my first drink all day. Honest."

"Daniela, sweetie. Do you know Natalie and Adrian?" asked Ruth, still bubbling. Apparently, she and my accuser knew each other. "Daniela is my dearest, best friend in the world. We've been through so much together."

197

"Yes, I know Natalie," said Daniela. "I'm her AA sponsor."

Needless to say, that put a damper on things. "Oh dear," said Ruth, her smile fading. "I'm so sorry." Her husband just sat there.

Daniela seemed heartbroken. "Natalie, why didn't you call? We could have talked through it. I know I shouldn't be disappointed. It's counter-productive." She turned to Monk. "When did it start?"

"It never stopped," said Monk. "I don't think she even made an effort." He might have elaborated on his point, but I punched him in the shoulder. I know, I know. I'm a mean drunk.

"You could be more supportive, too," Daniela said to Monk. "She needs you."

"I don't care if she drinks," Monk said. "She's been doing it forever."

"I'm not an alcoholic," I blurted out, speaking quickly so as not to be interrupted. "I know I said I was, but I said it just to fit in. The heat of the moment. We came for the cookies." I pointed. "Monk came for the cookies. I just followed him in. Why are you looking at me that way?"

"Geraldo?" Daniela was using her upper-class, imperious voice. My mother has the same one. "Take this away."

We both reached for the wineglass at the same time, Geraldo and I. His grasp was tentative. Mine was defiant.

You know how they warn you never to wear white when you drink red wine? This is the reason. In my last little defiant pull, Geraldo's tentative grip slipped and the Barolo lurched back toward me, streaming down the entire front of the sleeveless ivory cocktail dress that I'd been planning to wear at least once more, maybe twice. The glass itself went crashing to the floor, shattering into several large pieces. Everything stopped.

"I'm not an alcoholic," I insisted. I may have said it too loudly.

Diners at the surrounding tables were looking now. An elderly gentleman in a wheelchair leaned across to his wife for clarification. "Huh?"

"She said she's not an alcoholic," the wife shouted back, just in case anyone had missed it. I didn't even want to look in Malcolm's direction. My guess is I looked like an older, drunk version of Carrie at the prom.

From the opposite corner of the dining room, I could see Barry Gilchrist, chief operating officer of Ethersafe and a potential client of Monk and Teeger, Consulting Detectives. He was leaning across the table to his son, Gifford, the one with the zits and the braces, the girl-crazy thirteen-year-old who'd lied about the alarm. "She says she's not an alcoholic," Gifford repeated, informing the other half of the room. The kid looked positively vengeful.

19

MR. MONK REVISITS MEXICO

For most of the night, I lay in my lower bunk, blanket pulled up to my chin, staring at the outline of my red-stained dress hanging on the door. This was some mess I'd managed to get myself into—an impossible murder by a captain who was onto us now; a case of dangerous vandalism that we'd done absolutely no work on; a man I liked who seemed to be regularly lying to me about silly things; and, most aggravating, a ship full of people who considered me a sloppy alcoholic in need of an intervention.

Around five a.m. the throb of the engines ground to a merciful halt. Around six a.m. I heard Sonya and Beverly, the Bulgarian lounge singers, stumbling home to the crew quarters next door, and decided that I might as well get up. I crammed the ruined dress into my tiny wastebasket, then turned on my tiny TV and visited my tiny bathroom to try to repair some of the damage of a sleepless night.

The Sun Cruise Channel was showing a touristy video for San Marcos, the Mexican resort on the Baja peninsula where, according to the schedule, we should currently be docked. From the video, it looked like a nice town with plenty to do, including a bus tour of the old city, a zip line, a canopy walk, and donkey rides, all of which you could book from the excursion desk in the lobby. The video was followed by a scrolling list of the B. to Sea events for the day, which I promptly ignored.

When I finally opened the door to face the day, I literally bumped into Sonya and Beverly, who were standing in the doorway of their cabin. They were still in full makeup, dressed in their sparkly red gowns, drinking from foam cups what looked like instant coffee, with white plastic spoons poking out of the tops.

"Hi," I said.

"Hi," said Sonya. And then, just as I was passing them . . . "Hello? Look, we know you are friends with poor Mariah, so we say nothing." Her Slavic accent sounded stronger now than it did when she was singing "Tie a Yellow Ribbon" in the martini bar. "But you cannot stay here no more."

Beverly nodded in agreement. "We did not think it bad. But now . . ." She nodded sagely. I could smell the combination of Sanka and tequila wafting on her breath.

"Now what?" I asked.

"Now that the wagon has been fallen from," Sonya said, "it must be better for you staying with the passengers, yes? For safety."

Beverly continued. "If you collapse maybe,

God forbid, and choke on your vomit maybe, God forbid, and someone knows that we know you are living here against the rules . . ."

So this was it? I was being kicked out of the crew quarters for being an alcoholic? By these two?

"Fine," I said and started to slink away. "I'll be out of here today."

As opposed to Avalon Bay on Catalina, the port of San Marcos was large enough for cruise ships, with a good-sized dock that could handle two at a time. Today we were the only one.

It was a sunny, welcoming morning, and I was looking forward to getting off the ship. A lot of others must have felt the same way, because the gangway was crowded. At the front of the line was Malcolm Leeds, and I walked up to him to say hello—not to cut in line, just to say hello.

"Natalie," he said, looking surprised. He readjusted the faux-leather messenger bag over his shoulder, the one I'd admired a hundred years ago at the Melrose mansion. "Glad you're here." His smile seemed so forced. "I wanted to say hello."

"Wanted to say hello?" It seemed an odd turn of phrase, like we'd never say hello again.

"I mean after last night. Just wanted to make sure you're okay."

"Of course I'm okay," I said. "We should get

together for a drink." Ouch. I shouldn't have said that.

"Yes," he said. "When we get back on board. I'll leave a message." The man could not have sounded more insincere.

"Well," I said, turning away. I'd been wondering how Monk would ruin this relationship for me. Now I knew. "I guess I should go find Adrian." And I walked back down the line, just as they were opening the gangway gate, pretending like the moment had meant nothing.

I assumed Monk would be holed up in his cabin, cleaning a window or counting the specks on his ceiling tiles. But he was standing at the end of the line, trying not to feel crowded. As soon as he saw me, he lurched my way. "Natalie, where have you been?"

"Don't even start with the slugabed stuff," I replied. "I had a tough night."

"You mean from alcohol withdrawal?" I couldn't tell if he was joking or not. "Come on," he said, pointing to the sleepy town below us. For once, I noticed, he wasn't wearing his orange life vest. "The captain is waiting."

"Captain Sheffield?" I asked.

"Why would Sheffield be waiting in Mexico?"

"I don't know. Captain Stottlemeyer?"

"Why would Captain Stottlemeyer be waiting in Mexico?"

"Adrian!"

"Captain Alameda of the San Marcos police. He had someone leave a note under my door. I wonder if Lieutenant Plato is still with him."

Alameda? Police? As we got in line and made our way down to the pier, I racked my memory for the connection. I recalled one evening when Sharona and I were sitting down and trading war stories in her backyard in Summit, New Jersey. She mentioned an early case with Monk at a resort in Mexico. I didn't remember the details. Some death of a tourist? After a while, one impossible case gets jumbled up into some other impossible case. That's why I write them down.

I did vaguely recall a captain. According to Sharona, he was like a Mexican version of Captain Stottlemeyer, complete with receding hairline, cantankerous attitude, and bushy mustache. To add to the coincidence, his second-in-command had been the spitting image of Lieutenant Randy Disher, Stottlemeyer's number two at the time.

On that warm summer evening, over a few glasses of wine, Sharona was teasing Randy about having a Mexican doppelgänger. Randy Disher is currently the love of Sharona's life and the town of Summit's chief of police.

"Mr. Monk! Good to see you, old friend." Alameda waved from the pier. His smile was broad, not cantankerous at all. Of course, the man hadn't dealt with Monk in a decade and probably had fond memories of their exciting, successful case. "You look unchanged by the years. Still solving the murders of parachute jumpers who drown in midair as they fall?"

Oh yeah. That was the one Sharona mentioned. How could I forget!

Captain Alameda held out one hand to shake, and the other hand displayed a packet of American-made moist wipes. "You see? I remember. Where is the lovely Sharona?"

"Sharona left," Monk said as he shook the captain's hand, then accepted a wipe. "She has a life. This is Natalie. She doesn't. Where is your Lieutenant Plato?"

"Ah, he has a life, also. A police captain himself in Juarez, if you can believe. This is my new lieutenant. Miss Julia Rodriguez, meet Mr. Adrian Monk."

Lieutenant Rodriguez grunted and gave us both a firm handshake. She was tall and thin, with short, spiky black hair and a bit of an attitude. She also had a familiar quality to her, but I couldn't quite place it.

"Are you here to show us around town?" Monk asked. "We need to find some hermetically sealed, American-made oatmeal cookies. Our supply has dried up."

"I wish we could do so," said Alameda. "But this is a working day. Your captain has set up a communication with you at my office. Are you familiar with this thing called Skype?"

It seems Stottlemeyer and Devlin were desperate to get in touch. They'd been smart enough to figure out our itinerary and remember Monk's connection with the San Marcos police. Within ten minutes, we had made our way through the narrow streets back to the local *comisaria* and Alameda's tiny but tidy office.

Let me take a second here to say that no one looks good on Skype. Captain Stottlemeyer didn't. Lieutenant Devlin didn't. And I'm sure Monk and I looked equally creepy. All of us were crouched in front of computers, one computer in each town, staring into cheap fish-eye lenses.

"Finally," Stottlemeyer grumbled when he saw our faces. "I've tried e-mail, Natalie's cell, even calling your ship directly, which took some doing. Your ship's captain wasn't very helpful."

"He's not our biggest fan," I had to report.

Devlin laughed. "Really? I can't imagine why." Okay, now I realized who Lieutenant Rodriguez reminded me of.

"It wasn't my fault," shouted Monk, which probably had the same impact as my shouting, *I'm not an alcoholic.*

"Guys, forget it," said Stottlemeyer. "Business first. We ran into a glitch with the Melrose case."

"Glitch?" Devlin mocked. "The case fell apart. We had to release Portia Braun."

"What?" I was shocked. "Just yesterday, everything was fine. Malcolm Leeds told me that Lieutenant Devlin told him—"

"Leeds?" Devlin interrupted. "I haven't communicated with him since he left."

"Malcolm said you two talked yesterday."

"We didn't—not that I didn't try. Look," said Devlin, "who are you going to believe, me or some guy you met at a murder scene?"

To be frank, I had first met Devlin at a murder scene, but I guess that wasn't her point.

"You let Braun go?" Monk said. He pushed his nose to within an inch of the camera, thinking this would increase his impact. "But she's a killer. Like I said."

"We believe you, Monk," said the American captain. "But the DA wants more proof than a forged book at the bottom of a pond. Without a confession or something connecting her to the forgery . . ."

"My theory is the only logical one," Monk argued. "She should confess and save us the trouble."

"I agree," said Stottlemeyer. "But barring that . . . We were hoping Leeds could point us to a witness connecting her to the forgery. But his contacts with the few people in the area who could execute this kind of scam have turned up nothing."

"He didn't send you more?" I asked. "Malcolm said he sent you more sources to check out."

"Well, he didn't," said Devlin.

"It's a waste of time, anyway," said Monk. "You have to check out foreign sources."

Devlin scrunched up her forehead, which made her Skype face look even worse. "We were thinking local—because she didn't have access to the original, not until she arrived in the U.S. four months ago. Are you saying she planned this before leaving Munich?"

Monk didn't answer the question. "Concentrate on London. There are several legitimate sources that produce replicas of the Shakespeare originals for museums and libraries, that sort of thing."

Devlin kept her face scrunched. "Are you saying she ordered it long-distance mail order, like on Amazon?"

"Course not," said Monk. "That would leave a trail. This isn't the sort of thing she could carry off long-distance. Too many red flags."

"Okay," said Stottlemeyer. "We'll check England and France and Germany. Hell, we'll get Interpol to check all of Europe."

"Just make it England," said Monk. "Ireland, if you have time to waste. But concentrate on London. See if anyone produced two copies during the past few months."

"Two copies?" Devlin said. "Why two?"

"They don't have to be perfect forgeries," Monk said. "The paper is probably modern. I doubt they were created with the idea of fooling an expert."

Now it was Stottlemeyer's turn to make an

unattractive Skype face. "Monk, what are you getting at? Two copies of this Shakespeare book? Made in England?"

"What's your theory?" asked Devlin. "You have a new theory?"

"What do you guys care?" Monk was sounding petulant. He could get that way when you questioned the one thing he really knew how to do. "Theories don't count, right? A waste of time, according to the DA. Do you want proof against her? Do what I say and you'll get proof."

After that, there wasn't much to add. Monk had been insulted, and he wasn't going to hand out another theory until it was more than just a theory.

"All right," Stottlemeyer said. "We'll get on this instantly. Can you guys get off the ship and fly back? There's a nonstop to San Francisco."

"Give us a moment," I told them.

Monk and I looked at each other, thinking out our options. Then I covered up the lens and whispered. "We can't leave the ship now. What about Mariah? And the captain? And the vandalism?"

"You know we can still hear you," came Devlin's voice from the other side.

"Sorry," I said, and removed my hand.

"What do you say, Monk?" said the captain with a big Skype grin. "You hate boats. And we really need you. The mayor's office is pissed that we let our only suspect go."

"My boss informs me that we have prior obligations," Monk said.

"Prior obligations?" Devlin said. "What obligations? Something more important than murder? Natalie?"

"No," I had to admit. "Something exactly like murder."

Devlin threw her hands up out of the frame. "Augh, I should have known. It's always a new murder with you two."

"What?" I said. "It's not like we caused it. We just happened to be there. The same way you're always at a murder."

"We're homicide detectives."

"Children," growled the captain, like a father turning around in the driver's seat. "I'm sorry to hear about your murder, Monk. Anything we can do?"

"It's being called an accident," I informed them. "The ship comes back on Saturday, but they're going to need a sign-off from the SFPD before they can sail again. We're hoping you can make them stay."

"Do you have any evidence?" asked Devlin.

"I have it half figured out," said Monk. "The easy half."

Stottlemeyer nodded. "We'll keep the morning open. Meanwhile, we need to establish a better channel for communication on the Melrose case."

I agreed to keep my cell phone on as much as

possible—a billable expense—and to check the business center several times a day for updates—also billable.

"Did you at least put a tail on Portia Braun?" Monk asked.

A few reddish pixels hinted at a blush on the captain's face. "By the time I found out, her lawyer had already arranged her release. We lost her."

"Did you check the airports?" I asked. "How about trains or buses?"

They had checked, of course. But no trace.

"Well, keep trying," said Monk. "Meanwhile, arrange a police presence at the Melrose mansion, with emphasis on the library. Keep a guard there until I get back or drown at sea, whichever comes first."

"Guard the Melrose mansion? Why?" asked Stottlemeyer.

"No reason," said Monk. "Oh, and the Melrose son. Don't let him do anything about probating the will. Put everything on hold."

"Why?" asked Stottlemeyer again.

"No reason," said Monk.

Before hanging up, Devlin made a final, impassioned effort to get him to divulge his theory about London and the two forgeries. She was wasting her breath.

20

MR. MONK GOES SHOPPING

"What does Sumesa mean?"

"It means clean," I said. "Antiseptically clean. Super clean."

Monk and I were standing outside a Mexican supermarket looking up at the neon sign—SUMESA—which perhaps could be translated as "su mesa," your table, but which, for the sake of my sanity, I had translated differently.

"It looks fairly clean," he admitted grudgingly. This was the fourth grocery store we'd been to in San Marcos, and the first one I could convince him to walk inside.

This was how I was spending my day in an exotic tropical resort, Skyping with the police, then casing grocery stores to find American-made products wrapped in protective plastic. The next challenge would be smuggling the food back on board the *Golden Sun*. After that, I would have the task of finding somewhere to sleep, after having been kicked out by the Bulgarian party girls.

Monk took a wipe in each hand as he began pushing his cart. I followed at a distance as he made his selections from the shelves of Del Monte canned vegetables and, in the next aisle, Spam.

"You're going to eat Spam?" I asked in shock and awe. "You turn up your nose at my organic salads, and you're going to eat Spam."

"Nothing better," he said, and took an extra can just for good measure. "My mother served Ambrose and me Spam all the time. It's made in a U.S. factory, far away from all the dirt of nature, precooked to perfect edibility, sealed in a solid metal can—again avoiding nature—and comes out in a lovely symmetrical shape and exactly seven ounces every time. It's almost the perfect food."

"If it came in ten ounces, it would be perfect," I said. I haven't been at the man's side for a decade without knowing how he thinks.

"You don't know how many letters I've written to Hormel."

"I can guess," I said. And then something in the next aisle caught my own eye. "Ooh. I'll meet you at checkout."

When I joined him a few minutes later, he looked at my selections and frowned. "Natalie, I'm worried about you."

"Don't you start." I had picked out a corkscrew and the store's only bottle of California merlot. "Thanks to you, I can't have a drink anywhere on that ship."

"What are you talking about? Look at my old roommate, Darby. The ship gladly serves alcoholics."

"I'm not an . . ." Oh, what was the use! I shut my mouth and bought my wine. When it came time for him to pay, I didn't point out that he'd neglected to purchase a can opener.

We'd walked only half a block from the Sumesa, heading back to the *Golden Sun*, when I spotted four women from the ship, blocking the cobble-stone street in front of a souvenir vendor and his pushcart. Two of the women I recognized.

"Better hide your hooch," Monk whispered. I checked to make sure the bottle was fully inside the paper bag.

"Natalie, dear, how are you?" It was Daniela Grace, trying on a colorful scarf from the pushcart. Her eyes examined my face, like sympathetic X-rays, forcing me to clutch the bag even tighter. "You remember Ruth Weingart from the other night."

How could I forget! "Ruth. I'm so sorry for that scene. I'm not usually like that."

"We all have our moments," said Daniela. "The important thing is how you're doing today. Are you all right?"

I smiled and reassured them and filled up the awkwardness by making sure everyone was introduced. There was the thin, pulled-together Daniela and the taller, more matronly Ruth. The third friend was Sondra Winters, a gorgeous African-American, probably in her thirties. Rounding out their foursome was Lynn Sung. She was Asian with a Midwestern accent, probably the oldest of the bunch.

They were all friends from the Bay Area, and all four had persuaded their reluctant husbands to join them on this weeklong outing. "That's the great thing about a cruise," said Sondra. "You can ignore the hubbies and know they won't get into trouble. Like kids." Everyone laughed.

We spent the next few minutes immersed in small talk, all except Monk, of course. What lovely scarves! Isn't the food on the ship delicious! Isn't the weather perfect! We could have kept on going but were interrupted by a human bulldozer headed directly for us, weaving dangerously over the cobblestones.

It was Darby McGinnis. The potbellied man had just stepped out of a storefront bar, a Corona Light in each hand. He was mumbling angrily under his breath. "How can they not have whiskey? It's a bar, for God's sake." The six of us instinctively flattened ourselves against a stone wall, leaving the poor street vendor to fend for himself.

As the drunken man stumbled down the street, the women scowled.

"I'm not like that at all," I felt obligated to blurt out, still clutching my paper bag. No one replied.

"Excuse us," said Daniela, replacing the scarf on the vendor's cart. Her friends did the same. It had taken them long minutes to choose their favorites. Now they were rejecting them, throwing them back on the cart. "We'll see you later. Natalie. Mr. Monk."

"Half price. Two for one," the vendor suddenly offered. But the women's buying mood had been broken, and the four friends began moving like a pack down the winding street in the same direction as Darby. "Best bargain in San Marcos," the vendor shouted after them. His energy was wasted, and they all disappeared, Darby and the women, around a corner.

Monk had remained mercifully quiet throughout the encounter. Not even a peep about the wine bottle in the paper bag in my hand. "Thanks for not being yourself," I said. "I appreciate it."

"Hmm," he replied, not really hearing me.

"What's wrong?" I checked Monk's face. Something was bothering him.

"Are those ladies related to one another?" he asked.

"Related?" What an odd question.

"Are they sisters or something? I think they're sisters."

"Sisters? Adrian, one is African-American. One is Asian. And I think one is Jewish. So no, they're not sisters."

"Well, they look alike," he insisted.

"They do not," I said. "They're friends." Do friends start looking like one another after a while, I wondered, like husbands and wives or people and their dogs? "Maybe it's because they dress similarly," I suggested. "Or have the same hair stylist."

"Maybe," he said. But he didn't sound convinced.

Two hours earlier, when we'd first stepped onto the streets of San Marcos, Monk had been freaked out by the cobblestones. They were uneven and asymmetrical and made it hard to walk without stepping on a crack. But he'd gotten used to them fairly quickly, mainly because there was so much other disorder to distract him.

One of the main distractions here was traffic. An almost-constant honking of car horns ricocheted up the alleyways. Scooters and motor-cycles buzzed by everywhere, even on the side-walks. We had already witnessed two little fender benders.

"They drive worse than you." As usual, Monk had meant it as a compliment.

A few seconds later, when we heard an accident, the sound was different. The revs of the engine, the shouts of pedestrians, the crash of metal into something solid. More engine and tires. Finally, the screams for help.

It had come from nearby, maybe two blocks away, right by the San Marcos bus terminal. Monk and I both switched into cop mode and ran—he still grasping his bags of Spam, I clutching my wine. When we got there, the first thing I saw was Malcolm's messenger bag in the middle of the street. Directly ahead, a crowd was already gathering around the body.

"Nine-one-one is oh-six-six," Monk shouted.

"What?" I shouted back.

"For an ambulance. Dial oh-six-six." It was just like Monk to have the emergency numbers memorized. He probably knew hundreds of them all over the world. Just in case.

We hadn't expected to see Captain Alameda again. He and Monk had said their good-byes at the police *comisaria*, joking that they would meet in another ten years, the next time with even lovelier assistants. But next time turned out to be less than two hours later.

The San Marcos Civil Hospital was a frightening place, chaotic and broken and full of pain, not a place that I would trust to give me the best care. In Malcolm Leeds' case, it didn't matter. The man was already dead.

Monk couldn't stay in the emergency room. He was okay with death and injury and the sight of blood. It was the proximity to germs that made him queasy. As for me, I was just stunned. First Mariah, now Malcolm. For the first little while, I tried to cope by treating it as just your average, run-of-the-mill death. Nothing personal.

Alameda met us outside with the news. "Your friend stepped off a curb," he reported. "The car came straight down the hill and didn't stop.

A direct hit. He died instantly. The car kept going. The doctors always say 'died instantly' to make you feel better. This time it might be true."

"Any witnesses?" That was Monk. I was still too shocked to speak.

"Too many," Alameda said. "It was by the bus terminal. There was much coming and going and traffic everywhere. The witnesses agree on few things. It was a car, not a truck. A dark color—brown or black or green. And it was a tourist driving."

"How do they know it was a tourist?"

"The license plate for a rental car has orange stripes across the top and bottom. No one saw the number, but witnesses agree it had orange stripes."

"Good to know," Monk said. I could almost see him storing that factoid in his memory banks. "Is anyone checking the rental car companies?"

"Rodriguez is doing that. We may get lucky. Maybe not, if the car is undamaged. This is still your Easter period and there are many visitors."

"Spring break," I said, correcting him—the one thing I said the whole time.

"Spring break, yes. San Marcos is most popular with your San Francisco schools. Four or five nonstops a day in this season. Takes less than two hours."

"Can I examine the body?" Monk asked.

Alameda smiled. "I thought you didn't like our hospital."

"I don't like any hospital," Monk said, sounding more diplomatic than usual. For a split second. "But yours is especially bad. It's terrible. It's filthy. I'd rather die."

"Thank you," said Alameda. "So maybe you should wait until it is back on your clean American ship. I'll start the paperwork now."

It turns out when an American dies naturally or accidentally—and there was no evidence here to the contrary—the body is returned to the States. My first thought was about the ship's morgue. Would there be enough room? And would Malcolm be the last person to need it this week?

They were still talking about the body when a taxi pulled up to the emergency room curb. Captain and Mrs. Sheffield stepped out. "We came as soon as we heard," said Sylvia Sheffield. "This is so tragic."

I had called the ship right away, using the emergency number on the reboarding pass they hand out whenever you disembark. I had expected the Sheffields to arrive a little sooner than they did.

The Mexican captain explained the situation to the ship's captain and to its owner. In turn, they asked a few questions about the body's transfer. Had Alameda done this kind of thing before? Yes, more than you'd think. Could the transfer be done subtly and without fuss? Yes, of course. No gurney or body bag on the gangway? No, just a wooden box, like a supply delivery. Then Alameda said good-bye to us once again and left.

"Does Mr. Leeds have any relatives who need to be informed?" asked Sylvia.

"We knew each other slightly," I said, finding my voice again. "Malcolm's parents are dead, and there's no wife or girlfriend I know of. He has a sister in San Francisco. She's probably listed on the contact form." Before sailing, we'd all been required to list an emergency contact back in the States. I had listed my daughter, Julie. Monk had listed me.

"I'll take care of calling her," said the captain.

"Thanks, dear," Sylvia said. "Now, how do we break the news? Two deaths in one week? The last thing this ship needed."

"We don't say a thing," Sheffield decided for everyone. "Mr. Leeds was traveling alone. As far as the passengers know, Mr. Leeds disembarked in San Marcos and didn't reboard. It might be an illness. Or trouble back home. Things happen." He regarded us sternly. "Are we all on the same page?"

I had thought about this option, as I'm sure Monk had. He thinks about everything. On the one hand, it seemed disrespectful to let someone so warm and vibrant vanish from the face of the

221

earth without being properly mourned. On the other hand, he would be mourned by his sister and friends back in the city, and no one had really known him on the *Golden Sun*, except for me. And it would allow the cruise to continue as normally as possible.

"Same page," said Monk. I nodded. This was the moment I came closest to breaking out in tears.

Sylvia Sheffield glanced around. Their taxi was still waiting, but no one else was within earshot. "Do you think this was an accident?" she asked, looking at Monk. "I know it sounds crazy, but all these bits of vandalism . . . and now this."

During our working lives, Monk and I had seen so many accidents that hadn't been accidents. In this case, given the position and speed of the car, the direct impact without the squeal of brakes, the tourist plates, the quick disappearance of the vehicle, it looked bad. We hadn't shared any of our suspicions with Captain Alameda.

"I'm sixty-four percent sure it wasn't," Monk told the Sheffields.

Sylvia frowned. "Wasn't what? Wasn't vandalism or wasn't an accident?"

"Sixty-four percent that it wasn't an accident. And seventy percent that it wasn't part of the vandalism spree."

"Percent?" said the captain, tilting his head.

"We ask your opinion and you're answering us in percentages?"

"Yes, I am. A hundred percent answering you in percentages. It's sixty-four."

"That's just the way he talks," I said. "There's a better than even chance this was murder."

"Murder?" Sylvia gasped. "Who would want to kill one of our passengers? Do you think it might be drug related or a robbery? After all, this is Mexico."

"That's a ten-percent chance," said Monk. "Six percent for drugs and four percent for robbery."

"Are you just making this up?" asked the captain. "You're making this up."

In a way he was; in a way he wasn't. The numbers weren't exact but they weren't arbitrary, either. It was Monk's way of keeping all the possibilities open but keeping them in perspective. Don't ask me how it works.

"I'm a hundred percent sure I'm not making it up." Okay, now Monk was just being contrary.

"Fine," said the captain. "So, you're saying the odds are it wasn't an accident and the odds are it's not related to the things on the ship."

"Sixty-four and seventy percent respectively," Monk repeated.

"Do you know what happened at all?" asked Sylvia who was fifty percent confused and fifty percent frustrated.

"Not exactly," said Monk.

"But he's a hundred percent sure how Mariah Linkletter died." That was me. I couldn't resist throwing it in.

"Of course," said Sheffield's wife. "It was an accident."

Monk corrected me. "Actually, I'm at ninety-six percent, not a hundred."

Captain Sheffield sighed and threw up his hands. "Just tell me, Mr. Monk. What are the odds of you earning your money and getting to the bottom of this?"

"One hundred percent," said Monk.

"A hundred-percent guarantee," I agreed.

I wasn't quite sure what any of that meant, but we wound up with a great exit line. With those words ringing in their ears, Monk and I turned on our heels and haughtily walked away, Monk still clutching his two bags of Spam and me with my bag of wine.

21

MR. MONK'S MISSING LEG

We were among the last passengers to reboard the *Golden Sun*. There were still a few supplies on the dock to be loaded up the gangway, but I purposely didn't look. The last thing I needed was to make myself guess which box was holding the corpse of Malcolm Leeds.

It was pirate night, a realization I came to as soon as we stepped into the shipboard throng. The sound system was blaring some yo-ho-ho tune, probably from a Disney movie.

I don't know why cruise ships feel compelled to hold theme events, but this was ours. The two dozen or so kids on board were everywhere at once, outfitted in pirate hats and scarves and stuffed parrots. Three distinct groups were battling one another with plastic truncheons and rubber swords and all manner of semilethal weapons on loan from the ship's festive supply. Even the adults were in the swing of it, at least some of them, with plastic hooks and wooden legs and tankards of ale. A handful of wench-style blouses were being paraded around on female bodies that should have known better.

Thirteen-year-old Gifford Gilchrist was keeping

busy chasing his sandy-haired girlfriend up the stairs and around a lifeboat, singing a made-up song about booty and pillage. "Giff, be careful," his father warned, which might have sounded more convincing coming from a man without a wooden leg and an eye patch covering half of his pair of bifocals.

"Why pirates?" Monk asked. He had located a spot away from the action and magically had already found his orange vest and put it on.

"San Marcos has a history as a pirate port," I informed him. "At least, that's the pretext for all the fun. Everyone loves a pirate."

"I don't."

"Well, I do. They're sexy."

"Of course," Monk said. "And what's your favorite part of pirate life? I'd like to know. The murder, the torture, the rape, the kidnapping, thievery, destruction of property, cutting off of limbs, defiance of maritime law . . . ? I could keep on going."

"Be my guest."

"Pillaging towns, bad personal hygiene, promotion of violent behavior, sinking of ships, animal cruelty, setting a bad example for the youth of today, pirate booty . . . I could keep on going."

"Be my guest."

"The bad music played on concertinas, cheating at cards, lack of medical care or a retirement program. I suppose I already said murder. General sadism, sodomy, bad food, scary flags . . ."

I was fascinated to see how many more he could invent. But we were interrupted.

"I heard about Mr. Leeds." It was First Officer Lao. His only concession to pirate fashion was a red kerchief tied around the neck of his starched uniform. "What exactly happened?"

We found an empty game room on the lounge deck and told him almost everything we knew.

"It's like this ship is cursed," Lao said. "I don't know how we're going to survive."

"I'm going to need to examine Leeds' body," Monk told him. "Tonight's good."

"Whatever you need," said Lao. "I'll let the doctor know."

"Any more acts of vandalism?" Monk asked. "Not that I expect any."

"Actually . . ." Officer Lao hesitated, then shook his head. "No, it's hardly vandalism, but . . ."

"What?" said Monk. "If it's anything out of the ordinary . . ."

"It sounds petty, I know. But"—Lao laughed— "there's a wooden leg missing." I don't know what I'd been expecting him to say, but it wasn't this. "You know, one of those legs you strap on. Part of a costume."

It seems the pirate-night props and costumes had all been stored in a waterproof bin on the Calypso deck. Teddy, during the last cruise, while he was still assistant cruise director, had been in charge of putting things away. He was very organized about it, with every returnable hook and leg and feathered pirate hat checked off against a list.

Lao continued. "When Teddy opened the bin this afternoon to get ready, there was one wooden leg missing. That's all."

Monk was instantly intrigued. "A leg went missing between your last pirate night and this one? And the bin was locked?"

"Teddy probably miscounted last week, although he swears he didn't." Lao fidgeted. "I told you it wasn't anything."

"Does Captain Sheffield have a key to the pirate bin?" asked Monk.

"The captain has keys to everything."

Monk thought for a second, then left the game room for the lounge. He stood by the wall and waylaid the first wooden-legged pirate to stumble by. It turned out to be Barry Gilchrist, father of my thirteen-year-old nemesis. "Sorry," said Monk. "Can I see your leg?"

"You can have it," said Barry and sat down on a planter to take it off. "It's not terrible when you're just standing, but when you're actually trying to get somewhere . . . Has anyone seen Giff?" The last time I'd seen Gifford, he'd been chasing a girl, singing about booty and pillage.

I accepted his wooden leg and watched Barry walk off unsteadily, trying to revive his sleepy real leg, which had been tied back up around his hamstring.

Monk held the leg in a pair of wipes and examined its length and heft. Then he held it like a baseball bat and took a swing. I could tell exactly where he was going.

"Adrian?" I took out my iPhone and scrolled down to the pictures I'd taken yesterday in Dr. Aaglan's examining room. I pulled up the one of the wound on Mariah's left temple, enlarged it, and held it up next to the wooden leg. You could see where the wound narrowed slightly, like the narrowing of the artificial leg.

"There's your missing leg," I announced.

Monk nodded. "It must have taken some thought, given the confines of a boat. The man needed a blunt instrument that could mimic the impact of hitting your head on a wooden railing. And it had to be something he could throw overboard without it being missed."

"You're saying the captain killed Mariah with a wooden leg?"

"Another reason to hate pirates," Monk pointed out.

"So what do we do?" said Lao. "It's not like this proves anything."

"If we had the actual leg, we could check DNA—the smallest amounts of skin, blood,

maybe even prints. Wood is a good medium."
I was showing off my newfound forensic skills.

"But you say he threw it overboard," said Lao.
"So we've got nothing."

"We've got nothing," Monk echoed. "Except
now I know the murder weapon."

"And you know how he rang the alarm," I said,
"which you're not telling me."

"Because you're smart enough to figure it out
on your own, aren't you, Natalie?"

"Hold on," interrupted Lao. "You figured out
how he rang the alarm?"

"Don't ask," I said, shaking my head. "Mr.
Houdini here will tell us when he's good and
ready."

Monk rolled his shoulders in agreement. "What
I don't know is how Sheffield pushed the body
overboard without being there."

"But you're going to find out," Lao said.

"He always finds out," I said.

"Good." Lao looked relieved. "If there's anything more I can do, just ask."

"As a matter of fact, Natalie needs a room."

I had told Monk about my expulsion by the
Bulgarian party girls, but I never expected him to
actually be concerned. It was kind of touching.
"Thanks, Adrian. But they don't have any free
cabins."

"Sure, they do. One just opened up. He can get
you the key for Malcolm Leeds' room."

"What?" How he could even think . . . "I can't use a dead person's room."

"You're already using a dead person's room," Monk said.

"It's not the same," I argued. "Mariah was already my roommate when she died."

"Hold on." Lao turned to me. "You're staying in the crew quarters? You can't do that."

"You see, Natalie. You can't do that. What made you think you could do that?"

You're probably wondering how it could be any worse, sleeping in Malcolm's room instead of Mariah's. Well, you're going to have to take my word. Maybe it was the fact that I had started developing feelings for Malcolm and didn't want to have to face the reality of his abandoned room. Or maybe it was a cumulative thing. You take over one dead person's room and it's okay. You do it twice and it starts to seem like a ghoulish pattern.

Two more days, I told myself as I unpacked in cabin 562, just down the hall from my original digs. I couldn't decide if two more days was good or bad. Probably bad, since it meant we would either have to solve everything by then or see the murder scene and our suspect sail away.

Pushing aside a suit, a jacket, and a few shirts and pairs of slacks, I found room enough in Malcolm's closet for my skirts and blouses. Both sets of drawers were already full, and I didn't have the energy to try to make space. So I left the rest of my things in my opened bags lying on one of the beds. I took the other, hoping it was not the same bed he'd slept in the previous night.

The bathroom was easier. Malcolm's things were organized neatly on one shelf, leaving the other for me. I was mildly impressed that, in this day and age, any human being could take up only one shelf in a bathroom.

I stood there, staring at his shelf and my shelf, while a thought slowly dawned in my addled but still functioning brain.

Oh my God. I needed to find Monk.

I found him in Dr. Aaglan's office. The doctor was gone for the day, leaving Monk bending down over the tall, lean body lying on the examining table. It was the first time I'd seen Malcolm naked, and it was pretty much what I had expected to see, except for the dead part.

"He was a jogger," said Monk without looking up. "He played the piano and traveled a fair amount. He lived alone but had been married at one point. He's an Aries, not that he was a believer in that stuff, but his sister is."

I didn't ask him how he knew. "Why is any of this important?"

"It's not. I just like to stay in practice."

"Malcolm took his toothbrush," I said. "It wasn't in his bathroom."

"What?" Monk's head went up, like a gopher springing out of a hole. "Are you sure?" He didn't wait for my reply. "So that's why he was near the bus terminal."

"Exactly. Malcolm wasn't planning to return to the ship. I assume this pulls us up from sixty-four percent?"

"What are the chances that someone abandons ship and gets accidentally killed? This puts the murder possibility close to ninety. Eighty-nine percent, to be exact."

"What happened to his messenger bag? That might tell us something." The last time I'd seen the bag, it was lying on the cobblestones of San Marcos, not far from his body. "I'll call Captain Alameda," I said. "It could still be at the hospital or the police station."

"It's not," Monk said. "It's gone. Stolen, either by his killer or a bystander."

I had the same feeling but still intended to make the call.

Monk had moved away from the body and crossed to a black plastic bag filled with the deceased's possessions from the accident—his sandals and underwear and sunglasses. Some loose pesos from his pocket. No wallet or passport; they'd either been in his bag or had been stolen separately. Even Monk would have a hard time finding anything here.

"The deceased was slightly bowlegged. He

wasn't usually forgetful, but had been distracted a lot lately. He liked expensive things. . . ."

"Still practicing?" I asked.

"I like practicing. But you do need to call Lieutenant Devlin, as ASAP as possible. Fill her in on what's going down. Ask about the London connection. Oh, and one more thing . . ."

A minute later, I gladly left Monk with the body and made my way up to the lounge deck. The ship was once again at sea and our cell phones were useless. But the satellite phones in the business center would work perfectly, and they would be free, according to my arrangement with Captain Sheffield. I swiped my ship pass on one of the phones and started dialing.

"Amy?" It was after working hours and I was calling her at home, so I went with *Amy*. "Hope I'm not interrupting."

"Teeger? This better be good. I've had a long day, and I'm just sitting down with a glass of wine."

I had no sympathy. None. "Malcolm Leeds was hit by a car and killed."

I could hear her voice switch instantly into professional mode. "Was it an accident?"

I told Devlin everything I knew, which was probably less than Monk knew at the moment. "Did you get a chance to contact London about the fake Shakespeare?"

"It's only been a few hours," Devlin snapped.

"And they're eight hours ahead of us. But we made some progress. Interpol found a book restorer who says he made two copies for an American museum. A courier picked them up last week, he says. We're waiting for more details."

"So Monk was right—about London and the two copies."

"It seems so, although that shouldn't surprise us, should it?" Devlin paused, and I thought I could hear her take a sip of wine. "Does Monk think the Leeds death is connected to the Melrose case?"

"It's certainly possible," I said, which led me to my next question. "Did you locate Portia Braun? I know it's only been a few hours."

"Yes, we did," Devlin said. "Ms. Braun is old school chums with a German history professor at Holy Names in Oakland. Gretchen something-or-other. After we released Ms. Braun, she went to stay with Gretchen in her apartment in the Mission District. We tracked her down through Facebook. Braun posted a photo of the two of them last night."

"Good old Facebook. How did you get access to Braun's page?"

"Turns out Braun was Facebook friends with the victim, old man Melrose. We had legal access to his computer, so no laws were broken. Pretty cool, huh? My idea."

"Did you confirm it?"

"I called Gretchen at work. She confirmed it. We didn't want to make Ms. Braun too nervous, which is why we didn't do a check in person. What is Monk's theory?"

"He won't tell me. Could you go over and confirm it personally?"

"You think Gretchen is lying?"

"You won't know until you check," I said.

"You mean tonight?" Devlin paused, and I could hear the glug-glug of her wine leaving the bottle. Again, no sympathy. "Can I have my rotisserie chicken first? It's getting cold."

"If it's already cold, you may as well heat it up later," I said. "Monk would really like confir-ma-ion of Portia's whereabouts all day today, the sooner the better."

Devlin grudgingly agreed. "Fine. I'll e-mail you and text you as soon as I know."

After the call, I decided not to go back to the morgue. Monk didn't need me and I didn't need to be there. It had been quite a day and I didn't feel like eating, especially in the dining room, where some member of the B. to Sea Conference might ask me where Malcolm was tonight. I didn't feel I had the strength to lie.

Instead, I went outside and wandered around.

It was still dinnertime and the Calypso deck was pretty much deserted, the way it had been on the night Mariah died. I decided to make my way once around the ship's perimeter, starting at the three-o'clock position and meandering counter-clockwise. I was stopped more than halfway around, near the stern, between seven and six, by the sight of four women standing by the railing. Something about them made me step back into the shadows.

They were the four women from the street vendor's cart: Daniela, Ruth, and the other two. All were holding roses, red roses, like the ones from Mariah's memorial last night. Their words were drowned out by the breeze, but one by one they tossed their roses into the sea, then stood in a moment of contemplation, their faces still.

Monk had been right with his stupid comment this afternoon. Despite the different ages and races and heights and weights, there was something so oddly similar about these four women, something I couldn't quite put my finger on.

But the oddest thing to ponder was the full bottle of liquor at their feet, inches from the railing. From the shape of the bottle and the color, I assumed it was bourbon or maybe whiskey. What was my AA sponsor doing with an unopened bottle of the hard stuff?

I might have spent more time watching them from a distance and trying to figure it out, but the sight of the bottle reminded me that I had an unopened bottle of California merlot waiting for me in my cabin.

22

MR. MONK AND THE LADY PIRATES

I had only one glass of wine that evening—I swear. Then I fell into bed without dinner, exhausted but sleepless.

For the next few hours I lay there, drifting and thinking, the scene from the Calypso deck playing over and over. Four wealthy, married women by themselves in some sort of bizarre memorial, not all that different from the crew's memorial the night before, except for the bottle of whiskey. Did these women all have some connection to Mariah? If so, I was completely unaware of it.

I don't know what made me reach for Solomon Lao's vandalism report. An edge of it was visible in the smaller of my bags on the empty bed, poking out from under one of my two remaining pairs of clean underwear. Maybe I was looking for something to read or feeling guilty for having ignored our one paying case, even if we had been hired by Mariah's killer as a blatant distraction.

I sat up, turned on the reading light, and browsed the report's headings: Balcony Railing. Passenger Tender. Ice Sculpture. Mariah Accident. Bar Electrocution. I was on my second pass when

I focused on a list of names: Monk/McGinnis, Grace, Weingart, Winters, Sung. Next to each name was a cabin number: 457, 432, 444 . . . The cabins with the vandalized balconies, now all repaired.

It took me another few seconds to make the connection. Daniela Grace, Ruth Weingart, Sondra Winters, and Lynn Sung. The four best friends. And the only other cabins with the vandalized balconies.

The great thing about working for a decade with Monk is that you know a big clue when you see one, even if you don't know what it means.

Under normal circumstances, I would have knocked on Monk's door. But the sound of a vacuum cleaner told me he was still awake and might not be able to hear a civilized knock, so I used my key card, one of several that I'd been collecting over the past few days. Monk looked up from the perfect herringbone pattern of rug nap.

"Where did you get a vacuum cleaner?" I asked.

"You broke into my room at one a.m. to ask about vacuum cleaners?"

"No, you're right. I have other questions. Sit down."

"Just let me get in six more laps. Shouldn't be more than a half hour."

"No. Now." I switched off the small Electrolux and made him sit on his bed. "Those four women, the ones you say look alike? All of their balconies were rigged to collapse, just like yours."

I had expected some brilliant response, followed by "here's what happened." But he just stared blankly. So I told him about the secret memorial service just a few hours ago with the roses and the whiskey.

Monk still stared blankly, but this time he had a question. "What does Darby McGinnis do for a living besides drink?"

"Dr. McGinnis is a surgeon," I said, recalling Darby's statement at the business seminar. "If you can believe it. Cosmetic and reconstructive."

Monk stood up and marched up and down his own herringbone pattern, making a total mess of it, touching the far window and the doorknob at each turn, as if he were doing laps. On his sixth lap, he turned the doorknob and raced out in the hallway. I followed.

By the time we got down to level four, Monk had taken a key card out of his pocket. By the time we got to cabin 457, he had it ready to insert.

Monk recoiled as soon as he opened the door. He almost retched in horror. "What a mess."

It's true. Darby's cabin was a mess. But at least it was empty and no one was dead. Monk steeled his nerves and tiptoed, actually *en pointe* like a ballerina, to a stained blue blazer crumpled on top of a soiled section of carpet. "Tweezers," he demanded of me. "Or tongs. Or industrial-strength gloves."

"I get the point," I said, and without any protection whatsoever, lifted the jacket. Underneath it was a spilled bottle of Jack Daniel's, almost completely drained onto the floor. "Augh, it's worse than I thought," he said, and shot back out the door.

"Adrian, where are you going?"

I followed, of course—what else do I do?—down another flight to the Calypso level and out to the deserted deck. He was still way ahead when he rounded the last bend. "Stop," I heard him shout a few seconds later. "It's not too late. Don't do it."

I don't know what I was expecting to see. This was the spot where Daniela and her friends had been performing their little ceremony, although at the moment I didn't understand how that fit in.

There they were, all four of them, from early middle-aged to elderly, trying to heft the bloated, unconscious body of Darby McGinnis over the railing and into the churn of the Pacific.

"Put down the drunk," Monk ordered them. They didn't obey him as much as let Darby slip back onto the deck. He landed with a thud. "Good. Now step away from the drunk."

"We can explain," said Ruth Weingart, as though there could be some sort of innocent explanation.

"I know." Then Monk proceeded to do the

explaining for them. Meanwhile, I stood by, open-mouthed. And Darby? He remained crumpled on the deck, snoring.

All four friends, Monk explained, had had cosmetic procedures back in San Francisco. That's why Monk had seen the resemblance. Their sculpted eyes and noses and cheeks were all similar, all the product of a single surgical artist, Dr. Darby McGinnis.

But there had been a fifth, the friend Daniela had mentioned at the AA meeting, killed one horrible day exactly a year ago by their irresponsible, intoxicated doctor.

"We talked Samantha into it," said Daniela, taking up where Monk left off. There was so much sorrow in her voice. "She was happy with the way she looked. But no, we knew better. We had this great surgeon who worked miracles. And who cared if he enjoyed a cocktail or two after work or on the weekends! We all knew it. It was like a joke."

"Sam died the next day," said Ruth. "A combination of infection and lidocaine and painkillers. She tried to call Dr. McGinnis, but he was in the bar at his golf club and didn't pick up. The investigation blamed it on an accident, bad luck, a failure of communication. No charges were brought. But we knew better."

"I gave up drinking that same day," said Daniela. She looked at me. "By the way, Natalie, how is it going? I've been meaning to check in, but we've been distracted."

"Doing fine," I assured her. "Day by day."

"Good."

"So." Monk picked up the narration. "You learned McGinnis was coming to this conference and thought it would be perfect."

"It seemed like destiny," said Ruth. "On the anniversary of her passing. According to the books I read, it's easiest to kill someone and get away with it when they're someplace out of their element."

"Accidents happen on these boats," Monk agreed. "Boats are deathtraps. How did you get into McGinnis's cabin?"

Lynn Sung raised her hand. "My cabin was right next door. I told the steward I'd locked myself out, and he let me right in. No questions."

Monk nodded. "Of course, you couldn't unscrew just one railing. That would have been suspicious. So you unscrewed your own and hoped for the best. Your later stuff was even riskier, like the poolside bar."

"He was there every afternoon, drinking piña coladas, both feet on the footrail."

"Other people were there, too," I reminded them.

"I know," said Daniela. "We weren't thinking straight."

"You put innocent people at risk," I said. "What if one of them had died instead?"

"We're not experts at killing," said Daniela, in the understatement of the day. "McGinnis almost drowned when we sabotaged the shore boat in Catalina. We were all on board, standing guard while Sondra tried to hold him under."

"I grabbed onto him and pretended to panic," said Sondra with pride. "Screaming and pulling him. You know us black folk. We can't swim."

"It might have worked, too," said Ruth. "Except a guy from the crew pulled her off and dragged him back to the boat."

"Didn't he recognize you?" I asked. "Four of his old patients? You were stalking him all day today in San Marcos, right? Hanging outside that bar?"

"We thought that might be a problem," said Ruth. "But he's had so many patients. We were just paychecks."

"That's what gave us the idea for tonight," said Daniela. "His desperate search for a bottle of Jack Daniel's." She looked down at the twisted, snoring blob on the deck. "Don't worry. We didn't poison him."

"Then you can still get out of it," I said. "You're not killers. You're women in pain. And you proved you could do it. There's no reason to ruin your lives and your husbands'. Does Darby know you drugged him?"

"We left the bottle gift wrapped outside his cabin door," said Ruth. "A present from the captain."

"Then he'll never know—if we get Darby back to his cabin before he recovers. Adrian?" I looked at my partner. "Don't you agree?"

"I don't," said Monk firmly. "It's attempted murder. Plus destruction of property, aggravated assault, willful endangerment. You're like a bunch of female pirates."

"Adrian, please."

"We were hired to solve the vandalism. It's professional pride. Not to mention getting paid."

"Adrian?"

"We'll pay you to walk away and let us finish the job," said Daniela. "Fifty thousand." She said it like it was nothing.

"How much?" asked Monk, suddenly thinking it over.

"Fifty thousand."

"And you promise to get rid of him?"

"Adrian!"

He turned to me and shrugged. "This isn't a normal person, Natalie. It's Darby McGinnis."

It's never a good sign when I'm the sole voice of reason. "Adrian, you can't let them kill him."

"Party pooper." Monk sighed. The expelled air was mixed with a low groan and lasted about thirty seconds. "Okay, you're right." He turned to the women. "Sorry, girls. Natalie, get the captain."

"No!" shouted Daniela. She seemed about ready to faint. Despite the snoring drunk at their feet, they all looked so helpless.

"Hold on," I told Monk. "Maybe we can come to a compromise. Meet somewhere in the middle."

"You mean arresting only two of them?" asked Monk. "That hardly seems fair."

It took some more convincing, but I knew how Monk thought, and we eventually got it worked out. Darby would live. I would keep an eye on the news, just to make sure. But I trusted them now. This moment had been cathartic, and the impulse would pass.

"We won't try again," said Lynn Sung. Up until now she'd been the quiet one. "We just had to do something. We didn't care about the repercussions."

"Samantha wouldn't want you to ruin your lives," I suggested. And they agreed.

The hard part now would be getting Darby back to his cabin.

We tried several times, all six of us. But drunken flab is almost impossible to lift. And even if the man could be lifted and carried, there was no guarantee that we could get him there without being seen.

"How did you get him here in the first place?" I asked.

"He was still stumbling," said Ruth. "All we had to do was guide him along. Obviously, things have changed."

"Just leave him," Monk suggested. "He's woken up in worse places."

And that's what we wound up doing. It had been a long, emotional day for everyone. The temperature was well above freezing, almost balmy, and Darby's bulk would keep him from sliding under the railing.

Mission accomplished.

23

MR. MONK FILES A REPORT

That same night, before Monk and I even knew we were about to solve the ship's vandalism case, Lieutenant Amy Devlin had left the warmth of her rotisserie chicken and driven to a duplex apartment on Lexington Street in the Mission District, no doubt cursing me all the way.

Devlin was not subtle by nature. As a detective, she'd done some undercover work. But her hard-nose attitude was more attuned to throwing herself into a situation and getting it done, especially when it was late and she was hungry.

A more subtle detective might have knocked, politely introduced herself to Professor Gretchen Wilder, and made up some excuse to ask Gretchen's old friend and houseguest, Portia Braun, what she'd been up to today. Instead, Devlin made her visit short and unsweet. The fact that the women were about to sit down to a great-smelling dinner probably didn't help.

While Gretchen went back to set the table, Portia outlined her alibi. She had driven to Oakland that morning, she said, gone browsing at a few secondhand boutiques, driven back into the city for lunch, then out to Berkeley in the afternoon to catch a German-language film at an art house near the university. Her whole day. Alone in a crowd.

"You went back and forth across the bay twice that day?"

"Yes," Portia said. "I was feeling sort of aimless. Driving helps me cope. Is there a law against that?"

"Not yet," said Devlin. She thought about asking Portia to describe the plot of the movie, but Devlin had once seen a German art house film and knew there probably wasn't much to describe.

On her way back to her car, Devlin stopped to peer inside Portia's car, the one she'd been leasing during her California stay. Suctioned onto the windshield was a FasTrak pass, which gave the lieutenant an idea.

Back home, while chewing on her tough, warmed-up chicken, Devlin used her police ID to check the secure section of the Bay Area Toll Authority Web site. Portia's story seemed to check out. According to her FasTrak, she had traveled across the Bay Bridge at 9:05 a.m., then again at 11:39 and 1:47, and finally back home at 5:57 p.m.

Early the next morning, Monk was standing over my shoulder, reading Devlin's lengthy, poorly typed e-mail. No one else was in the business center at this time of day, so we felt free to speak.

"Did you really think she flew down to Mexico, killed Malcolm, and flew back?"

"It's less than a two-hour flight," said Monk. "And, given the fact that she was planning the theft of a six-million-dollar book, the woman probably has a fake passport."

"But why?" I asked. "Why would she fly all that way to run down the guy who helped get her arrested? If she's that vindictive, she should have run you down." But I guess I already knew the answer. "You think they were in on it together, don't you?"

Monk shrugged, his way of saying yes. "It's not unreasonable they would have met, two rare book experts in a city the size of San Francisco. She would have told him about the Shakespeare folio, and it would have been tempting. But their plan went wrong. Melrose died and Mr. Leeds was brought in by the police to authenticate the volume."

"That's just a theory," I said. I couldn't help feeling defensive.

"But it explains why Malcolm Leeds never responded to Devlin's calls, and why he took his toothbrush, and why someone in a rental car would run him down in Mexico."

"Except she didn't," I said.

"I didn't say it was a perfect theory," said Monk, and led the way out of the business center.

Today would be a day and night at sea, as the

Golden Sun raced north toward Pier 35 in San Francisco. The salt air was already a little cooler, or so it seemed.

I had scheduled a meeting late in the morning with Captain Sheffield and his wife in their quarters on the navigation deck. We had only a few minutes to spare, so I avoided taking Monk through all the distractions of the pool area. Instead, we cut through the lobby to the main staircase, where we happened to see Darby McGinnis slumped at the breakfast bar, nursing a cup of coffee. My eyes met his for just a second. I felt so guilty—and curious—about last night that I had to stop and say hello.

"Natalie. Monk," he murmured. You could see from the way he sat that the man was in pain. His face seemed to have a few new bruises.

"Darby," I said. "What happened? You look . . ."

"Terrible," Monk said, completing my thought. "Like you had an alcoholic blackout and woke up on the deck this morning without remembering how you got there or anything. Am I right?"

"Pretty much," said Darby in a feeble chuckle.

"Good," I said. "I mean, it's good that nothing worse happened. I mean, you could have fallen over a railing." Shut up, Natalie! "But you didn't."

"It's the second time this week," Darby moaned. "First time, I felt like I was suffocating. This time, I felt all these hands. . . . I'm thinking it

251

may be time to do something. About my drinking."

That was good to hear. Finally. "They have meetings on the ship," I said, pointing across to the meeting room by the T-shirt boutique. "Friends of Bill W. Every day at four. I'm sure they'd be glad to talk to you."

"You mean AA?" He laughed. "Jeez, I'm not desperate. Just thought maybe I'd stick to beer for a while."

I had spent an hour that morning writing up a short, evasive report. I knew it would be a thankless job. But writing useless reports is one of the obligations of running a business.

Monk and I sat across from Dennis and Sylvia Sheffield at the coffee table in their little suite. Each was reading a printed copy. Neither looked pleased.

"You're saying you solved the case," said the captain, indicating the lead bullet point on page one. "And yet"—he flipped to page two—"you don't state what happened or who was behind the various acts. People could have died."

"People did die," Sylvia pointed out.

"Yes," I allowed. "The good news is that neither death had anything to do with the vandalism." That's one of the things I learned from *Business Management for Idiots*, page forty-seven. Always mention the good news, even when there isn't any. "The Mexican police ruled Mr. Leeds' death an accident. Miss Linkletter's death looks like an accident, too."

"It looks like one," interjected Monk.

"You're obviously protecting someone," Sheffield said. "Who?"

I ignored the question. "Would you prosecute the vandals if we told you their names?"

"Are they employees?" asked Sylvia.

"No," I said.

Sylvia frowned. "Then no. Probably not. Publicity in this sort of thing is never good."

"And we can assure you that those events were unique to this cruise. The motive didn't involve the *Golden Sun* company, and it won't be repeated on future trips."

"Then why won't you tell us?" asked Sylvia. "We said we're not going to prosecute."

"Was it teenage kids?" asked the captain. "A disgruntled employee? No, you said it wasn't an employee."

"Sorry," I said.

Monk and I had thought it over. We agreed that a killer isn't the best person to trust with anyone's secret, especially the secret of four rich, vulnerable women who'd made a horrible mistake.

"So we're exactly where we were before," said Sheffield. "If we hadn't hired you, the results would be the same. In fact, there's no proof you did any investigating at all."

"But we did," I assured him. "And you have the peace of mind of knowing it's over. It won't happen again. Guaranteed."

Looking back, I probably shouldn't have used the word *guaranteed*.

"Guaranteed? Fine. So where are the results?" Sheffield shook the flimsy three-pager. "Don't you think we have a right to hear your results?"

The whole meeting had been a long shot. Necessary, yes, since we'd agreed to report back. But I was all set to walk away empty-handed. Until Monk interrupted Sheffield's latest little rant.

"There are a few things we did figure out that aren't in the report," said Monk. "For example, the wooden leg . . ."

"Wooden leg?" said Sylvia.

"Page two," said Sheffield, shaking his head in disgust. "Some passenger didn't return a pirate costume."

"We know what happened to the leg," continued Monk. "And the chunk from the ice sculpture."

"What?" Sheffield snorted. "That damn ice sculpture? Is this how you were wasting your time?"

Monk was smiling, as close to smiling as he got. More like a smirk. "We know who chipped it off and why he did it. This happened an hour or so before Mariah Linkletter went overboard. It has nothing to do with your case. But if you really want to know . . . about the leg and the ice?" He paused dramatically. "Mrs. Sheffield?"

Sylvia Sheffield glanced over to her husband.

"What do you say we pay half?" Dennis Sheffield said. "Half the agreed-upon fee. It's worth it just to get rid of them."

"Darling?" Sylvia looked confused. "Why should we pay them anything?"

I never saw a checkbook come out of a drawer so fast in my life. "Well, we did hire them," Sheffield explained as he reached into his pocket for a pen. "And their time is worth money."

Two minutes later, I was following Monk down to the Calypso deck, waving a check and watching the ink dry. "Did you just blackmail him?" I asked, trying to keep up with him. "Because it sounds like you just blackmailed him."

"Nonsense. I had no idea he would offer us money. I just wanted him to realize we're not dumb. Well, I'm not dumb."

"I'm not dumb, either."

"Really? Then tell me, Ms. Teeger, why is he afraid every time we mention the ice?"

"For the same reason you're afraid of milk." Okay, that was a silly answer. But I had to say something.

Monk had led me to the Calypso deck, past the CREW ONLY chain, to the spot where the man overboard alarm rang three days ago. Together we stared at the red bell and the little red hammer poised an inch and a half away. "Ice," he said simply, expecting me to fill in the blanks.

I did my best.

"Okay. Sheffield slipped a chunk of ice between the hammer and the bell. Then he pulled the alarm. When the ice melted, the bell rang and the electrical contact was made."

Monk nodded. "Very good. Remember the bird drinking from the puddle on the deck? How else would freshwater wind up here?"

"But how did Sheffield time it?" I asked. "There's no way he could know how long it would take for the ice to melt."

"He didn't know," Monk admitted. "He just had to make sure he was around people every moment for the next few hours."

"And how did he dump the body?"

This was the big problem, you see. The ringing of the bell and the dumping of Mariah's body had to be coordinated. The two couldn't have happened more than a minute or so apart.

"I don't know," said Monk. "How much time do I have? Three or four days?" He knew better. If anyone was counting the hours until he hit dry land, it was him.

"The trouble is Sheffield knows the ship," I said. "And he controls it, from the top of the smokestack to every inch below deck."

Monk looked puzzled. "What do you mean, below deck? This place has a basement?"

"Yes, Adrian. This place has a basement."

24

MR. MONK GOES DEEP

"Why are you still wearing a life vest?"

"Am I wearing a life vest?" Monk answered the man, tightening the straps on the piece of orange vinyl. "I didn't realize. It feels so comfortable."

"He's joking," I said.

First Officer Lao pretended to laugh. "That's the cleanest vest I've ever seen. How did you get it so . . . ?" He went in for a closer look. "Wait. You had your name printed on the back?"

"It's not printed," I explained. "It's indelible marker. He just has very precise handwriting."

"You realize, Mr. Monk, that you're going to have to return that."

"Or I could just buy it," said Monk. "My vest back home isn't nearly as nice. For one thing, it doesn't have a whistle." He touched the red whistle hanging from his shoulder. He had disinfected it and wrapped it in two layers of clear plastic.

"Why do you need a vest back home?"

"Don't ask," I said. That's my explanation for a lot of things with Monk. Personally, I've seen him use his home vest only once, in the midst of a monthlong drought, standing on the roof of his little apartment building on Pine Street. As I said, don't ask.

We were with Solomon Lao in his bachelor quarters below deck, just a few turns of the hallway from where I'd spent two memorable nights. He had just rummaged through his drawers and come upon a green key card. "This opens everything," he said, "even the captain's quarters. But please don't."

"We won't," I said, not quite sure if I meant it. "We're interested mainly in below deck. Right?"

"Right," said Monk.

"Good. Because if the captain knew, I'd be thrown in the brig, lose my job, and probably be prosecuted."

"A cruise ship has a brig?" Monk asked.

"A cruise ship needs a brig," Lao answered.

"Good to know," said Monk. "What else does the ship have?"

"Do you have a map?" I asked.

"For the crew areas? No. But there are two levels below this one. The first has the engine room, laundry, anchor access, electrical room, and desalination plant. The one below is basically ballast, water storage, and the stabilizers. I wouldn't go down that far if I were you. There's nothing to see, and it can be dangerous."

"We've been in a ballast tank on a submarine," I told him. "It wasn't fun."

"What were you doing in a ballast tank on a submarine?"

"Drowning," said Monk.

"We were dealing with another homicidal captain," I said. "He's now serving life at the naval station prison in San Diego."

Lao chuckled until a second later when he realized that we were serious. "Holy Mother Mary. Believe it or not, that makes me feel better." He checked his watch. "I have to get back on top for my shift. Be careful."

Monk and I began on the crew level. There wasn't much to see, just a lot of tight corridors and cabins, interspersed with the lounge and cafeteria and a small disco bar that always seemed to be full and noisy. Monk kept his arms folded across his vest to avoid contact with anything.

"What are we looking for?" I asked as we started our second loop around the ship.

"I'll know when I see it," he said, then headed toward the down staircase.

On the lower level, the lights were dimmer and the throb of the engines louder. I could see Monk tensing and drawing himself even more tightly in. It was hard enough for me. And I'm not claustrophobic.

The laundry room was toward the stern, full of steel industrial-sized machines and the smallest, most compact workforce I'd ever seen. Four of them were working nonstop and no one looked over five foot two. Like a factory of overheated Oompa Loompas producing clean sheets and towels instead of chocolate.

The electrical room was small and not much to look at. Hundreds of switchboxes lined the walls, all with labels. Here, I walked behind Monk, keeping a careful eye on his hands. If there was one switch facing down when Monk felt it should be facing up, the temptation might prove irresistible. The last thing I wanted was to be stranded at sea with no electricity and five hundred people blaming me for the short circuit.

Next was the engine room. It was huge and high-ceilinged and hot with the friction of moving parts that were hidden under the light green housing of six engines, each the size of a Mini Cooper. A low, perforated steel catwalk ran between the two rows of three. Monk stood right inside the steel door, frozen. I could see the panic forming in his eyes. I was surprised he'd made it this far.

The engine room was too loud for us to hear each other, so Monk motioned me up to the catwalk and mimed for me to look around. And I did.

What was he expecting me to see? What could Mariah's death possibly have to do with the engine room? But we knew that Sheffield's advantage was linked to his knowledge of the ship. And Monk's OCD made him determined to check out everything.

I was concerned about letting him out of my sight. Between the noise and the claustrophobia, he was barely holding on. But I focused on the six engines, found nothing unusual, and walked down the six steps on the far side of the catwalk—only to find Monk gone.

I didn't blame him for fleeing this mechanical chaos. I blamed myself. But I wasn't really nervous until I stepped back into the hall and saw that he wasn't there waiting for me.

"Adrian?" I shouted into the dim, metallic subbasement. "Adrian? Adrian? Mr. Monk?" I felt in my pocket for the key card, then realized that he had it, not me.

I don't know how long it took. Long enough to look everywhere I could. Back to the switch-boxes. Back to the Oompa Loompas. The engine room had been locked behind me, but I slammed my fist on the door and called. Next, I headed down to the lowest level and the locked stabilizer room and the tanks. "Mr. Monk?" I didn't want him refusing to answer me on a technicality. "Adrian? Mr. Monk?"

After that, it was two levels up to the crew quarters. That wasted five more minutes. Then down to the engine level. Then back down to the ballast level and another full circuit. Had he fled to the passenger area? Had he accidentally locked himself away? Was he catatonic in a corner? I made one more circuit, listening for the whistle from his life vest. If he was in danger, he would unwrap and blow the whistle. I knew him. Why wasn't he blowing the whistle?

Finally I collapsed near the stern of the crew level, by a wall of critical-looking pipes and gauges. When the phone above me on the wall rang, I knew it had to be him. But it wasn't.

"Natalie." It was First Officer Lao, calling from the bridge.

"Is Monk there?" I asked.

"No. Listen to me."

"How did you know I was here?" Then I glanced up to the camera winking in the corner. "Oh, okay."

"Natalie." There was an urgency in Lao's voice. "Captain Sheffield was in the communications room. He must have seen you on the monitor."

"Is he still there?"

"No, that's what I'm saying. Sheffield raced right out and down the stairs. I caught a glimpse of him on a monitor, entering the crew area. He must be after you. Have you seen him?"

"No," I said. "Wait. Are you by the monitors now? Do you see Adrian? Where is he?"

"I don't know. But when I saw you, I knew there was a phone."

"Go check the other cameras," I told him. "Where's Adrian?"

There was a slight, nervous pause. "They're not

working. When I got into the communications room, the cameras on the engine level and the ballast level were turned off. I can't turn them back on."

"What do you mean?"

"Sheffield must have done something. Natalie, I'm sorry. But we're blind down there."

I was still adjusting to the news that Captain Sheffield had seen Monk on the monitor, sneaking around. He knew where Monk was—which was more than I knew—and had gone running off to do something about it. That's when I heard the alarm bell. It was a familiar sound to me now.

Man overboard!

"What's happening?" I asked.

"It's the pool deck," Lao informed me before hanging up and starting his list of emergency procedures.

Except for the time of day, midafternoon, this was almost exactly the same situation as three days ago. First Officer Lao was at the helm. I was in the crew quarters again, maybe thirty yards from where I'd been before.

The other alarm bells joined the fray, and once again the six Mini Cooper–sized engines ground to a halt. Three stewards came running out of their quarters, pulled on their life jackets, and scrambled up to their stations.

Once again the engines went into reverse as I scrambled up the stairs myself, this time heading up to the pool deck toward the rear of the ship. By the time I made it to the pool, the engines had stopped. By the time I'd pushed my way through the crowd, the massive anchor chain was rolling off its spool.

"I did it," Gifford Gilchrist shouted for everyone to hear. "This time I really did." The thirteen-year-old stood by the red alarm, in the middle of the crowd, beaming at his father.

I was one of fifty passengers at the starboard railing, staring into the choppy ocean swell. Unlike the others, I knew what to look for. An orange life vest. Thank God for the life vest. And sure enough, there it was, bobbing down the length of the ship.

Empty.

At first I couldn't believe it. How could anyone or anything have gotten that off him? He'd been wearing the damn thing 24/7 since the lifeboat drill. My second thought was *Maybe it's not Monk.* Maybe all of this fuss was because some eager, desperate-for-attention teenager saw a floating vest and wanted to cement his reputation. King of the alarm bells.

"There he is," the woman beside me said. I followed her pointing finger to a man in a brown wool jacket, barely floating on the waves. He was facedown in the water. And he was Monk.

Two decks below, a trio of stewards was already swinging a lifeboat into the water.

"You see?" Young Gifford was at my side, staring straight up at me. "I am a hero."

"Thank you" was all I could say. I just stood there and said thank you, like he had just passed the salt or held open a door for me. Like nothing I had just seen could possibly be real. Then a sense of panic suddenly gripped my chest and I bolted, scampering down to the lower deck.

Dr. Aaglan was standing by when Monk's motionless body was finally lifted out of the lifeboat. "Three?" he mumbled, shaking his head. "I don't think we have room for three."

"He's not dead," I snarled, not knowing if it was true or not. "He can't be."

25

MR. MONK TAKES A NAP

If Monk had actually died, I probably wouldn't be writing this. I'd probably be catatonic, staring at the walls, blaming myself for luring him back onto the ship in Catalina. For not taking better care of him. For not being nicer and more understanding.

Monk, it turned out, wasn't dead. But he wasn't conscious. And the gash on his left temple was frighteningly similar to the one on Mariah's.

I followed Aaglan and the stewards and Monk on the gurney down to the infirmary. At the landing by the elevator, we ran into the captain. "Who is it?" he demanded. "What happened?"

I wanted to say, *You know damn well what happened: You got Monk's vest off and pushed him overboard.* Instead I just said, "He's alive."

As we rolled into the elevator, Solomon Lao appeared on the stairs, on his way down from the bridge. "Call the coast guard!" I shouted. "We need a medevac."

"That's the captain's prerogative," said Lao, eyeing Sheffield, who was still on the landing, frozen in place.

"Call them now!"

I don't know how I did it, but I took control. Captain Sheffield couldn't have been happy that Monk was still breathing. Dr. Aaglan was fairly clueless. And First Officer Lao was required to obey the captain. I was the one who had to keep the captain out of the infirmary and preempt any attempt he might make to delay the air rescue.

I stayed by Monk's side until the helicopter arrived from the coast guard air station at LAX. It hovered over the ship's largest open area, the pool deck. Hundreds of passengers and crew looked on from a distance as I squeezed Monk's hand one last time. Then I cleaned his hand with a wipe and adjusted the straps across his body so that they were all lined up evenly. Even unconscious, he would want that.

I could barely hear my own voice above the chop of the flying wind machine. "You'll be all right," I promised. It was a promise I knew I couldn't keep. "And I'll catch him. Don't worry. I'll catch the bastard." A promise I intended to keep.

Lao was standing next to me. He signaled the chopper, and we watched together as the rescue gurney and my partner were drawn up into the bay. The fact that Monk didn't instantly wake up and start to panic told me he must be in pretty bad shape.

The next hour or so passed in a fog. I went directly from the pool to the poolside bar and was the first in line when they reopened for business. I ordered a glass of white wine and sat there defiantly, back to the bar, elbows on the counter, waiting for anyone to try to take it away.

The idea of Monk's dying was unthinkable. He'd been through so much. This man with a damaged soul and a hundred phobias had survived so many attacks over the years and faced down so many killers. And now, on what seemed to be just another case . . .

I left my half-finished glass of wine and went inside to the business center to call Adrian Monk's next of kin.

"Leland? It's Natalie." Okay, Captain Stottlemeyer wasn't technically next of kin. But Monk's brother Ambrose was incommunicado, on his extended honeymoon in an RV somewhere in the continental U.S. And Stottlemeyer was closer than anyone else in our lives.

"What happened to Monk?" He could tell from my tone.

I started to explain. But he didn't need to know the whole case. "What the hell happened to Monk?"

I told him the basics—concussion, in the water, lack of oxygen. "They're flying him to Good Samaritan in L.A."

"I'm catching the next flight," said Stottlemeyer. "You talk to Devlin. She'll hold the fort and give you everything you need in San Francisco. What about you, Natalie?"

"What about me?"

"Are you going to be okay? Do you think your life's in danger?"

I hadn't even thought of that. Now I thought. "I don't think so. Adrian's the one who was close to figuring it out. I don't think the bad guy sees me as a threat."

"Well, that's his mistake. People underestimate you."

"I hope it's his mistake," I said. "I need him to make one."

"What about the ship's captain? Is he on your side?"

I had to laugh. "The captain is, in fact, the opposite side."

I took a few minutes here and explained to Stottlemeyer the basics, in case neither Monk nor I survived our lovely six-night cruise. It felt a little like when I made out my will a few years ago, speculating about how life would have to go on without me. It's not a pleasant feeling.

"I gotta call the airlines," said the captain, turning back to practical matters. "Is Ellen flying down?"

Damn. I hadn't even thought about Ellen. "I'm calling her right now," I said. "She and Adrian had a little falling out. But I'm sure—"

"Oh," the captain interrupted.

" 'Oh' what?" I asked. *Oh* is never good, not in that tone of voice.

269

"Nothing," Stottlemeyer lied. "Okay, not nothing. I happened to walk past her store this afternoon. It was all closed up in the middle of the day."

"Oh," I echoed in response. Maybe Ellen had flown off to take care of business in New Jersey, I thought. But then she had an assistant, Suzie, to keep the Union Street shop open. You don't close a storefront for no reason, not when you're paying that kind of rent. "I'll give Ellen a call."

I tried Ellen's cell phone a few times. Each time it rang and rang and went to voice mail. Either she was away from her phone—odd behavior for her—or she was screening her calls. The third time, I left a message, saying it was important and to call Captain Stottlemeyer as soon as possible. I didn't want to say anything scary. I didn't even want to think it.

That evening, I dialed room service and had dinner delivered. I forget what it was, something light and simple. Then, antsy in my cozy cabin, I went up to the Calypso deck and started walking, doing slow, steady laps around the ship.

One more day, I thought as I lapped. Another day at sea, to discover whatever Monk might have discovered. When we woke up the day after, the gangway would be down at Pier 35. The *Golden Sun* would be turned around in a few hours, refilled with passengers, and cruising into international waters by that afternoon, this time up to Vancouver.

• • •

When the business center opened at seven, I was waiting at the door, phone number in hand. I found the bureaucracy at Good Samaritan to be mercifully efficient, and once I explained my relationship with the patient and dropped a few names, they patched me through to a very tired-sounding doctor at the ICU.

"I've been on the phone with everyone from the San Francisco mayor to the ex-governor. You guys should share information. Start a Facebook page." I was glad Stottlemeyer had told so many influential people and that they were taking it so seriously. Monk would get the best care. On the other hand, I needed to hear it personally—and right now.

His first words were not reassuring. "A medically induced coma," I repeated. It didn't sound any better when I said it.

"It's not an unusual procedure in drowning cases," he told me. His voice was flat, as if he'd already said this a dozen times. "We use barbiturates. The coma reduces the rate of activity in the brain and the amount of blood it uses. This decreases the intracranial pressure, and we might be able to avoid brain damage."

"Avoid brain damage." I ignored the word *might*. "So we can expect a full recovery?"

"God, you're worse than the mayor." He sighed and I almost felt sorry for him. "A full recovery is possible, yes. And if I can anticipate your next question, Ms. Teeger, it could take as little as a few days or as long as a few months."

I don't recall much else of what he said that morning. But I do remember giving him a piece of medical advice. "Is Adrian in a private room?" I asked.

"It's part of an IC unit," he said, "but it's curtained off to make it private."

"Well, keep it as private as possible. And keep everything in his line of vision clean and symmetrical. I know you run a clean hospital, but make it extra clean. And symmetrical. The same number of rings on each curtain, that sort of thing."

"Ms. Teeger, the man's in a coma."

"It doesn't matter. He'll know."

I added on another call to my account, this one to Captain Stottlemeyer at a motel just down the street from the hospital. He confirmed what the ICU doctor had told me, and I confirmed that there'd been no change since last night.

"Did Ellen call you?" I asked. "I don't have any reception, so I left her a message to contact you."

"Not yet," said the captain. "When she does, I'll try to break it to her gently. Thanks for the heads-up."

We exchanged a few more words of encouragement and strategy. Then I reluctantly had to say good-bye. I was alone now, on someone else's turf, playing the game of cat and mouse that Monk had always been so good at.

From the business center, I went for breakfast in the cafeteria, feeling slightly better than before. Monk was getting the best of care. Stottlemeyer had my back. And the fruit salad looked better than it normally did.

I like to think of myself as a sensitive person, sensitive to my surroundings. But even a self-involved gorilla could have figured out people were talking. My few acquaintances among the passengers were giving me a wide berth on the food carousel. They huddled in small groups, their heads close together, their eyes trying not to glance my way.

Sitting by myself at a corner table for two, I returned to my old trick of shutting out the ambient noise and isolating voices across the room. I didn't expect the gossip to be positive or uplifting, so I guess I shouldn't have been offended. Still . . .

"On a calm sea like that? How can you fall overboard?" "The weird guy with the life vest." "My dad says the captain says it was suicide." "He took off his vest before he jumped." "Is he dead? I heard he drowned." "They say his alcoholic girlfriend went back to drinking."

I lost my appetite for the fruit salad and pushed my tray away. If I kept this up, I'd be the only person in the history of cruise ships to lose weight.

Dr. Aaglan began his office hours at nine. I arrived around nine fifteen and found I wasn't the first. Captain Sheffield was in the examination room. They both saw me as soon as I walked into the waiting area.

"There she is," said Aaglan, and waved for me to join them. "I was telling the captain that I haven't been able to get a report from Good Samaritan. The doctors won't talk about Mr. Monk's condition."

"Natalie, you placed a call to the hospital this morning," said Sheffield with a concerned expression. He was demonstrating that this was his ship, that I couldn't hide anything. "What did they tell you?"

"He's in a coma," I said. I put on a brave face and held back the tears that weren't there. "They think he might not make it." I let my voice crack. Not too much, I warned myself.

If Monk recovered before Sheffield could make a run for it, then it was straight to jail for attempted murder, even if we never solved the Mariah case. But if Monk died or stayed in a vegetative state, Sheffield would be off the hook, hounded only by the ace detective's drunken female partner.

Stottlemeyer and I wanted Sheffield to feel safe, not to run or be stupid, hence our instructions to the hospital staff and my Oscar-worthy moment.

"That's terrible," the captain murmured, although I could sense his relief. "When you get a chance," he added, "Sylvia and I would like to meet with you. Whenever you get a chance."

Dr. Aaglan waited until we were alone and the door was closed. "Is he really in a coma?"

"Yes," I said, perhaps a bit too forcefully. "Do you think I'm lying?"

"I don't know," said Aaglan. "I'm not American-born, so I misconstrue. But something odd is going on. You first ask me about pregnancy. Then the captain asks about pregnancy. Mariah's dress had this long stain. And now Mr. Monk's life vest has a stain just like it. Both he and she had head wounds. Then the captain comes in and asks if I have possession of your friend's vest. I say no, but . . . ."

"Whoa, whoa," I said. "Back up. Adrian's vest has a stain? From yesterday? Do you have the vest?"

Dr. Aaglan opened the long drawer beneath the examination table and pulled out an orange vest, still wet and smelling of the sea. "The stewards brought it in with your friend."

It was Monk's all right, from the evenly matched buckles to "Adrian Monk" printed in a ridiculously neat hand with a black Sharpie. Running diagonally was a greasy stain combined with a crease that hadn't been there before. My first reaction was to retrieve my iPhone and take a picture, just as I'd done with the dress.

"Maybe I'm too suspicious," said Aaglan. "It was dirty before?"

"No, trust me. This vest was not dirty."

"Then something bad is going on."

"Something bad," I confirmed.

26

MR. MONK
SHRINKS HIS BRAIN

I don't know what I'd expected from Sylvia Sheffield. A short meeting full of sympathy for my partner and friend? Perhaps a hundred dollars off my next *Golden Sun* cruise? I certainly didn't expect to get called on my money-back guarantee. By the way, I don't believe I ever said *money-back*.

"We hired you so there would be no more incidents," said Sylvia. She was obviously the one in charge. "That was your job and you guaranteed us."

"Do you know what happened to Mr. Monk?" asked Sheffield, with a straight face.

"Not everything. It wasn't a suicide attempt and I don't think it was an accident."

"Do you have any idea how this is affecting our passengers?" asked Sylvia. "Two overboard incidents in a week? Two emergencies where we had to grind to a halt and drop anchor? They're in the business center right now, Facebooking like crazy. The office is already getting calls from the press."

I wanted to point out that both of these

"incidents" had been caused by her husband. But really, how do you phrase something like that? "It's not our fault" was the best I could do.

"You said you knew who was responsible," said Sylvia. Her husband squirmed.

"The vandalism wasn't connected to the overboards." Even as I said it, I knew she wouldn't believe me.

Sylvia rolled her eyes. "I'm afraid we're going to have to insist. We need someone to take responsibility. Otherwise, the *Golden Sun* will be branded as dangerous. Or a jinx, which is even harder to combat. Electrocutions, capsized tenders. And I'm not even counting the death in Mexico. Once that becomes public knowledge, God knows . . ."

"We need answers," said Dennis Sheffield.

If you're looking for a textbook definition of irony, this is it. A killer scolds me for not identifying the killer, even though he knows that I know. But what could I say? If I stood up now and pointed a finger at the captain, what would it get me? Even less credibility with his wife.

"Are you saying this is my fault?" I decided to go with indignation. "My partner was a victim. On your ship. He very well may die."

"That's why you need to tell us," Sylvia said. "If you know who's responsible . . . What if something more happens, something you could have prevented? How would you feel then?"

I was an inch away from telling all. "There won't be any more incidents," I promised instead.

"You said that last time," Sylvia reminded me.

"What Sylvia means is we're stopping payment on the check."

"What?" But I wasn't surprised.

"You're lucky we don't sue," said Sylvia. "If you could have prevented this last incident, you should have told us. The damage to the ship's reputation and the cost of lost business could run into the hundreds of thousands, maybe millions."

"But we're the injured parties," I pointed out. "My partner's in a coma."

Sylvia shook her head. "No, dear, our business is the injured party."

I can't begin to tell you how maddening this was. Completely, want-to-take-her-by-the-throat-and-strangle-her maddening. So self-absorbed and blind to her husband's guilt. So oblivious to the suffering of others. Although . . . in the teeniest of ways, I understood her point.

Our problem was that we'd accepted the job under false pretenses, investigating Mariah's death as part of the vandalism case. And now that we'd made that connection in Sylvia's mind, I couldn't very well separate the two cases, not right now.

Anyway, that was the highlight of my day.

I spent the rest of our last day at sea pretty much to myself. Somewhere in midafternoon, I stopped pacing the decks long enough to have a cup of tea. First Officer Lao must have been following me, because he passed by my table as soon as I sat down.

"Whatever you need, I'll do it," he said, and slipped a calling card under my saucer. "I always have this phone with me and it always works." Before I could even mutter a thank-you, he was gone.

As I watched my tea grow cold, I reviewed the few facts that I had to cling to. Monk had gone somewhere after running out of the engine room. This location was probably important, as no one had seen him since, not until he was floating in the ocean without his vest.

Another fact. The matching stains on Monk's life vest and Mariah's dress couldn't be coincidental. If I could discover the source of the stain, I would probably have my answer.

Before dinner, I made a final visit to the satellite phone in the business center. Monk was still in his coma. The swelling in his brain had gone down and the doctors were encouraged. Stottlemeyer was still at his bedside, carrying on a one-way conversation, occasionally checking up with Devlin about their cases, and becoming quite the expert at Angry Birds.

Ellen still wasn't answering and still hadn't responded. I left another message, saying it was important and Monk needed her. Of course, that's what I'd said earlier in the week, before she flew down to Catalina and we sent her away.

On the other hand, Lieutenant Devlin was answering. She picked up on the first ring. "Any breakthroughs?" she asked.

"Not unless you count taunting as a breakthrough."

"Geez, get a move on." Always the diplomat, that Devlin. "What time does your gangway open?"

"Eight a.m.," I said. "It leaves port again at five. But you can always refuse to sign off. That'll give us an extra day."

"It's not that easy. Their lawyers are already pressing the department with the paperwork. We need a good reason to deprive them of their ability to do business."

"How about a restraining order? Or a provisional warrant?" These were all things I'd learned in my PI studies.

"On what charge?" Devlin asked. "Allowing people to fall off your boat?"

"There was a shipboard death. That warrants an investigation of some sort."

"I'll talk to Judge Markowitz." Mary Markowitz was our favorite cop-friendly judge and a big Monk fan. "But even if she grants a restraining order, there's nothing to keep Sheffield from going on the lam."

"I think he feels safe for now," I said.

"Good. Just in case, I'll have Markowitz standing by. Try to have a breakthrough."

"I'll do my best."

"See you on the pier at eight."

"Oh." Speaking of women waiting for us on the pier . . . "Have you heard from Ellen?"

"Monk's Ellen. Why would I hear from Monk's Ellen?"

"I'm trying to get in touch with her."

"You mean she doesn't know about his condition?"

"She might have gone back to Summit."

"I'll check her house," said Devlin. "As if I don't have enough to do."

That was Devlin's way of being gracious. "Thanks."

27

MR. MONK'S FAVORITE WORDS

As soon as I heard the ship engines stop, I woke up. Technically, I guess I was already awake.

The previous evening, I'd packed up my luggage and left it in the hall. Then came the big chore, packing up Monk. I had a team of stewards bring his eight huge suitcases up from the "executive VIP dry cleaning suite," otherwise known as the hold. I dusted them off, packed them as neatly as I could, knowing that whatever I did, he would call my efforts irredeemable and throw everything out. At least, I hoped he'd be able to do that. And soon.

Looking out to my balcony, I could see through the shadowy mist the familiar outline of the Transamerica Pyramid looming above the pier. I don't know exactly when I packed up my toiletries and left the cabin for good. Probably around six a.m.

I grabbed a quick yogurt and a plastic spoon from the cafeteria, then headed for the gangway. Even though it wasn't yet open for passengers, I felt I needed to be there.

I was standing by the railing when the wooden

box from Mexico was wheeled out from the lower gangway, just above the level of the pier. A tall, thin woman in her thirties stood out there with Captain Sheffield, her eyes focused on the approaching box. Were her eyes also hazel? I wondered. I felt bad that I didn't know her name. Malcolm had mentioned his sister only once, but he'd spoken of her with real affection.

A man in a black suit came forward to officially claim the body and take it out to the street, probably to a waiting hearse.

Fifteen minutes later the scene was repeated, this time with a black body bag instead of a box. I imagine this had all been carefully timed. It wouldn't have been diplomatic to bring out both corpses at once.

The captain was still on the pier, this time with a man and a woman, probably about my age. The woman leaned against her husband, but she didn't seem to be crying. I could envision her, twenty-three years ago, listening to Mariah Carey songs on old Sony headphones as her unborn daughter kicked at her belly.

When the captain used the lower gangway to reenter the ship, I breathed a sigh of relief. At least he wasn't on the run.

"Was that Miss Linkletter?" someone asked.

I looked around to see a scraggly line of passengers milling around, waiting for the gangway to open. Daniela Grace and her three friends were at the railing beside me, each holding the straps of a Chanel or a Louis Vuitton carry-on. "It's so sad," Daniela added. The others murmured in agreement.

"And how is poor Mr. Monk?" asked Ruth Weingart.

"He's in a coma," I said, and watched their faces fall—as much as was physically possible for those faces.

"Oh no," said Sondra Winters. "He's such a nice man." It might have been the first time I'd heard Monk described as nice.

"He kept us from doing something terrible," added Daniela.

"Although we do feel more empowered now," said Ruth. "Just knowing we could have done it—for Samantha."

Daniela pulled a card out of her Chanel. "Please let us know if there's anything we can help with."

"The law offices of Grace, Winters, and Weingart?" The name was very familiar, perhaps from some long-ago case. "Is your husband a criminal attorney by any chance?"

"I am," said Daniela, "along with Sondra's husband and Ruth's husband."

"I'm a retired judge," said Lynn. "That's how we all know one another."

"What?" I had to laugh. It would be my one good laugh of the day.

"I know," admitted Lynn sheepishly. "You couldn't pick four worse assassins."

"If you're lawyers," I said, "you should work to revoke Darby's medical license. So no one else dies."

"Absolutely," said Lynn. "We were discussing that last night."

"We would love to hire you," said Daniela. "You and Mr. Monk, of course, whenever he recovers and gets back to work."

"I'm not sure what we could do to revoke Darby's license."

"No, I mean on other things. Do you ever work criminal cases? On retainer?"

"Of course," I said. "We would love to—when things get settled." What a coup! Well worth the price of the trip. "Thank you, Daniela." And I slipped her card firmly into my pocket.

Daniela fixed on me with her matriarchal smile. "My only condition is that you stay with the AA program and give up drinking."

Lieutenant Devlin, a detective I didn't know, and a young ADA arrived a few minutes later at the bottom of the gangway. They showed their IDs to the guard and climbed up the ramp to meet me.

The detective—introduced as Sergeant Hollo-way—and the ADA—Amanda Weber—went off to do whatever interviews and paperwork the situation required, while Devlin stopped to talk.

"You're sending in a sergeant?" I asked.

"Do you want to spook him by sending in the big guns?"

"No. But you're so much better. . . ."

"Do you think I could learn anything in an hour that you couldn't learn in four days?"

"No." Okay, she'd proved her point.

"So, how can I help?"

It had just turned eight, and a steward was removing the chain from the gangway. A flood of eager passengers began to funnel around us and down to the pier. As they passed, I could hear more than one of them joke about making it home without falling overboard. It was all done in good humor, which served only to irritate me more.

"I need to get off," I told Devlin. "Maybe I'll think better on dry land."

"You mean you've got nothing?"

"Don't rub it in," I said, then began pushing my way through the crowd.

We didn't stop to deal with luggage, but went straight to the spot by the fire hydrant on the access street to the Embarcadero where Devlin had parked her red Grand Am. It was a 2005 model, one of the last ever made.

After a few blocks, I asked her to stop. I didn't want to get too far from the *Golden Sun*, just far enough. I could still see it out of the passenger-side window, the whole length of it, from our current spot on the abandoned part of Pier 32.

"It's got to be something simple," I told myself, although I'm sure Devlin was listening. "Some spot on the ship where—"

My monologue was interrupted by Devlin's phone. She checked the display, pushed a button, and held it up between us. "Talk to me."

It was Sergeant Holloway. "Lieutenant?" He sounded nervous. "I may have made a mistake."

"What mistake?"

"I was interviewing the captain and I may have let something slip."

"Talk to me," Devlin said again.

"I may have let it slip that Monk is in a medically induced coma, rather than a normal coma. I guess there's a difference."

"There is," I said, having Wikied the subject thoroughly during the last two days. "A regular coma is chancy. You may come out of it, you may not. A medically induced coma is a procedure."

"Oh," he said from the other end. "And this is important?"

"Yes," I shouted at the phone. "It means Monk can be brought out of it and testify, which is exactly what we didn't want the captain to know." I glared at Devlin, then at her phone.

"Maybe he doesn't know the difference," Devlin said, then turned to the phone. "Holloway, how did Sheffield react?" asked Devlin.

"He said he had an appointment in the city and we could continue the interview later. Then he walked out. That's why I called."

"He's going to run," I said.

"Should I stop him?" asked Holloway. "Can I? Legally?"

"Follow him," said Devlin. "Ask him to stay for further questioning. Make it sound like he doesn't have a choice. Go. Go." And she hung up. "He's not going to stay."

"Can Markowitz get us a material witness order?" I asked.

"I doubt it," said Devlin. "But I'll try."

Devlin got back on the phone and I got out of the Grand Am. *How infuriating,* I thought as I began pacing the abandoned pier.

The *Golden Sun* was three blocks away, its profile mocking me, daring me to figure it out. The morning mist was just starting to lift, and a glint of sun sparkled off the anchor. For a crazy split second, I panicked. The anchor was up! Did that mean they were about to set sail? Was Sheffield going to use the ship as a gigantic getaway car?

It was idiotic, of course. Ships don't drop their anchors in port. They use them when parked in the middle of a bay, like in Catalina. Or for emergencies, like dealing with high winds or a man-overboard situation or . . .

Bingo!

Devlin was still on the phone with Judge

Markowitz when I pounded on the driver's-side window. "Tell her we need a search warrant for the ship."

"Excuse me, Your Honor." Devlin lowered the window and placed her hand over the receiver. "For the whole ship? That's a fishing expedition."

"No, just one room. Let me talk to the judge." I reached over and grabbed the phone. "Good morning, Your Honor. It's Natalie Teeger, Mr. Monk's partner."

"Of course, Ms. Teeger," came a soft voice. "How is Adrian? I heard about his accident."

"He's recovering. Still unconscious, I'm afraid. But I just figured it out. I know how it was done and I need a search warrant."

There was a pause. I could almost feel the excitement from the other end. Or maybe that was my excitement. "You know," she said, "Adrian has never disappointed me. I've gone out on a limb with him dozens of times, and he always pulls through. I remember this one case. He asked for a search warrant at a cattle ranch. He was literally looking for a needle in a haystack. My clerk thought I was crazy to okay it, but . . . ."

"Excuse me, Your Honor. This is an emergency."

"Right. Sorry." Judge Markowitz cleared her throat and got serious. "Ms. Teeger, I am familiar with the details of the case as outlined to me by Lieutenant Devlin. Please state the location for the requested warrant and your reason for needing it."

"Thank you, Your Honor," I said, then followed up with Monk's three favorite words in the English language. "Here's what happened."

I was the one driving back up the Embarcadero access road to Pier 35. The road was jammed with vehicles going in the other direction, passengers from the ship now on their way home. Occasionally, they would try to pass in my lane. But you don't play chicken with a woman who has just solved a murder.

Meanwhile, Devlin was in the Grand Am's passenger seat, waiting for a copy of the signed warrant to download to her phone. Also arriving would be a material witness warrant for Captain Dennis Sheffield, meaning we could hold him until we had grounds for his arrest.

The captain's black Mercedes was easy to find. It was in a private parking spot right at the foot of the gangway. Making it even easier was the sight of Sergeant Holloway leaning into the driver's window. He looked up and seemed glad to see us.

The same couldn't be said for Dennis Sheffield.

28

MR. MONK AND
THE BEDSIDE MANNER

"When you ran out of the engine room, did you know?"

"No. I just had to get out of there. All the noise and smell and the heat. I was waiting for Natalie out in the hall. And then I saw the door marked ANCHOR ACCESS and it came to me. Obvious."

Monk was sitting up, the top half of his bed at a forty-five-degree angle, the sheets weirdly unwrinkled, as if the bed had been made with him already in it. He paused here for a drink of water. Four perfectly square ice cubes and a straight, clear straw.

"You used my all-access key to get in," I said.

"I used your key," he confirmed. "It was just going to take me a minute."

So that was the simple but annoying explanation. While I'd been scouring the lower decks, going up and down three flights shouting his name, he'd been right there, in the anchor room next door.

Two days after that, I'd been in the anchor room myself with Judge Markowitz's warrant. It was a largish space, near the very point of the prow and almost completely occupied by a long, massive chain wrapped around a series of interlocking spools. On the outside wall was a steel access panel, held in place with a row of simple bolts.

Monk took another sip of water, then didn't like the level and motioned for me to fill it up to the line in the red plastic tumbler.

We were gathered around his bed in a private room, still at Good Samaritan—Stottlemeyer, Devlin, me, and an LAPD officer we'd borrowed for the occasion to record our statements and take notes.

"Here's the thing," said Monk. He was looking tired and maybe a little confused. "Here's the thing that occurred."

"Here's what happened," I prompted.

Monk had been awake for a day and a half now. The doctors warned us that recovery wouldn't be instantaneous, that there might be gaps in his memory, and that his mind might not be exactly the way it was. That was scary. Not that Monk's mind was ever a perfect specimen. But it was perfect for him, and I was used to dealing with it.

"Here's what happened," he said. The sleeves on his brown checkered pajamas were uneven, the left a full three inches higher on his arm than the right. He didn't seem to care. Stottlemeyer had noticed this, too.

"Here's what happened," Monk repeated, trying to mentally find his place again. "Captain what's-his-name met with Mariah what's-her-name that night, probably in the anchor room," said Monk. "Secret rendezvous."

"That would have been Monday, your second night at sea," stated the LAPD officer. "And the name is Sheffield. Captain Sheffield."

"Correct," said Monk. "Sheffield. Whether he knew she was pregnant with his child doesn't matter. Somehow he got the liquor into her system. There are ways of getting liquor into people, aren't there, Natalie? You should know."

"I'm not an alcoholic," I shot back, then grabbed the officer's arm. "Strike that. The question and the response."

Stottlemeyer nodded. "Strike it."

The officer made a note and Monk continued. He seemed to be recovering strength. "Captain Sheffield brought the wooden leg with him, so we know the act was premeditated."

"Premeditated," mumbled the officer.

"After he killed her, Sheffield unscrewed the bolts to the panel, giving him access to the anchor. What he did then was brilliant, although I hate to glamorize the work of a cold-blooded killer. Can you erase the word *brilliant?* Just say *nifty.*"

The officer made another note. "What he did then was . . . nifty."

Monk considered. "Maybe you should say *diabolical.*"

"I like *nifty*," said Stottlemeyer, wrinkling his mustache just a touch.

"We'll stick with *nifty*," Monk said. "It was nifty the way Sheffield wedged her body on top of the anchor. From there he went up to the crew section of the Calypso deck, placed the chunk of ice in the alarm bell, pulled the lever, and went to dinner. He made sure to stay in the public eye all the time. His second-in-command, the Asian guy . . ."

"First Officer Lao," I reminded him.

"Right. First Officer what's-his-name did the rest, although he didn't realize it. When the ice melted and slipped out of place, the alarm bell rang. The Asian guy followed the rules for 'man overboard.' He took the ship back to the coordinates and dropped anchor. The falling anchor dumped the girl's body into exactly the right position."

"We have a statement from Gifford Gilchrist," said Devlin, for the record. "The boy recants his story about pulling the alarm, although Barry Gilchrist made us put into the record that his son did pull the alarm for Monk."

"I appreciate it," said Monk and went on. "If I had it to do over, I probably wouldn't have tried that stunt with the vest. What was I thinking?"

The stunt with the vest had been Monk's way of testing his theory in the anchor room. He'd deduced that the long stain on Mariah's dress had come from her being wedged along the anchor top. To this day, I'm not sure how he did it, but while I'd been frantically looking for him, he had managed to remove the bolts, swing the panel in, and have access to the open sea.

Directly below him was the anchor, protected by a curved barrier from the onrush of salt wind. There was only one way Monk could think of to replicate the stain, so he removed his life vest—the one he'd stubbornly refused to remove even when in bed at night—and wedged it in the same place along the anchor.

After that, he had very little memory of events, except that Captain Sheffield had stormed his way in. There was a struggle near the open hatch to the anchor. The next thing Monk recalled was waking up four days later, after his brain had returned to its normal size. Normal for him. At least I hoped so.

Monk glanced down at his sleeves—and still didn't straighten them. "Did you guys figure this out? I forget."

"Yes, Adrian." Apparently he had some problems with short-term memory. "I figured it out. Judge Markowitz got us a search warrant. We sent in the best CS techs. They found Mariah's fingerprints, blood spatter traces, DNA, even a thread from her dress wedged in a steel seam behind the anchor."

"So you don't even need my statement."

"We need it, Monk," said Stottlemeyer. "We're indicting both for murder and attempted murder."

"Good. Glad to hear it. Can I go back to sleep?" He reached for the remote control on his bed.

"Sure," said the captain, giving an affectionate squeeze to the shoulder of Monk's pajamas. "Good job, buddy. You earned it."

"No," said Lieutenant Devlin and grabbed for the remote. "You can't go to sleep."

"I can't?" Monk whined. "But the captain said I earned it. You heard him say I earned it. No backsies."

"I'm sorry, Monk," said Devlin, gently prying the remote from his hand. "But as long as you're awake and running on all cylinders, I need to ask you about the other case."

"But Leland said I earned it."

Stottlemeyer twitched the corner of his mouth. "Sorry, old buddy. Devlin's right. We've got officers working overtime per your instructions. And the mayor's calling me once daily, like an alarm clock."

"It's the Melrose case," said Devlin, trying to prompt his memory. "The German woman who killed Lester Melrose? Right before you left? Portia Braun?"

"She didn't confess?" Monk asked, irritation breaking through his fatigue. "Usually they confess."

"She didn't confess," Devlin assured him. "In fact, we had to let her go."

"Let her go?" Monk drifted into wordless thought. For a few seconds, I thought he was falling asleep. "But she didn't leave town. Of course not. She wouldn't."

"Because of her inheriting the Shakespeare?" Stottlemeyer asked. "That's not true. An inheritance can be handled long distance."

"No, no. You don't get it." Monk paused dramatically. We waited for something more, something brilliant . . . "I'm sorry. What is it you don't get?"

"How to solve the Melrose case," said Devlin. "It's been ten days. Portia Braun is still staying with her professor friend in the Mission District. And we have a twenty-four-hour presence on the Melrose library. I'm not sure why."

"Why do you have a guard on the library?"

"Because you told us to," said Devlin. "You told us to keep a presence until you got back or you drowned at sea." She winced. "I didn't mean that. I mean, that's what you said. But I wasn't taking it literally."

"And did I drown at sea?" asked Monk. "Did I?"

"No," admitted Devlin. "You didn't."

"Good. Just checking." He closed his eyes. "Good." And he was asleep.

29

MR. MONK MISSES A BEAT

It was after midnight. The four of us had been twiddling our thumbs in the darkened Melrose library for nearly two hours. Amy Devlin and I were quietly pacing, careful to keep out of each other's way. Monk sat perfectly still in a leather wing chair, while Stottlemeyer was in the matching one. From what I could see, he was the only one actually twiddling his thumbs.

"This is ludicrous," Devlin whispered. Monk tried to shush her but she didn't care. "I don't mind wasting a night. Part of the job. But this is disrespectful." She was referring to the fact that Monk had arranged this whole midnight event, or nonevent, without informing us of what to expect.

Stottlemeyer had removed the police guard from the mansion this morning. Jeremiah "Jerry" Melrose, heir and executor, had finally been given permission to let his father's estate go into probate. And the only two residents, Jerry and Smithson the butler, had been instructed to remain in their parts of the house with the lights out.

"Reminds me of the old days," said Stottlemeyer. He sounded a tad wistful. There had been a time, toward the beginning of their relationship, when Monk would purposely keep everyone out of his mental loop. I'm not sure if it had been a matter of trust with Monk or his flair for the dramatic, but the last moments of a case would often be like this—with the police and me waiting in the dark, waiting for Monk to spring some sort of unfathomable trap.

Rather than being insulted like Devlin or amused like Stottlemeyer, I was concerned. I knew the man better than anyone. "Adrian. Come here." I took him by the elbow. He let me guide him out of the wing chair and into a corner. "What are you doing?"

"I'm solving the case," he said. "Just a little longer."

"You could have solved it without a production," I said. "Why are you being this way?"

"I don't know," he said, and the catch in his voice proved he wasn't showing off or being dramatic. He was scared. "It comes and goes. Sometimes everything is clear and sometimes it's not. Ever since I woke up . . ."

"You mean from drowning?" I didn't know what else to call it. That's what he called it himself.

He nodded. "Like tonight. I know who's going to walk in. But when I start to explain it inside my own head, it gets hazy."

"Have you told this to the doctors?"

"Yes. But"—he seemed pleased with himself—"I was careful to state it as a hypothetical. You know. What if someone happened to wake up after a drowning and a medically induced coma, and his mind was hazy. I don't think they knew I was talking about me."

"What did they say?"

"They said it's not uncommon. Probably temporary."

"Of course it's temporary. It's been only a few days. Being through all of that and now being back home . . . I'd be hazy."

"Yes," Monk said. "But you're not expected to be brilliant every single minute. In fact, you're not expected to be brilliant at all. In fact, people expect very little. . . ."

"Okay, I get it." I wasn't insulted. After all, Adrian Monk was defined by his genius. It was how he defined himself. I didn't want to think about how that might have changed. "I'll help you through this one. No one will know."

"You?"

"Yes, me. I've seen you do this hundreds of times. Just tell me who we're expecting. And please don't say Malcolm Leeds, because that would really freak me out."

Monk had his mouth open to give an answer. But we were interrupted by a dot of red from the security system panel. Ten seconds of steady red followed by maybe fifteen seconds of flashing red. Then it flashed off. Someone had just come through the front door and switched off the alarm.

The captain and lieutenant had seen it, too. Without a word we shrank into the dim corners. I thought I could hear the soft tread of footsteps on the staircase, but it might have been my imagination.

A minute later, the library door eased open, then closed with barely a squeaky hinge. This time I heard the footsteps and the click of a table lamp.

It was Portia Braun, revealed in the soft glow. Not unexpected, I had to admit. Except that she was carrying a dead ringer of Malcolm's faux-leather messenger bag over her shoulder. We watched from the shadows as she tiptoed across the room to the leather-bound Shakespeare on its stand by the window. I guess it was Devlin who turned on the other lights.

"Good evening, Ms. Braun," said Captain Stottlemeyer. "Mind if we look inside your bag?"

You could see the fight-or-flee response surge through her before she settled on a third, more sensible option. Surrender. Her shoulders slumped as Lieutenant Devlin put the bag on a table and, at a nod from the captain, opened it. There in a cotton-padded interior, taking up almost the entire bag, was a twin to the Shakespeare folio on the stand.

"The second fake," said Devlin. "The spare from London."

"No," Monk announced. "The six-million-dollar original."

That statement was enough to throw everyone for a mental loop, except for Monk and probably Portia.

Had the book on the stand been a fake all along?

If so, had Malcolm Leeds been part of the swindle when he authenticated it? If not, how had the book been switched out and why? And was that Malcolm's bag on the table? Or a twin? All three of us were asking these questions aloud until Monk held up a hand. It was time for him to do the thing he did best in the world.

"They were in on it together," he explained.

Okay, this was disappointing. Not totally unexpected, just disappointing.

"I knew from the first time I met Leeds. Or maybe the second time. Was it the first or second time?" Monk was looking at me. Helpless.

"How did you know?" asked Devlin.

"Um." I could see his eyes wander. "It was something Leeds said."

I began reviewing everything Malcolm had said in front of Monk that day, like someone else's life flashing in front of my eyes. And then it hit me. "He said Portia was from East Germany."

"Yes," Monk agreed, his mind back on track. "She taught at the University of Munich, so one might assume the woman was Bavarian. But

Leeds mentioned she was East German, even though he supposedly never met her before."

I nodded and tried to take over. "Portia and Malcolm met here in San Francisco. Some mutual friend probably introduced them." I was just spitballing, looking to Monk to contradict me. "That's when they came up with the plan to substitute a fake. After the theft, Portia would use a new passport to disappear, and Malcolm would never be under suspicion to begin with. How am I doing?"

"Good," Monk said. "And it was Leeds who arranged for the copies to be made in London."

"Yes, London," said Devlin. "How did you know we should look at London?"

"I knew because of . . . his watch. Something about his wristwatch."

"Are you okay, Monk?" asked the captain.

"I'm fine." Monk rolled his shoulders. "I'm just giving Natalie a chance."

I said, "Thanks," and kept thinking.

I thought back to one time I'd seen Malcolm's Rolex. "Malcolm had just gotten back from a trip to New York, so he said. But his watch wasn't three hours off. It was more. Am I right? Adrian?"

"Right," Monk said, remembering. "His Rolex was eight hours off. That means England. It's not the only country in that time zone. Theoretically, the copies could have been made in Spain or Portugal or West Africa. But since Shakespeare

303

wasn't Spanish or Portuguese or West African . . ."

"Got it. But why two copies?" Devlin asked.

"Why not?" I said. "Everyone needs a backup. It's logical to have a backup." I knew this was how Monk thought. Backups for everything. If Monk had a better reason for this last deduction, he didn't say.

Stottlemeyer eyed us. "What's with all this back-and-forth? A tag team match?"

"I'm just trying to contribute," I said. "Do you want to go on, Adrian?"

"Why don't you?" said Monk.

"Thanks," I said. But nothing was coming to mind. For a crazy second, I looked over to Portia.

"Don't expect me to help," she said, her mouth curling in a sneer. "I'm no good with silly fairy tales."

I plowed ahead anyway. "The original plan went wrong. Circumstances forced Portia to return the real folio and toss the copy in the lily pond—and kill Lester Melrose."

"It was just luck how Leeds got involved as your consultant," said Monk, "although there aren't that many rare book experts. Leeds came in and did his job. On the second day, he came prepared. While we were arresting his partner, he stole the Shakespeare book again and replaced it with the second fake."

"You mean when our backs were turned?"

Stottlemeyer was stunned. "Right here in this room?"

"He had his messenger bag with him," I said, recalling the moment well. "And the rest of us were busy with Ms. Braun's arrest."

"Right under our noses?" You could see how angry the captain was with himself. But how could he have suspected that his consultant was one of the bad guys?

Devlin turned to Portia and grinned. "Did you see what Leeds was doing? Damn, that must have galled. You get handcuffed for murder, and he's right across the room stealing your prize."

"I don't know what you're talking about," said Portia. That comment alone set my mind at ease. We must have been right on the money.

"Malcolm Leeds knew he had a limited window to disappear with his prize." Monk seemed focused again and on a roll. "That's why he needed to cozy up to Natalie and get me distracted."

"Yes," I agreed before listening. "Hold on. What? Cozy up to me?"

A smirk is not Monk's most attractive look. "I told you he was using you, Natalie. And I believe your response was 'Shut up.'"

"Shut up."

"You shut up. When you two met, you kept bragging about how I couldn't get on without you. That's why he wanted you on that cruise, to keep me off balance."

"Shut up."

"Captain. Natalie's telling me to shut up."

"Boys and girls, that's enough," growled Stottlemeyer. "Let's just say, for sake of argument, stop arguing. Okay?"

We stopped. "Good," said the captain. "Now where were we? All right, Malcolm takes Natalie to Mexico for whatever reason. He double-crosses his partner and jumps ship with the book. Is that right?"

"Right," I said. This part was pretty straightforward. "Malcolm didn't expect Portia to be released. But she was. It was easy for her to fly to San Marcos, follow him from the dock, kill him, grab the book, and fly back. All that remained was for her to replace the book—yet again—and inherit it legally."

Devlin and Stottlemeyer were both smiling, amused by the whole process. If there weren't two murders involved, it would be pretty funny, you have to admit. Four different substitutions—first putting in the fake, then the original, then a different fake, then the original again.

I was grateful that Portia hadn't chimed in about Malcolm using me as a patsy. Despite my volley of "shut ups," that detail had the annoying ring of truth.

"That is the most atrocious fable. I never went to Mexico." Portia was wearing black-framed glasses tonight and looked even more like a scholar. "My car pass shows me going over the San Francisco bridges that day, several times."

"Huh," said Stottlemeyer, unfazed. "That's funny." He cocked his head. "It's funny you should mention the FasTrak pass. Most people give an alibi by mentioning witnesses or business or friends. You went straight for the FasTrak."

"It's true," said Portia. "You can check my pass."

"We did," said Devlin. "Unfortunately, we didn't check your friend's pass." I could tell that she was mentally kicking herself for being so sloppy. "We'll do that first thing in the morning." She took out her iPhone and checked her notes. "Your roommate, Gretchen Wilder. She teaches across the bay. She must have gone back and forth that day, several times. It would be very curious to see if her FasTrak and yours crossed at exactly the same time. Wouldn't that be weird? Almost like both passes were in the same car."

"It would be a fascinating coincidence," said Portia. She was less belligerent than a moment before, but still belligerent. "But this would not prove I went to Mexico. I'm certain you have already checked the airlines? Yes?"

"Yes," Devlin admitted. "Nothing under your name."

I couldn't believe this woman was still trying to get away with it. "What about this?" I asked, pointing to the messenger bag on the table.

"This belonged to Malcolm Leeds. In Mexico."

"No. This is mine," said Portia, hardly skipping a beat. "When Mr. Leeds was here, I admired his bag. I went out and bought one just like it. In cash," she added before we could ask. "I don't remember where."

All right, this was downright rude. Any decent killer would have confessed by now.

The captain was just as frustrated as me. "Ms. Braun. We have you on a charge of breaking and entering."

"I plead guilty to that, although, in my defense, no one ever confiscated my house keys or changed the code. Is that a felony?"

"We also have you in possession of stolen property."

"Property that I am about to inherit."

Despite her talk, I felt that we had her, at least enough for a grand jury and an indictment. We could probably find a witness at the car rental place in Mexico. But this woman had proved slippery before.

The room fell silent as the three of us, perhaps even four of us, waited for Monk. This would be the moment when he would do something big and clever and just nail the murderer to the wall. It didn't happen.

"Monk?" Stottlemeyer finally asked.

Monk kept his face a blank, then leaned over from his feet, like a mime in a sideways windstorm, until he turned his head and his lips were an inch from my ear. "A little help?"

I'm not saying I'm a genius detective, although I am getting better. But I am a fairly visual person, and it was the memory of what I'd seen—or hadn't seen—in Malcolm's bathroom on the *Golden Sun* that flipped the switch.

I whispered one word in Monk's ear, then watched as he began to lean back, recovering from the imaginary windstorm. When he was fully vertical again, Monk walked over to the faux-leather messenger bag on the table. He slipped on a pair of plastic gloves from his jacket pocket and began to rummage inside the bag.

It took him a while. But when his hand came out, it was holding a small blue cylinder, a bit thicker than a pen and maybe two-thirds the length. He held it up for all to see.

"Toothbrush!"

30

MR. MONK STARTS FRESH

"So, you're going to walk into her shop? Just like that?"

"I'm going to walk into her shop." Monk seemed as determined as you can be when you're marching down a busy section of Union Street and avoiding every crack in the sidewalk.

"Even though the shop's name is Poop and it's filled with poop?"

Monk's toe hit a crack. He powered through the injury, limping for the next block or so. "It used to be poop," he said, trying to convince himself. "Now it's just dead organic matter. Like a corpse. I'll try to think of it like a corpse."

"Ellen will be so impressed."

"Enough to talk to me again?"

"We won't know until we try."

This had been Monk's idea. Since we'd been back in town, we'd been busy. There had been evidence to gather in the Portia Braun case. The woman still hadn't confessed. But the DNA from the travel toothbrush had proved to be Malcolm's, and Aeromexico had found a Hanna Blitzer who had taken two flights that day—to

310

San Marcos at seven a.m. and a return to San Francisco, arriving at five fifteen.

Devlin's doppelgänger, Lieutenant Julia Rodriguez, was working on witnesses at the car rental company, while Stottlemeyer was in contact with his twin, Captain Alameda, to work out the details of the two murder indictments. Things were looking pretty good.

Meanwhile, Monk had been sleeping twelve-hour nights and improving every day. He was also learning how to give himself sponge baths, since it would be a while before he'd be ready to use a bathtub.

For my part, I'd been reconnecting with my daughter, Julie, catching up on her career plans and her boyfriend plans. I was also spending time with Daniela Grace, my AA sponsor. She had dragged me out to a few more meetings.

I know this is weird. But it made her feel better to think I was an alcoholic and needed her. And it helped me to stay in touch with the facelift quartet. True to their word, they had stopped trying to kill Dr. McGinnis and were working to put him out of business. He was currently under an injunction preventing him from practicing while the AMA review board interviewed other patients.

"You know, Ellen may be back in New Jersey," I said as we crossed to the north side of Union Street.

"I know. But she's not answering my calls. If I go into her shop, I'm sure her hideously deformed assistant will tell her, and Ellen will be impressed enough to call." By *hideously deformed,* Monk meant that Suzie, a sweet Berkeley graduate, had a half-shaved head and a few piercings and tattoos.

We almost passed the store without seeing it. That's because the bright, retro neon POOP had been replaced by a FOR LEASE sign taking up nearly the entire window. Behind the sign, the shop was dark and nearly empty.

Monk and I stood silently, two great detectives trying to make sense of the obvious.

"Should I go in anyway?" Monk asked. "I was all prepared to go in."

"I don't think it matters."

"Maybe she's getting out of the poop business to spend more time with me."

"Yes. That would explain why she's not answering your calls."

"No, it wouldn't," Monk said before getting the sarcasm. "Oh."

We stayed another minute, as though the sign would suddenly change back to POOP or Ellen Morse would suddenly open the door and come out and explain herself.

This second thing is exactly what did happen. Ellen seemed just as surprised as we were when she walked out of her ex-store and found us lingering on the sidewalk.

"Adrian. Natalie." She bit her lip and blushed. "I was going to call."

"After you got back home to Summit?" I asked.

Ellen didn't acknowledge the sarcasm. "This store hasn't been working out," she explained. "You know that."

Ellen had confided her business concerns to me a few months ago. But I'd thought that her fondness for Monk, combined with the reward money that we'd shared with her from our last case, would have convinced her to stay.

"Not working out? I didn't know," Monk said, which was true. He handles the possibility of change even worse than he handles change itself, so I'd kept all of this from him. "You can't leave."

"Unfortunately, the good people of San Francisco disagree."

"Ellen, please. Why didn't you tell me?" he moaned. "I could get all my poop-loving friends to come in and buy your poop."

"Do you have any poop-loving friends?" Ellen asked.

"Ugh!" Monk shuddered. "Crazy talk. That's a figure of speech. But look. I'm going to walk into your store."

"My inventory's already on its way back to Summit."

"Good. That makes it easy. Look, I'm walking in."

It was no use. Ellen had probably made up her

mind that afternoon on the tender, heading back alone to the dock in Catalina. It wasn't just the business, of course. It was Monk. And, to a lesser degree, me. As long as she was here in our city, she would be tempted to forgive everything and start over and pretend that the next time it would be different. She deserved better.

"I saw on the news that the girl was killed, the one you were trying to save." Ellen smiled sadly. "I'm sorry."

"But I caught the guy," said Monk, as if that had made everything right. "Actually, Natalie caught the guy. I was busy at the time, drowning."

"What?" said Ellen. "Drowning?"

"I almost died," Monk confirmed. "You can ask Natalie."

"He almost died," I said.

"He almost always almost dies," said Ellen.

That was weirdly true. For someone with so many phobias, Monk did spend a lot of time on the brink of death. Ellen had no way of knowing that this brink of death had been a lot closer than most.

"I don't mean to seem callous, Adrian, but if that news is supposed to make me want to stay . . . it's doing just the opposite."

"It wasn't all that close," Monk clarified. "I was just in a coma."

"A coma?" This caught her off guard. "I'm so sorry. Are you all right? I had no idea." She reached out to touch his shoulder but stopped herself. "I should have answered your calls. It was selfish and mean of me. I don't know what to say."

"It was a short coma," Monk told her. "Very relaxing."

"Adrian," said Ellen, "I think being involved with you would be worse than being with a cop. A cop has backup and procedures to follow. A cop has regular hours and probably doesn't get into as many wild situations. And a cop gets to retire. I would have that to look forward to."

"Retire? How can I retire? The bad guys aren't going to put themselves away."

It was exactly the wrong thing to say. But true. As long as there was the chaos of murder staring him in the face, there would be Adrian Monk, trying to clean it up.

From Union Street, Monk and I took a silent, thoughtful stroll to Rassigio's, not far from the Pine Street apartment. Along the way, I texted Tony Rassigio, the owner, warning him. This would give him time to make sure everything was spotless and to change the board of health rating card in his window from A to AAA. It was a fake sign made just for Monk, but the result was that we now had a restaurant he would go to.

It was early, a little after five. Tony unlocked the door, led us to the only table Monk would sit at, and brought us new menus, fresh from the printer, not yet touched by human hands. I immediately ordered a glass of white wine and wondered when I'd stop feeling guilty about ordering one glass of wine.

"So good to see you, Mr. Monk. I was hoping you'd come in." Tony seemed even more solicitous than usual as he scurried off to get my chardonnay and a bottle of Fiji Water for Monk.

"It's all your fault," said Monk.

"My fault?"

"Yes. If you hadn't known Mariah Linkletter was going to get killed, I would have gotten off the ship with Ellen, and everything would be normal."

"First off, you're not normal, Adrian. Second, if you hadn't stayed, people would have gotten away with murder. Mariah's killer and Malcolm's killer. And Darby McGinnis might be dead."

"That's not helping your argument."

"Okay, forget Darby."

"We can't keep everyone alive," he said with a careless shrug. "Or solve every case."

This sentiment was unusual coming from him, the man who had practically invented the idea of obsessive perfection.

"So, looking back," I asked him, "knowing what you know . . . would you have gotten off the ship with Ellen? Is it okay to let killers go unpunished? Mysteries to go unsolved? If the result is you get to have a 'normal' life?" It was one of our rare philosophical moments.

"Would Darby be alive or dead?"

"Forget Darby."

Monk made a face and rolled his shoulders. He sighed. "This is what we do."

I had to sit on that for a moment. We waited in silence for Tony to return.

"Excuse me, Mr. Monk." The restaurant owner delivered our drinks, then cleared his throat, as if about to run down the daily specials. "Please. I need your help with my son, Tony Junior. He's dating this girl. I looked her up on the Internet, just to check, and she's been dead for six months. The exact same girl."

Talk about bad timing. "Tony, is this a case you want us to work on?" I asked.

"Yes, please. I showed my son this girl's obituary online but it doesn't bother him."

"Tony, I'm sorry. But it's a Saturday. Adrian and I are in the middle of some personal stuff. If you want to set up an appointment . . ."

"Of course, of course," he apologized. "I can come by your place tomorrow."

"Tomorrow is Sunday," I pointed out, "when normal people don't work. You can come by Adrian's apartment on Monday. At nine. Will that be okay?"

"Of course, of course." Tony continued to apologize and thank us as he took our order

317

and retreated back into his AAA-rated kitchen.

Monk sipped his Fiji and stared at me over the rim. "Aren't you interested in the dead girl?"

"That's not the point. The trouble with us, Adrian, you and me, is that we let work become an excuse. We ignore our lives. And because we're helping people, we think it's all good. Meanwhile, we're getting older and we don't have any friends. . . ."

"We have each other."

"Don't depress me. What if you were here tonight with Ellen instead of me? Would you suddenly ignore her and start working on Tony Rassigio's problem? You probably would. Or what if I was here with a boyfriend?"

"You mean a boyfriend who's not a crook?"

"Yes, let's say I had a boyfriend who's not a crook or a soon-to-be murder victim. Would I ditch him to go work on a case with you?"

"I hope so."

"Well, that's got to change. We've got to pretend our lives are as important as a double homicide in the Castro. More important. That's the only way we're going to wind up happy instead of alone and lonely, chasing down bad guys in our motorized wheelchairs."

"So what do you suggest?"

"First, you have to decide if you care enough about Ellen to change your ways and win her back."

"I think I do."

"Good. We'll work on that. Meanwhile, I have to set limits. I can't be at your beck and call twenty-four/seven. I need an activity. Maybe I'll train for a marathon. And I need to spend time with Julie before she moves away for good."

"I should get an activity, too," Monk said, warming to the idea. "Maybe curling. That involves a broom."

"Sounds wonderful. I'll come to all your matches."

I let the image sink in for a minute. Monk seemed to be giving it a lot of thought. Well, he was giving something a lot of thought. "Do you think it's stolen identity?"

"Not if she has the same face," I replied. "And why doesn't Tony Junior care? If I showed Julie her boyfriend's obituary, she would care. A lot."

"I wonder if Tony Junior has a job."

When Tony Senior emerged from the kitchen a moment later, I motioned to him. "All right, Tony," I said, following it with a sigh that could have supported the weight of the world. "You win."

The man's face broke out into a grin as he grabbed an extra chair and headed for our table.

Center Point Large Print
600 Brooks Road / PO Box 1
Thorndike, ME 04986-0001 USA

(207) 568-3717

US & Canada:
1 800 929-9108
www.centerpointlargeprint.com

DATE DUE